LOVE
contract

Passion Always
HAS A BOTTOM LINE

A LOVE@WORK SERIES NOVEL

PAX SINCLAIR

ISBN: 978-1-7336445-4-9 (Print Edition)
ASIN: B0843SF5ZF (ebook Edition)

Printed and bound in the United States of America
First printing February 2020

Red Kettle Ink

Published by Red Kettle Ink
2010 El Camino Real #1151
Santa Clara, CA 95050

www.paxsinclair.com

Book Cover by Uniquely Tailored
www.uniquelytailored.com

Acknowledgments

I want to thank my wonderful beta team.
This is a better story because of your help and support.
Thanks Ash, Lucie, Maureen and Pearl.

Table Of Contents

CHAPTER 1

The Interview

I make a U-turn, just barely making it through the yellow arrow light, and nearly careen into a red Tesla. That a-hole of a driver had, like a fish, gotten in front of me when he made a right turn. He's probably thinking it's his right to cut me off because he has a trendier car than me. The flat of my hand hits the steering wheel with a frustrated thump. I groan as pain shoots through my hand. I hate these jumped-up Ford Focuses. Traffic at 9:15 a.m. in San Jose is a beast and I'm going to be late.

I crane my neck to see addresses on the buildings and try to keep an eye on the stop-and-go traffic in front of me. "Goddamn it, it's got to be around here somewhere," I say to no one. I check the clock on the dashboard. I'm quickly burning my twenty-minute cushion trying to find this freaking place. The GPS app on my phone, which is sitting in my cup holder, is directing my progress. The male Aussie voice that's giving me directions just landed me in front of an auto dealership.

I should have done a dry run and made sure I knew where this place was before today. Chalk it up to arrogance. I was born in this valley and know every freaking nook and cranny from Morgan Hill to San Francisco and beyond. I've forgotten that they're building up every spare inch of this place. "Okay, people," I say, trying to calm myself before I do something stupid. "I just need to find a building on North First Street, and no one will be harmed in the process." I brake and make a hard right into a parking lot to text the recruiter who set up my interview. When I look over at the building I've parked in front of, I realize glory-be-hallelujah if it's not the place I'm looking for. I swing into a visitor's spot and kill the engine. I grab my bag and tablet and speed-walk across the parking lot. My heart is pumping at a manic pace to the clacking of my heels on the pavement.

Just before I get to the lobby, a guy walks out of the building and takes a few steps away from the door. As I get closer, I register that he's a tall hunk of gorgeousness. Mr. Sexy catches me going full throttle towards the entrance and doubles back to open the door as I sail into the lobby, a "Thanks" thrown over my shoulder as I pass him. He gives me a deep, rumbled "No problem" that has contained laughter underneath it. I ignore him.

I'm nearly out of breath when I reach the security station. A bored, rail-thin male, somewhere south of sixty with a black tie that seems to be wearing him, stares up at me while his fingers tap something on his keyboard. "Welcome to Drachen Technology."

I smile, only because I'm winded and need a second. "I'm here to see Nina Madrone, I--"

"Name," he says, not stopping his typing.

"Kellis Ivarsson."

"Driver's license, please."

I fish in my purse, open my wallet, and hand him the license while taking in the lobby. It's an ultra-modern reception area of glass and steel that says, *Yeah, we're a bad ass technology company in Silicon Freaking Valley.* The colors are stark grays with splashes of cold blues. Behind the gleaming white enamel security station, the familiar dragon logo of Drachen Technology, a multi-national company headquartered in Germany, reigns with dark dominance, seeing all.

The security man slides a badge and my license toward me. "You'll need this to enter the offices. The badge is only good for the day. Ms. Madrone will be down shortly."

I retrieve the badge and my ID. I lean forward to see Robert Benson on his name tag. "Thank you, Robert," I say and follow it up with a smile.

He doesn't look up from his screen. "You're welcome, Ms. Ivarsson."

I'm looking for a seat, when I notice the man who opened the door is still standing outside, watching me through the glass. He gives me a ghost of a grin, then nods. I don't manage a smile, but I return the nod. This brief exchange seems to be enough for him. He begins striding down the path to the parking lot. I could ask Robert who he was, but I decide it isn't an option. After my epic break-up with Tim, I'm not about to run after a man, no matter how hot he looks. I've sworn off men, at least for a while.

The black leather sofa I settle on looks nicer than comfortable. I've made it here with five minutes to spare. I pull out my cell phone and run through my texts. There's one from my sister Chloe, who asks me to pick up pizza after I get off work. I'm working, but as a volunteer in the evenings at a local job club in an adult education complex. I teach a series of classes on how to find a job. I make a mental note to cover knowing where the interview is located beforehand.

"Kellis?"

A woman holding a folder is walking towards me in slim navy pants and a tailored pale pink shirt. I'm guessing she's in her thirties. Her dark hair sweeps her shoulders as she moves, but it's her large cornflower eyes that you notice when she draws near. "Nina?"

"Yes, welcome," she says, extending her hand.

3

We exchange a handshake.

"Do you need anything before we start? Water or the restroom?"

"I'm good." I follow her into an elevator that takes us to the level below. She taps on the light to reveal abandoned cubes with equipment still in them. It's clear no one has occupied these seats for a while. We walk through the center row of cubicles, heading for a glassed-in meeting room. To the left of the space is a large area with two screens, video equipment, and about fifteen rows of chairs. Nina observes me looking at the area.

"We use this space for our all-hands meetings," she says, flicking on a light to illuminate the section. "This building is actually the headquarters for the company in the Americas. We have twelve other sites around the country, including Puerto Rico. A few sites in central and South America."

"Is this floor used for storage?" looking at an old calendar that's still tacked to the outside of a cube.

"This housed a division that was sold almost two years ago. Many of the employees now work for the new company. Drachen hasn't decided if we will acquire another business or find a smaller space." She pushes open the door to the meeting room. A couple of monitors sit on the table. Nina frowns and picks up a monitor, and I grab the other.

"Just place that one over here," she instructs. "Sorry, I cleaned this area; someone must have sneaked in here for a quick meeting." She sighs. "Please have a seat."

I settle in, and my nerves jump to attention. Remember, I chide myself, what you'd tell your candidates in prep: 'Don't think of this as an interview, think of it as a chat with your friend.'

She opens her folder to reveal my resume and application. "I'm the manager of staffing and a few other related functions. When the team reviewed your resume, we were impressed with your background. Your company closed a few years ago. Why did you stop recruiting?"

4

If I was considering a recruiter with my background, that would be my first question.

I sit straighter to radiate confidence. "I recruited for several large corporations in the Valley. When the recession finally hit the tech community, my clients stopped hiring, and I was forced to close shop."

That was the diplomatic way of describing some of the darkest times in Silicon Valley. Companies were posting jobs with no intention of hiring. They used the time to cut the fat, pare down benefits, and lay off non-essential workers in an effort to ride out the storm.

Nina glances at my resume. "You were a business consultant for the last few years?"

"Yes, and I enjoyed it, but I want to continue my career and I think Drachen would be a great place to begin again." I stop talking. Number one rule of interviewing is to answer the question, then shut up and wait for the next one. I've had a few candidates that I've prepped for interviews ignore my rule and talk their way out of a job.

She levels her gaze at me, not satisfied with my response. "Why not re-open the business?"

"That's a fair question." I say, validating her concern. "I've been out of staffing for a few years. The players are different, and new industries have emerged. It takes time to pipeline new candidates and find client companies. I've done that and was successful, but I'm looking for a new challenge."

"If you were hired here, you'd have to do some of what you've outlined." She says this with a slight challenge in her voice.

I contract my stomach to stop the anxiety that's beginning to build. "It's different." I come back with more conviction. "As Drachen's recruiter, I can pull from your enormous database of applicants that have already shown interest in your company. My direct access to your hiring managers would help me to pipeline the right candidates. I'd be building on an established foundation. How could I compete with the resources of a multibillion-dollar company?" I have before, but she didn't need to know that part; best to leave that information out.

The left side of her mouth quirks up. I've scored a point. Rule number fifteen: forget about your nerves and observe your interviewer. Unless they're a poker player, you can always gauge where you stand. We chat for an hour, discussing the company and her expectations for the position. After my last answer, Nina produces her phone and checks it. "Sorry, my time went over a little and I'm late for a meeting," she says, making a few taps on her cell.

I start to gather my stuff, grateful that I asked for an early interview and now I'll have hours before my class to relax.

She glances up from her phone. "I'll send the next interviewer down. I've let Haley, our coordinator, know. She's managing the interview today. She may come down to check on you. Let her know if you need anything."

I stop collecting my things. Wait a minute, what?

She must have responded to the surprise on my face. "Didn't Candice tell you? You have four interviews."

No, and I'm going to kill that absent-minded recruiter. She assured me I'd be speaking with the manager when she arranged this meeting. It was supposed to be a quick hour with Nina Madrone, who I researched to an inch of her life. Candice broke rule number five: know who you're going to speak to before the interview so you can do your research.

I drop my bag and plaster a smile on my face. "Yes, she did," I lie. "I was going to ask where the restrooms are on this floor."

Three hours later, I'm escorted back to the lobby. I'm surprised it's still daylight.

CHAPTER 2

Pizza Pizza

The pizza box is threatening to tip out of my outstretched hand as my purse slides from my elbow to the wrist. The fingers of my other hand are trying to push the key into the lock. I manage to open the door to the house without incident. The TV is on, every square inch of the living room floor is taken up with stacks of paper, and there's no one in sight.

"Chloe," I yell, pushing the door closed with my hip. "I've got pizza, come out."

"I'm on the phone," comes the reply from her bedroom.

I place the pizza box and my purse on the kitchen table. Chloe arrives in an oversize T-shirt, jeans, and no shoes. Her dark hair is pulled back into a ponytail. Even with no make-up, I've seen guys give her a second look. She has big brown eyes and a full mouth like our mother. She's much shorter than me and carries her weight in her hips. That full mouth is now frowning at me.

"What?" I say, trying to figure out why my big sister is disapproving.

She points to my bag. "Your purse doesn't belong there."

"It's only going to be there for a second."

"That's what you said about that box in the corner two weeks ago, and it's still there."

I pick up my bag and head for my room with my sister on my heels.

"How did the interview go?"

"It was fine," I say and pitch my bag on the desk and kick off my heels. My sister sits on the foot of the bed cross-legged. I pull off my shirt and skirt. I take a T-shirt from a pile of clean clothes I've yet to fold and push my head through the opening. "Did you wash this in hot water?" trying to get it over my chest.

My sister looks at me critically. "No. Do you think they've grown? Maybe you could transplant some of what you've got on top down to your butt. It might balance you out so you don't look like you're about to tip over," she says, smiling sweetly.

I give her the evil eye and pull on my sweat bottoms. I look like my dad, Zach Ivarsson, who's over six feet. He's a professional bowler who always places in the top five on the money board. My first childhood memory is of my father encouraging me while I pushed a bowling ball down an alley.

I have long, dark hair like Chloe, but I usually wear it in a braid down my back. I'm tall, but not as tall as my dad, with long legs and long limbs. I loom over Chloe, who's displaying a grin like she's ready to burst. I place my hands on my hips; I'm not letting her get away with the old taunt.

"Dear sister," I say, "you're just mad because you're blessed with mosquito bites and have boob envy."

Chloe's eyes widen, then she rocks back on the bed holding her side, laughing. "Good one, Kel," barely getting the words out. "I still say you should be a comedian or at least write comedy."

"I'm glad I keep you amused. Let's eat, I'm starving." I walk out of the room, her laughter trailing me.

I hand my sister a cold beer and she gives me a napkin. I drop into a chair. The open pizza box is wafting heavenly aromas. I pull out a wedge and shove a big piece of Johnny's Pi Explosion in my mouth, and I'm finally a happy camper.

"Kel?"

"Hmmm?" I swallow and I'm about to take another bite.

Chloe looks down at her chest and considers. "Do you think I have mosquito bites?"

"No, you're just right."

She tilts her beer up for a drink. "I spoke to Gwen next door,"

I stop chewing and swallow. Chloe always knows what's going on in the court. The neighbors volunteer all kinds of information to her because my sister has an honest face. "What's the earth-shattering news? Did someone get an electric lawn mower?"

She ignores me. "Gwen, Tom and the kids are moving by the end of the week. He's got a job in Colorado. They're renting the house until they decide whether to sell."

That means new neighbors. I'm going to miss Gwen and Tom, but not their three yappy dogs. I point my pizza slice toward the living room. "Why're there stacks of papers in there?"

She looks over as if she's forgotten the place looks like a how to be a hoarder training video. "I've got to put together a report for the counsel."

Chloe works as an analyst for small city government. Her boss is a councilman who doesn't know how to turn on the copier. She's always stuck with administrative tasks, although they've got two perfectly good admins that have been there since the Clinton administration. "How many trees did you kill as a result of this report?"

"Several, but to their credit, it's recycled paper. I'm not going to bore you with the city's intrigue. It's really too stupid to repeat. Tell me about your interview."

I recall the story between sips of beer and bites of pizza. "They seem to be nice people, although I was consigned to an underground lair during my interview."

She takes a drag on her beer, then stifles a burp. "Sorry." She looks surprised by the noise. "If they offered you the job, would you work there?"

I shrug and close the pizza box. "I've never worked for a company that big. I ran my business alone for a long time; it might be nice not making every decision. Yeah, I think it might be interesting."

"Did you see any cute engineers?"

That's Chloe, always trying to help my pathetic love life.

"I only talked to females. Wait a minute, I take that back. I did talk to a security guard." I'm not going to tell her about the hottie outside of Drachen's reception that stared holes into me, or she'll never stop asking questions about him.

"I was talking to Candice, your recruiter, when you came in. Why didn't you tell me you asked her to find you a job? I haven't talked with her for ages. She says they want to offer you the position."

I sit back in my chair. "Why didn't you tell me this earlier?"

"I know you." She sniffs. "If you hated the place, you'd have taken the job anyway. I wanted to know how you felt about them before I told you, in case I had to talk you out of taking the offer."

"I would not," I complain, then stop. "Okay, you're right. But in my defense, I need the money; I'm dipping too far into my savings. I would need to take something soon."

She waves a hand toward me. "Those big companies are famous for luring you in with money, perks, and benefits, then working you like an indentured servant. Your soul will die if you take something you hate. You're too much of an entrepreneur to survive in a corporate culture."

That's enough of my big sister telling me how to run my life. Just because she was right about my ex-boyfriend doesn't mean she's allowed to make my decisions. "Careful, you're sounding like Mom."

She doubles down and lets the comment sail right over her. "You're not the corporate type; structure is going to make you insane. I say open another business, or better yet, work for Mom. She'd love that."

"You're crazy," I say, defending my position. I might not be the corporate type, but I want to try. Maybe a success at Drachen will erase the failure of closing my company. "If you can do it, I certainly can, what's the big deal?"

Chloe reflects. She's never talked seriously about her work. She usually entertains me with stories of dysfunction, entitlement, or courage. "I thrive in a bureaucracy. The bigger and more convoluted the better. But that's me. I don't want to blaze new territory, I'm happy to be the unassuming cog in a city government wheel. Besides, if I took the city seriously, I'd have opened a vein long ago."

CHAPTER 3

First Day

I follow Nina down a row of cubes, getting the who's-this-person stare from the cube community. At least I'm able to make it to a floor where it's populated with people. We've been walking around poking our heads into offices for Nina to do impromptu introductions to the executives and the CEO. We halt at her office, something small with one wall glassed that affords her the back view of a bank of cubicles. She can see her staff, if they step out of their boxes.

"I'm glad you're here. The rest of the team is anxious to meet you," she says.

What rest of the team? I thought they'd sent everyone downstairs to grill me during the interview.

She opens a drawer. "I have some information I want to share with you." Pulling out an Excel sheet, she places it on her desk.

"Sorry to interrupt," says an excited woman with a blond pixie cut. She has the wide-eyed look of an intern in a black sweater, short plaid skirt, and tights. "You asked me to tell you when they're ready. Everyone's in the conference room."

Nina nods at the new comer. "Kellis, this is your coordinator, Haley. She sits in front of you. Haley will show you how things work here. We'll eventually need another recruiter and I hope working with you will help with her training. We plan to find her replacement once she's ready to take the new role."

"Great to meet you," Haley says with a wide smile.

"You as well," I return, grateful I have someone to help me with staffing.

Nina pushes away from the desk. "We can finish our meeting later. Let's leave now; you're invited as well. This little get-together will give you a chance to see us informally."

We enter a conference room filled with balloons and crepe paper stuck around a sign that says: *Double the pleasure, double the fun, double the joy with a girl and a boy*. About fifteen people are seated around a conference table chatting. In the middle of the huge table is a cake frosted pink and blue. More people are milling about in small pockets.

"Abigail's having twins," Haley says. "Ah, there aren't enough seats for the three of us; let's stand here near the door, and we can grab chairs from another room once the party begins."

"I'm taking that empty seat at the front," Nina says. "I'll introduce you around when Abigail arrives."

A few seconds later, two people are engaged in a heated discussion outside the closed door. A male is pleading with a woman, trying to convince her someone needs her report now. It sounds like he's losing the argument.

"Oh my God," Haley says in an exasperated whisper, "she's leaving... open the door."

Others are silently urging me. "Go ahead," someone whispers. "Open it now!"

I grab the handle and give it a quick jerk. A very pregnant Abigail and the man are staring at me. I don't know what to say; I step back to reveal the people in the room, who jump up and scream "surprise!"

Abigail's mouth drops open. She covers it with her hand and shrieks. Laughter erupts, and she makes thank yous to the room while she takes in the decorations. I think she's going to cry until Haley moves forward and places an arm around her.

I stay by the door. I only know Nina and Haley. After the excitement calms down, I'll attempt to introduce myself to some of the approachable ones, if Nina or Haley forget about me.

"You must be the new recruiter," comes a male voice from behind me.

I face the man who'd arrived with Abigail. I hadn't paid attention to him before, but now I have time to really notice him. He's Mr. Sexy, the guy who opened the door for me the day I interviewed at Drachen. This time, he gives me a real smile and extends his hand. "I'm Matt."

I look up into blue-gray eyes, a wisp of dark hair falling onto his forehead, light stubble on a strong jaw, and I almost forget to shake his hand. I wonder if he recognizes me from the day I was here for my interview. I stretch out my hand and shake his palm. An electric shock shoots through my fingers. We both recoil.

"Sorry," he's looking at his flexing hand, "that's never happened before."

I recover first. "No worries. I'm Kellis, by the way."

He steps closer. "Then you're the new recruiter. Great, we're going to be working together. I supervise the production line in the South San Jose facility. We're adding a temporary night shift and I'm going to need help staffing that crew."

God, he smells good. I know he's speaking, but all I can do is look up, breathe him in, and nod. He's in a pair of dark jeans and a dress shirt. That isn't unusual around here; I'd met the CEO and he was wearing something similar. There's no ring on Matt's finger, but that doesn't mean anything.

"I'm in the office today for a meeting," he breaks into my thoughts. "But when you settle in, I'd like to set up a meeting with you to see the facility and tour the production line."

It might be nice working with a hot production supervisor. Then I remember another rule that doesn't even have a number. It's my dad's when I first started working and he'd notice I was getting a bit too excited about a co-worker. "Kellis, don't get your honey where you get your money," was his stern warning. It's a stupid rhyme, but it sticks in my head when it looks like I might be wandering into dangerous territory with someone who should be off limits. He warned me dating someone at work never turns out well and it's usually the woman that gets hurt. Matt stops talking. He gives me a curious look. I smile and nod. Idiot me lost the thread of the conversation.

"Okay, I'll catch up with you later," he says. "It's nice meeting you." Matt faces the crowded conference room. "I'm late for a meeting,"

"Ah, can't you stay for cake? It's chocolate, your favorite," a woman says.

"You're right it's my favorite and, believe me, if I stay, I'll eat half that cake, but I can't." He turns his attention to the very pregnant woman. "Abigail, sorry about the ruse."

She beams. "Good one, Matt, I owe you for this."

"Well, if you want to pay me back, Abby," he spreads his hands wide, "Matthew is a nice name for a boy."

The conference room gives a collective groan. He throws a wave and strides out of the door.

Nina moves me around the room, making introductions to the HR department. It'll take a couple more interactions with them before I remember everyone's name. Nina finally excuses us, and we stroll back to her office. This time, she instructs me to close the door to intruders.

"I see you've met Matt," she takes her seat.

I swipe my notepad from the chair and sit down. "Yes, he asked me to help him staff a night crew."

"That's some of the information I want to share with you. It's a priority project, along with another."

"Is he the night supervisor for the production facility?"

Nina wrinkles her nose. "Supervisor? He's the CEO of Dark Star. They're a subsidiary of Drachen Technology. He sold the company a few years ago but maintains the management of the company."

That's about the time I left the business. So that's Matt Westmore, one of the Valley's whiz kids who started a company out of college, found angel investors, and soon began to eat the lunch of all his competitors. That would have been another company I'd have gone after as a client, if I was still in business. They paid their vendors well and, in the company's early days, their partying and beer busts were legendary. They were one of the last companies of that era.

"The project I'm concerned about is for a VP from the home office, Kurt Heinrich," she says searching the paperwork on her desk. "He's a rising star who's been assigned here to expand this region. He'll be heading the R & D division. He might bring some personnel with him, an admin or possibly a manager, but it hasn't been decided. While we wait on that decision, he needs to fill out the rest of his team. You'll be working on the hiring of about six new team members." She pushes the sheet toward me. "This is a list of the jobs; the business partner assigned to his team has already worked with him to write the job descriptions."

I pick up the sheet and scan the information. "Is he available if I have questions?"

"That can be arranged. He isn't due in the US for another three weeks, but he'd like to start interviews next week on some of the sales positions."

I glance up from the sheet. "Does that mean we FaceTime?"

"Something like that. We have video equipment set up in a few of the conference rooms. You can have meetings and interviews

17

there." She sits back in her chair. "I'll warn you that it gets a bit tricky. Munich is nine hours ahead of us. The sweet spot for you to meet with him will be 6-8 a.m. For him, it will be 3-5 p.m."

I grimace.

"He's made an exception for you; he's notorious for holding early-morning meetings. Unless you'd like to meet at 11 p.m. for his 6 a.m. meetings." She sighs. "Ah, the joys of midnight meetings. Just be glad we're not working on joint hiring with the Bangalore team."

I'm not a morning person; it wasn't a problem when I managed my company. A lot of recruiting is done after work; at least, it is for me. Candidates seem more receptive after an unhappy day at work.

"You're meeting with him tomorrow at 6 a.m. Haley will go over how to use the video equipment. Good news is that you'll become a pro at it."

CHAPTER 4

Munich Calling

*T*here are only a handful of early birds working this morning on the main floors, but no one is here in the dungeon.

Blurry-eyed and sipping from a mug of coffee, I try to wake up enough to be alert for my meeting with Kurt Heinrich. Thank God Haley walked me through the set-up yesterday; it seems straightforward, so I should have no problems. I tuck my folder of notes for the meeting under my arm and move inside the small conference room. I turn on the light and discover someone has used this room for a meeting after we cleaned. No one is outside the room; there's no one around to hear my complaints. Later, I'll post a sign, warning under pain of death, not to use this room to scare any would-be meeting room wreckers. There's no reason for this carnage; there are enough spaces to choose from around here.

I check my phone. I have seven minutes to move monitors and cups off the table and re-set up the video console. I deposit the cups in the trash and notice a large coffee spill on the table. I don't have time to find a paper towel to wipe it clean. I place my mug near the puddle to remind me to avoid it and test the console. I dial the number to the bridge to call up Kurt's conference room, but no picture appears. I pull the cheat sheet from my training session with Haley. I've followed her instructions and all the lights are flashing except for the one next to the picture icon. Maybe it's the connection? I push the chair aside, drop to all fours, and crawl underneath the table. I try to sort out, from the tangle of wires, which is the right one. There's no one to ask. I feel like an idiot until I see the plug and shove it into the power strip.

"Guten Morgen, Ms. Ivarsson," comes a disembodied voice. "I assume that's you, but I can only see your backside. Did you lose something?"

Shit. There's a big thump when my head hits the table's underside. Great, I'm going to have a goose egg on my head. I crawl out to see the image of an impeccably dressed man peering down at me. The feed is clear. I'm sure he can see me just as well. He's seated in a conference room. The diffused, after 4 p.m. lighting makes him look like a black and white photograph. His dark, trendy European suit with the tie artfully loosened is just enough to signal this is the end of his day.

I slip into my chair. "Good afternoon. The equipment wasn't working." I give him a tight smile to show I'm not fazed by our awkward introduction, but his blond GQ features are not pleased.

"Are you alright? It sounded like you hit your head. Are you well enough to continue?" His English is impeccable, like the rest of him. He must have learned it from an English non-American native speaker; there's only a slight German accent.

I want to rub my head, but I stifle the urge. I think a slight headache is beginning. I hope it isn't the result of a concussion. "I'm fine. How has your day been?"

"Good, Ms. Ivarsson. Did you receive my notes on the types of candidates I'm expecting?"

And the small talk and bonding period is now officially over; it's time to get down to business. "Yes," I say, eying my folder a distance away. I lean out of my chair, resting my forearm on the table to retrieve the paperwork and pen. I slip back into my seat with the folder, but as I pull my arm away, a brown sticky stain blights most of the sleeve of my white shirt. I drop the file on my lap and keep my arm down.

"You seem to be having a bad day already. I hope that coffee wasn't hot." There doesn't appear to be a lot of sympathy, in his bored tone, just a statement of fact. "I can call someone to help you if you're injured. If no one is there at this time of day," he glances at his watch, "I'm sure emergency services would respond."

Now he's just being an ass. "Thank you, Kurt, but I'm fine."

He appears to be ruffled. My tone was not unprofessional, and didn't I say thank you?

"As you wish. Are there any questions?"

"No, not at the moment. How can I contact you if I need to discuss candidates, interviews..."

"Ana Warner is my administrative assistant. Her details were in my notes to you. She'll handle communications between us. Are there any more concerns?"

"No."

"Auf Wiedersehen, Fraulein Ivarsson." He nods and cuts the feed.

I stare at the blank screen. "Okay," I mumble, "I think that went well."

The dark brown stain on my sleeve is now beige after my visit to the restroom. My team hasn't arrived yet. Haley will be in at eight and Nina at nine. IT is still working on my computer. Since I don't have access to the Drachen intranet, I decide to read through company marketing materials and notes from meetings on internal procedures.

A little after eight, Nina appears at my cube. She places her laptop case on the floor and adjusts her bag on her shoulder.

"I came in early to treat you to breakfast and discuss your meeting with Kurt. I've also got some new information on the night crew staffing for Dark Star. There's a place across the street. We can go there. How did it go? All sweetness and light, I hope?"

"Is it legal to fire someone via video conference?" I say.

Nina scrunches up her face. "Ouch, was it that bad? Never mind." She waves her hand to stop me. "Let's go now before the seats are all taken."

The little breakfast spot is filling up with diners. Nina throws out some cheery hellos to some of the people that are standing in line waiting to order. It's a warm, bright morning. We're lucky to find a table outside. I relive my meeting with Kurt for Nina's benefit between bites of muffin. I admit I tell the story with a little more embellishment. I'm channeling my mom's flare for drama. She valiantly tries to stifle a laugh at some of my tale, but a stray giggle manages to escape a couple of times.

"Have you ever met Kurt?" I ask.

"No, I almost slipped into your meeting this morning to meet him. I'd heard he looks like a blond footballer, or what they call a soccer player here. He doesn't look the corporate type. Someone said he should be on the cover of something with those smoldering looks. He's actually followed in the German press. I was just curious."

"I think he's good-looking, but I was too busy trying not to look incompetent while I was on all fours."

"Wait. You say he appeared ruffled after you said 'thank you, Kurt?'"

I nod. "Yes, I said thank you. It was difficult, but I think I managed to be sincere. Aren't they polite in Germany?"

"I should have warned you, but this company is a stickler for formality in the workplace. In the Munich office, everyone uses 'Miss,'

'Mrs.,' or 'Mr.' to address one another, even the higher-ups. We've had transplants from headquarters. The managers don't even address their secretaries by their first name. That would imply a personal relationship. When they established an office in America, that bit of protocol didn't go well here, so we are an exception. But Kurt is from that culture, so he's probably expecting to be addressed as Mr. Heinrich or Herr Heinrich."

"Jeez, the way he's acting it's more like he's expecting Your High Holiness." Nina raises an eye brow. I'm reading slight concern. "I've worked with a lot of hiring managers in the past," attempting to calm her fears, "and most of them were great, but you always have a few problem children. I can do this," I assure her. "I'll kill him with kindness and dazzle him with results. I usually win everyone over in the end."

"I know it's crazy, but for the sake of peace, call him Mr. Heinrich, not Herr Heinrich; that could sound condescending since you're not a native speaker. Oh, and pronounce his name with the 'i' long and the last 'h' silent. Like Heinrick. It's not the German pronunciation, but that's what he prefers."

I take a sip of my coffee. "Sure, I can do that, Mr. Heinrich it is."

"Look on the bright side. He'll call you Ms. Ivarsson, so you'll still be on equal footing."

I look doubtful.

She pushes her untouched coffee to the side and reaches for a folder from her case. "I'm giving you paper until your computer is ready, then you can pull this information off the SharePoint. I've already given you permission to access this on the server."

I take the paper from her. "What's this?"

"Details about the night crew for the production site. I've already had a call from Matt asking when you can visit. I told him as soon as your computer is ready, which should be today. You have a ten o'clock appointment tomorrow to meet him and tour the production line."

The list of jobs looks pretty standard. If he isn't like Herr

Heinrich, I might stand a chance of keeping my job. "Got it, ten, tomorrow. Do you have any advice about Matt?"

Nina glances around the restaurant, thinking. "He has a charismatic personality," she says, like she is ticking off points on a list. "He's able to get the trust of people quickly. He seems very nice, but he didn't get where he is by not watching the bottom line. As long as you produce, and keep it low-key, you should have no problem with him."

I place the sheet in my folder. "What do you mean by low-key?"

"Around here, we call him Matty Ice, you know, like that quarterback. Do you follow football? I mean European and American. You've got to around here; it will make you seem like one of the boys when Cup finals rolls around and they're all in the lunch room watching a game."

I just look at her, wondering how I got so lucky. I know who Matty Ice is, but she knows him too and now I'll have someone else to talk to about sports.

"It's his style of leadership," she continues. "He doesn't like prima donnas or drama. We think it's because of his five-year marriage with that crazed supermodel Jena. She probably burned the drama right out of him. You know she has five memes? Three are from her saying 'please' and rolling her eyes." Nina demonstrates.

I chuckle. I've seen the memes. Nina does a scary good imitation of the drama queen of supermodels. I glance at the paper again. Nina is closing her briefcase with a snap. I smile. "There should be no problem staffing the night crew,"

CHAPTER 5

Dark Production

The production facility is located on the border of San Jose near Communication Hill in an industrial park. I thought I'd been everywhere, but this is part of the south side I haven't visited much.

The receptionist buzzes me into the office. I wander through a long hall with small offices on either side of the corridor that house the supervisors. Heads shoot up or eyes follow me as I walk past open doors. People in locked facilities are always a bit on edge when they see someone new walk around unescorted.

Wendy, Matt's admin, is on the phone when I arrive at her desk. We've met over the phone. She called to confirm this appointment and give me directions.

She leans away from her computer, pushes her glasses further up her nose, and smiles. "Matt's on the phone, but he says to send you in as soon as his light blinks off."

I look around for a seat in case it might be a while. I select the middle chair in a bank of seats against the wall. My laptop and purse are on my lap. I'm taking in the industrial surroundings, when I notice my knee is bumping nervously against my laptop. Wendy looks up at the sound I'm making. I shrug and stop. Other than the brief meeting at Abby's baby shower, I haven't spoken to Matt. I've taken meetings with dozens of execs, but this is Matt Westmore. I wasn't nervous at the baby shower when I thought he was a production supervisor; it seems I am now.

"Kellis, good to see you again," Matt calls from the door. "Come in. I hope this place wasn't too hard to find. Sometimes we lose visitors on the way up the hill. Let's sit here." He motions me to a small table with four chairs. I take a seat and retrieve my laptop to pull up the information Nina and I had discussed.

"What's your deadline for this project?" I'm waiting for the Drachen's launch page to come up.

"Two weeks ago, but I'll settle for from today. How quickly can you begin interviews for the production line?"

"That depends. Will you be interviewing, or will it be me?"

"Hal will--" A man with a thinning combover and a slight paunch appears at the doorway. His curious gaze settles on me, his mouth slit into a tired smile.

"Wendy said to go in."

"Come in," Matt calls. "You can close the door. Kellis, this is Hal Lavery, my newly promoted night supervisor."

I extend my hand. "Good to meet you," he says and takes a seat.

"As I was about to say, Hal will be conducting the interviews with you. If you could do the pre-screens and pass on your recommendations to Hal, he'll choose who he wants to interview."

I nod.

"I was talking to Nina before you came. She understands we're in an emergency situation with hiring this crew. I've convinced her to let you work out of this office a few days a week. There's a vacant space a few doors down; you can use that while you're here. I hope you can start on this project today?" He gives me a searching look.

Nina was right. He's nice enough, but he knows what he wants. I hadn't anticipated that I would split my time between offices. Working here should dampen my attraction to him. He might be Mr. Sexy, but he's not Mr. Perfect.

"That's no problem," I say. Kurt isn't in the US yet and I can schedule the Germany interviews for the crack of dawn and still be here for a full day.

"Great, you come highly recommended by Nina. While you're here, Wendy will do the administrative tasks for you. Hal will give you a tour of the production site. It'll give you a chance to talk about the project. If you don't mind, I'd like you to come back to finish our discussion."

Matt moves to his feet while I close my laptop.

"Leave your things while you're on the tour. They're safe enough here."

I follow Hal out the door. We walk into a small changing area. A woman is standing in back of a counter. "Hi Rita," Hal says to the older woman. "This is Kellis, from HQ; she's the recruiter that will be helping us hire a night crew. We need to get her suited up."

I'm issued my clean wear, which is the most unflattering look. Clad all in white, looking like mad scientists, we walk among the machinery as Hal explains each function. I'm about to ask him a question when I feel another presence. On the other side of the glass enclosure, Matt is leaning against a cube, arms folded and watching the tour. It's a little awkward. He's the CEO of Dark Star... you'd think he would've had a call to jump on or a meeting to attend. I acknowledge him and he smiles back. I'm half listening to Hal while I unobtrusively keep Matt in my line of vision. He appears to have parked himself there for the duration. The tour takes no more than ten minutes. During that time, Matt talks to a few people who wander by and use the opportunity to get his ear. When he isn't engaged with someone, his gaze always comes back to us. During the last part of the tour, Hal moves me to the last station, where some of the crew are seated doing a task that requires small tools for final assembly. We are hidden behind machinery. When we move back, Matt is gone from his observation point.

I return to Matt's office. Wendy is away from her desk, but Matt's door is open. He's studying something on his desk when I tap on the door frame. He glances up, face still in deep concentration until he realizes with a grin it's me. My heart skips at his unexpected attention. I pull my eyes away to my laptop on his desk, embarrassed that I have a strong physical attraction to him.

"What did you think?" he says, not noticing the effect he has on me.

I walk into the office and close the door. "Impressive. It's easy to see why Drachen is the leader in their industry. He settles in his chair as I take a seat, glad to have something solid between us.

"Do you know the history of Dark Star?"

"About as much as anyone in this valley. Nina talked about your company becoming a subsidiary."

"It was a good move for both of us; now we're the engine that drives Drachen's production. Our client is demanding more with a quicker turnaround. This is why I wanted to speak with you. We're barely meeting our production goals. I want you to understand how important it is that we find the right people."

I'm back on solid ground. On a scale of tricky hires, production personnel aren't that difficult to find. I feel confident I can deliver easily.

"I just received new objectives; our client is the government. They've informed me of additional requirements. Not only do we need to find workers with a specific skill set, but they must have an active secrets clearance." My stomach drops. He offers me the paper he was studying. "Here's what we need."

I want to scream some choice expletives. These are engineers, and the pool with this skill set is small. "Please tell me I can look anywhere for these candidates and there are at least incentives I can offer to get them here?"

"HR is working on it and we'll get the okay we need. This is a long-term contract; you can offer at least five years of work."

Matt pushes away from his seat to settle at the front of his desk. The barrier between us is gone. I'm in his orbit, enough to notice the sensual curve of his mouth and his hard, lean body.

"We work as a team here," a slight note of seduction in his voice. "You won't be expected to manage the entire process alone. I'll be working closely with you to get this project done. Is there something you need from me?"

His meaning is clear. If I don't do my part, I'll let the team down, but what he's really saying is that I'll disappoint him if I fail. Good move to bring this to a personal level to get me invested in the work. Nina was right, he's a charmer.

It's still going to be difficult working with Matt if I can't see him as another hiring manager. I glance at the paper, determined not to let my attraction get in the way of my job at Drachen. "Yes, you can help," I say, taking charge. "I'll need strong coffee, cream, one sugar and all the names and cell numbers of your contacts in the industry."

It's well after midnight when I push open the door to the house. Chloe left a few lights on for me so I don't bump around in the dark. After dropping my purse and case and sliding off my heels in the living room, the kitchen is my next stop. My sister left some unidentifiable food in a pot. At least it's something; a couple of potatoes are floating in brown gravy. Instead of looking for a spoon, I open the fridge, push the yogurts aside, and pull out a brown ale. Collapsing into a seat at the kitchen table with my prize, I twist the bottle to a satisfying whoosh. I take a long drag of the cold brew, look up at the ceiling, and sigh. I'm grateful this day is over so my brain can slow down.

"This is the fourth night you've come in after midnight." Chloe's standing in the door, adjusting her robe's sash, drawing it tighter. She stifles a yawn.

I'm still gazing above at a crack that needs repair. "What's in the pot?"

"Stew. It's Mom's recipe."

I grimace.

"Don't worry, it's edible. I didn't use cornflakes. She called earlier. We had a chat, but she left you a foretelling."

I get a familiar niggling of dread when I hear the word foretelling. "Why didn't she leave me a voice mail?" Chloe just looks at me with a *please, this is Mom face*.

I take another drink. Mom never leaves predictions. It's more dramatic to deliver the news in person or through a herald. Mom's a psychic. She uses most forms of divination, but her talent lies in the Tarot. She's dabbled on and off reading for family or friends but didn't turn professional until after the divorce.

"She said she needed to pull cards for you. It was a short spread. Something about two men and a woman that'll disrupt your life. If left unchecked, one or all will cause irreversible damage. Nothing is as it seems."

That's Mom being dramatic. The two men had to be Kurt and Matt, because I kicked Tim out weeks ago and had heard he'd already found a new girlfriend to irritate. But the only woman that could fit that description would be Nina. She didn't have an agenda; we were becoming friends.

"Are you sure she said disrupt?"

Chloe tries to think in her sleepy state. "Now that you mention it, it could have been destroyed."

I take another drink, regretting I asked for clarification.

Mom's predictions have to be viewed on a sliding scale. Disrupt or destroy could mean a threat of epic proportions, but more than likely it's that I had to work late on some project. "Nothing is as it seems" is her tag line. She used it as the title of her first book.

"You need to talk to Mom. You might be lucky and get details, but don't count on it."

I might consider booking a session with her to get on her calendar. She has clients that pay a premium for her advice. She founded Madre Luna, an institute in the hills of Los Gatos for people to explore spirituality and divination in a spa resort setting. But of course, the jewel in the crown is the psychic hotline. Our family of six struggled to make ends meet on Dad's bowling earnings. But when Mom took over the family finances after the divorce, it was a big house, private schools, and vacations that coincided with book tours and TV spots. I still can't figure out how she managed to earn a doctorate in Philosophy between raising us and managing a growing empire.

"I'll call Mom later. I need to catch up with her; maybe she can find some time to have lunch."

Chloe moves to the fridge, filling a frosty glass with water. "Why are you so late?"

My stomach rumbles on cue. I stare at it; apparently liquid sustenance isn't enough.

"I'll get your dinner," she says. "Start talking."

"Nothing earth-shattering. I'm working on two big projects with two demanding hiring managers. I've been on the phone most of the evening."

"Who're you calling this late at night?"

"I was talking to Ana, Kurt's admin, from the Munich office. I don't talk to Herr Heinrich much, so she keeps me updated. You're right that it's too late to call anyone in the US, but I was also running searches to identify potential candidates. I'm running out of time. I'm seriously thinking of coordinating a kidnap attempt to get these engineers in here."

She places a steaming bowl of stew in front of me. It smells edible, but I frown at it. "Am I supposed to scoop this up with my fingers or does a spoon come with this?"

"Ha ha," she says and produces a spoon and a paper napkin. "Here, although it might have been funnier watching you eat cavewoman style." She takes a seat across from me. "You always suggest desperate measures, but in the end, you get it done. I think you like the drama like Mom."

I shove some of the food in my mouth. Chloe is lying; this is her creation. Mom's talents were never in the kitchen. "Kurt's hires are going without a hitch; thank God. Maybe that's why I don't see much of the big scary man unless he has to growl at me about something that displeases him; other than that, he's quiet. He's due in the US in a week, then he can growl at me in person. The last hire for him will be his second-in-command. That'll be difficult; he hasn't liked anyone I've suggested he interview." I glance at the half-empty bowl. There's an unexpected hint of thyme in this savory stew. I'm surprised this warm comfort food is really good. It might be hard to stop after one bowl.

CHAPTER 6

What Do You Do?

I've just settled a nervous candidate and introduced him to Herr Heinrich. It's 9:00 a.m. here. It's a reasonable time to ask a candidate to interview, but Ana warned me Heinrich grudgingly agreed to the 6:00 p.m. meeting his time.

I shut the door as Kurt is beginning his interview with the candidate when my cell signals a text. 'Where are you?' is all it says from Nina.

I text back, 'In the lower level, interview for Kurt. Why?' She's texting something back. The little dots vibrating on the screen are making me anxious.

'Come to the large conference room on the first level now, no time to explain.'

I skip the elevator for the stairs, my heart pumping from the message as I race up to the next level. My heels are clacking on the steps, the sound echoing in the deserted stairwell. I try to figure out what I've done to warrant an immediate summons. When I get to the main floor, a good portion of the cubes are deserted. I walk quickly, heading for the north end of the building. As I approach the door of the room, Nina slips out, concern on her face as she looks around. She grabs me by the arm and urges me into the room. All of HR is jammed into the space. We receive furtive glances, but the room's attention is focused on a woman at the end of the conference table who is speaking. Her eyes watch me as Nina and I park ourselves on the opposite end of the room, our backs to the wall.

The woman finishes her sentence. "And I expect everyone to be on time when I call a meeting," directing the comment to me.

I start to speak, but Nina intervenes. "Kellis is our new recruiter; she was left off the email blast and wasn't aware of your invitation."

The woman appears unconvinced. "Don't let it happen again."

I stifle an urge to ask who this woman is and why she would call a meeting. "It's been fixed," Nina offers.

The woman nods.

Maybe she's someone visiting from Munich. She sounds American, but that doesn't mean anything; some employees from the Americas are promoted to work in the home office, especially the ambitious ones that want a leadership role in the company. No matter, I'll only have to endure her for a few days at most. I'm lucky, I move around between here and Dark Star.

I must have missed most of her talk because we're dismissed after a few more questions. Nina and I are the last to file out. I'm anxious to find out who this woman is. "Nina, Kellis," the woman calls after us. "I'd like an update on the Heinrich and Dark Star projects. Let's talk in my office." She strides confidently ahead of us as we trail behind like obedient ducklings. She's almost as tall as me, and her navy suit is tailored and expensive. Her auburn hair is pinned in a chignon. Her make-up is flawless on pale skin that shouldn't spend any time in the sun.

I text Haley as we're walking, asking her to monitor the interview downstairs.

We slip into what I thought was a vacant office. A few unpacked boxes sit on the small meeting table in the corner. There's an empty box on the floor near her large executive desk. She's unpacked some photos and mementos. There are a couple of photos of small dogs, her standing with a conservative politician, in sunglasses leaning against a white sports car, and a few scattered awards. Maybe the family photos would come later?

"Kellis," Nina says, as we take seats, "Allison Mackey is the new VP of Human Resources." She's trying to stave off some of the most obvious questions I have. I smile at her.

She nods, sizing me up.

I give her the same gaze, *yeah, I'm taking your measure too*. It's reminiscent of two cats circling one another, trying to find the most vulnerable spot to scratch. I'll have to ask what happened to Jack Rogers, the VP Nina was reporting to.

Allison slips into her seat. She grabs a small rubber green alien doll from her desk and begins squeezing it as she talks. "Munich has told me you're in charge of the hires for Kurt Heinrich. What's the status?"

I've run upstairs without my laptop; I'd have to look confident and wing it. "The hiring for the sales and application engineers should be completed today. Mr. Heinrich is interviewing the last candidate now. The only hire left is the second-in-command, the senior manager's position."

Her gaze travels to the window; the day promises to be gray. Her silence is a little too long. She pitches the doll on the desk and smiles. "It's my stress reliever." She indicates the green doll. "I hear they are pleased with the candidates, so I'm pleased. But I understand you weren't so successful with the senior manager's position."

"The process is still ongoing. The hiring manager will be here next week to conduct the final round of interviews."

35

"Have you hired for manager level in the past?"

That's a loaded question. I'm sure she reviewed my resume; she knows the answer. "Yes, all the way to senior manager."

"But no executives, is that right?"

"No, no execs." watching her roll something around underneath that perfectly coiffed hair. I hadn't wanted to do executive recruiting; that's a whole other animal.

"Because it's the second for an executive VP, I consider it an executive search. This position is a high priority. I've contracted a firm that specializes in these hires."

"But," I begin to protest. I see Nina shoot me a warning glance to shut up. I guess I'm used to managing my own firm and handling high-powered clients on my own. "I've already begun the process. Kurt--"

Allison's eyebrow arches.

"Mr. Heinrich has identified who he wants to speak with, and I've already contacted them to conduct prelims." Allison turns to Nina for clarification.

Nina leans forward on the arm of her chair. "Prelims are preliminary interviews. Kellis conducts them. It's a short, friendly interview. She's gaging interest, finding out if the candidate is a fit for the company/team… even salary range is discussed."

"But you're not technical? Why would you conduct an interview?"

"The technical portion of the interview is left to the team," I say.

Nina interrupts before Allison can frame another question. "Gathering this information helps us when it's time to craft an offer to the candidate."

My guess is that Allison never worked on the staffing side of a business. Most people think we just stick an ad online and hope for the best. Looks like we'll need to carefully educate her about our roles.

Allison swings her chair around. She eyes the green man on her desk but decides not to pick it up. "I'm sure for what we're paying Exigent, they have some kind of prelim they conduct. As for the work you've already completed, I'm sure the firm will be grateful for your legwork. Please turn over all notes and schedules to your coordinator. She'll assist them with any support on our side. This will free you up to concentrate all your attention on Dark Star."

Did she say Exigent, that high-priced executive search firm that has the highest retainer in the industry? They're new on the scene, formed by three execs from two of the powerhouse talent acquisition firms. She's right about what Drachen is paying them, and they keep that money whether they're successful or not.

There's light tapping on the door.

"Did I get the meeting time wrong?" We turn our attention to Matt Westmore's tentative grin. "Did Jack move his office? I got a message I had a meeting with him."

Allison moves her gaze down his body like a predator sizing up lunch. "That meeting would be with me." She springs to her feet and skirts her desk, extending a hand. "I'm Allison Mackey, the new VP of HR. Jack was kicked upstairs to Munich. Managing HR was only a temporary assignment for him until they found a permanent replacement. I guess the announcement hasn't gone out yet. Please come in. We're just wrapping up. You're just in time. Kellis is about to give us a status on Dark Star's staffing."

Matt acknowledges Nina and I, then takes a seat. They all stare at me. They're waiting for a report that isn't going to make me look brilliant. There've been some glitches with the hiring. A candidate we thought was a good fit decided that he didn't want to move to California. Matt and I are scheduled to meet over his concerns later this afternoon. If Allison is unsatisfied with my handling of Dark Star, she might replace me. Matt clears his throat. "If Kellis doesn't mind, I can give the status."

Allison leans in, anticipating the report. I wonder if she already knows about the candidate declining our offer and is looking forward to Matt complaining about how I wasn't able to find the people he needs. Nina is chewing her lip, worried. I've already let her know about the problem. Chloe was right, I'm not cut out for corporate. It looks like I'm going to be working for my mother after all.

"We selected a candidate," Matt says, "but he declined our offer..."

My phone zips. I glance down at a message from Haley. The candidate I left to interview with Kurt is leaving and asks to speak with me. I look up to see Allison's annoyed face. "I apologize for the text, but we're running interviews today. Haley is managing the process while I'm gone but a candidate has asked to speak with me before he leaves. This is a potential hire for the Heinrich team."

I didn't return to my cube upstairs; instead I hid in the dungeon in an abandoned office I use as a makeshift base when I'm conducting phone interviews. I thought about calling Nina, but they were probably still in the meeting deciding how best to get rid of me. I'm too deep in thought to notice a tall man standing in the door tapping lightly.

"Haley told me where to find you," Matt says, sliding into the chair across from me without an invitation. He looks around, taking in the small, abandoned office. Everything about it looks makeshift. It's decorated with secondhand everything, useful things that aren't shiny and new any longer. "I like what you've done with the place."

The joke falls flat, but I nod and look around. I don't think he's here to fire me; I'm sure Allison wants that pleasure all to herself.

"That was an interesting meeting," he muses.

I say nothing, waiting for him to get to the point. Our regular meeting is scheduled for the end of today at his office. There's something on his mind. If he wanted to cancel, he could have done that over the phone.

"I've never met Allison before, but I know her reputation. Let me back up. I know the man who mentored her, so if she's adopted even a tenth of that man's managing style you're in for a rough ride."

"Thanks for the warning."

"I sense you're new to corporate life?"

"Is it that obvious? Before this, I owned a staffing company."

He leans back in his chair. "I know it's different when you're not the one in charge. It can be pretty Darwinian, like an episode of Survivor."

He didn't need to point out that I was in way over my head.

"Since you're not higher up on the food chain, you'll need allies. People who'll come to your defense and make it harder to push you out."

"I haven't been here long enough to form alliances. I'm a contractor, so she can dismiss me at any time. I work here at her pleasure."

"I didn't know about the contract part, but the rules still apply. Make it difficult or inconvenient for them to disregard you. You do have an ally. Nina was fighting hard for you after you left."

"What happened?"

"That's right, you didn't hear my report. Alexander did decline the offer, but a Drachen employee is interested in the position. She's more than qualified and her current project is ending. I want to move her over to the open job and I'd like you to backfill her old position."

"Then why is Nina fighting for me?"

"Allison thinks you should have known that Alexander wouldn't have taken the job. She looked over your notes. You indicated he had declined to discuss the job initially but later called to say he was interested. She thinks that's a red flag you ignored."

"I'm not to take candidates at their word when they contact me about interest in a position?"

"Something like that. I told her you did bring it to my attention and that I made the decision to pursue him, but I don't think she was

39

convinced until Nina said it was proper to advise me, but to follow my wishes."

"I like Nina, she's a great boss, but she's middle management and not able to fend off someone like Allison, so basically, I have a cheerleader."

"I fought for you too."

He sits there unaffected by the earthquake-inducing statement. This is Matt freaking Westmore. We've been working together for the past few weeks, but I never thought he would think I was worth saving. Either he likes my work or he dislikes Allison Mackey. "Thanks, I think?"

"Before you get too excited, there's a selfish reason why I defended you. We've gone through three recruiters in the last year and all of them were disasters. You've been quick, efficient, and intuitive. I like that. And I'm not about to start over again with someone else."

"You did this for self-seeking reasons?"

"You betcha." Matt stands. "I expect to see you later today at our meeting. We need to discuss the backfill."

I sit for a little longer after he leaves, daydreaming about Matt saving me from the clutches of Allison. Then I remember my mother's prediction that I'd have to watch out for two men. And I'm willing to bet that Matt is one of them. But I can't deny this persistent fluttering in my stomach when he's around. Although I've noticed no matter how much time we spend together, I don't get the impression that he has the same feelings. My father's words come back to me: "Don't get your honey where you get your money, daughter." What can I say? Forbidden honey is so sweet. My cell rings. I'd almost forgotten that Kurt normally calls after his interviews to discuss the candidate.

"I have to say that the last candidate you suggested was decent enough. But he didn't have much charisma." Kurt's voice is going in and out.

I head to the stairwell that leads to the back parking lot in search of a signal.

"He had all the answers, but his personality is somewhat lacking."

Kurt sounds like Henry Cavill when he's talking to me, his audience of one.

"I often wonder why people like him climb the corporate ladder. But I bet if I dig deeper, he probably has a family tie. Ms. Ivarsson, are you still on the line?"

He launches into another diatribe before I can take a breath, but I interrupt him anyway. "Yes, I'm still here. If you would like us to dig a little deeper into his background, that can be arranged. That will have to be a job for the next recruiter."

There's dead silence. "What are you saying? Ms. Ivarsson?"

Ah, that got a little of his German accent to make an appearance.

"Are you tired of the project already or have you decided to abandon me?"

He always makes everything about him and his world. "No, I've been taken off the project. You'll be working with Exigent, an executive search firm."

"This position isn't for an executive. Why would an executive firm search for a senior manager's position? Is this Rogers' idea?"

"Rogers has returned to his old duties. They've hired Allison Mackey as the new permanent VP."

"I wasn't told about a new VP or this change in staffing. Are you sure you didn't do something?"

Now he's just being irritating. This is probably for the best. Maybe Exigent would have better luck working with Herr Heinrich. "No, I didn't do anything," I shoot back with more irritation than I should. "I wasn't asked about the decision or about the firm that would be doing the search. If you have any questions, I suggest you talk to Allison Mackey."

"I plan to, Ms. Ivarsson." He clicks off.

CHAPTER 7

Candy

Normally, I make the commute to South San Jose just after the morning traffic. But I have to be at Dark Star for a 6 o'clock meeting and I'm fighting my way through the evening traffic.

Wendy is packing up her desk when I arrive. She informs me that Matt and Hal are on a conference call and it might be a little while before they'll be free. She sticks her head inside the office and motions that I'm outside waiting.

The office occupants are sparse on this side of the building. Crews in the clean room run 24 hours, so the building doesn't appear to be deserted. I sit on a chair checking my emails when the office door opens.

"Sorry about the wait, Kellis. We were on the phone with a client and it ran long." I walk by him into the office to take a seat at the small table, where I greet Hal.

"I've already filled Hal in on the last hire for the special project.

He agrees that Marianne Davis would be a good addition to the team and we just found out that she's a contractor who is finishing up her assignment. The job she's leaving doesn't exist any longer; lucky for us there'll be no position to backfill."

"Then why are we meeting?" That popped out before I could censor the question. "I mean, I'm always glad to work with Dark Star, but if I have no more staffing duties..." I trail off, noticing the two men with amused looks on their faces.

Matt grins. "Who says there's no more staffing to be done for Dark Star?" He looks at Hal, who shrugs. Matt eases back into his seat. "We've just completed hiring for the government project but there are always new hires and new projects. I haven't spoken to Allison yet, but I'm going to make sure you are here permanently, at least a few days out of the week, to work with our team."

Hal nods an agreement.

I'm glad. I enjoy working with Hal; he's taught me a lot about production.

"We've had our hands so full with staffing the government project that we haven't had a chance to introduce you to the rest of the employees in this location. We're having a celebration party next week and would like you to come. It's important that you be a part of the Dark Star culture."

This was still a wasted trip; he could have told me this over the phone.

"I know I asked you to come out here at the end of the day for a meeting, but what I really wanted to do is to thank you for all the hard work that you've done to staff our team in record time. Hal doesn't know this, but I wanted to invite you and Hal to a dinner tonight so we can relax and have our own celebration before the next onslaught of hirings. What do you say, do you both have time tonight so we can now go to a nice restaurant? Your choice."

Hal is already shaking his head, declining the offer. "I'm sorry,

44

I can't. My wife and I are going to a recital for one of the grandkids tonight."

"That's okay, we can plan for another night."

"Don't change your plans on my account," Hal says.

Matt turns his gaze on me and I almost do a little shiver. "Would you like to go out to dinner? I'd like to thank you for your work, but if you have other plans, I understand."

Plans were for someone with a life. I had nothing for tonight and possibly the next three months. But he didn't know that. Chloe's voice is in my head saying don't be an idiot. Accept it. I can't forget he defended me in front of Allison, a dinner with him is the least I can do. "Sure, I'll have dinner, no problem."

The restaurant isn't ready to seat us, so we wait. We're the only people seated at the end of a long ebony bar. The bartender asks me what I'm having. I'd prefer a beer, but it doesn't seem right to chug a bottle of brew in an upscale restaurant. The bartender takes pity on my indecision and creates a cocktail for me after a few questions. Matt orders a whiskey.

The mango-infused drink is like sweet sunshine and I make a mental note to ask him what it's called. Matt tips his glass toward me in a quasi-toast.

I mimic the gesture and take another sip.

"Have you always lived in this area?" he says.

My throat constricts. I nearly choke. I grab the napkin coaster thing and place it over my mouth. It's too early to talk about my quirky family. Matt slides his coaster napkin over to me in case mine isn't enough. I give him a raspy thanks and grab that too.

"Sorry if that sounds like a cheesy pick-up line. I'm out of practice at small talk."

"No, it's fine. I'm from this area--"

His phone rings. He pulls it out of his jacket and frowns. "Sorry, I need to take this; it has to do with work."

Matt slides off the stool, talking in a low, agitated voice out the door. I sip my drink for a while, waiting for him to return. I finally drain the glass. The bartender scoots over. "Another?" he asks.

"Yes, but make this a virgin." This is still work and I'm not getting drunk with a hiring manager. I need a clear head to make my family appear normal.

The bar is starting to fill and the volume of conversations is increasing as groups take their seats. I hate sitting alone at a bar. It feels like I'm waiting around for a hook-up. I watch people through the mirror in the back of the bar and stretch out my drink for as long as I can, but there's no sign of Matt.

The hostess has already come over twice to tell me our table is ready. After she returns for the third time with a *you need to take this table now or I'll give it to someone else smile*, I reluctantly follow her to café-size tables along the distressed brick wall facade. She indicates a chair sandwiched between two tables where couples are already seated. There's only one place setting. I shimmy into the tight space, nearly bumping the man in back of me. I'm close enough to notice the man's woodsy aftershave. Why do upscale restaurants think they need to place you five inches away from people you don't know? "There should be another plate; I'm dining with someone," I call to the hostess' retreating back. She halts and turns, not pleased.

"The reservation is for one."

I throw her a look. "Please set another place… my companion will be arriving soon."

Her cold, bored gaze holds mine for the briefest of seconds. "I'll have a table set immediately."

I try not to listen to the hushed conversations from the other tables. I don't have a problem dining alone, but I wouldn't have chosen this place for a solo dining experience. A livelier restaurant would be a better choice. The key is to ignore the pitying glances of others, but then again, I'm not alone. I sigh, why does stuff like this happen with someone you barely know? I search the dining room. Matt still hasn't returned. Maybe it's time to call a car and make my escape. I slump down a little to reach underneath the table. I rummage inside my purse, trying not to disturb the guy in back of me.

"Kellis?" comes a bewildered male voice. Conversations abruptly stop near me.

I'm concentrating on my fingers curling around my phone. "Got it," I whisper, then look up from my hunched position. Tim, my ex, is looking down at me with a self-satisfied grin.

"Thought that was you." He's focused on the one table setting and shakes his head. "Having dinner alone? Couldn't find anyone to keep you company?" The fake sadness is irritating.

"Go away," I say, straightening up and vigorously swiping at my phone.

Tim slips into the vacant seat at the table. He can be thick as a board sometimes. He's a big handsome hottie and sex with him was mind altering. That's why our relationship lasted six months longer than it should have.

I set down the phone. "What part of go away did you not understand? Didn't I say it in English?"

The grin turns into a smirk, "Same old Kellis… why am I'm not surprised you're here alone?" He drops his voice to a stage whisper. "I still miss that feisty vixen in my bed." He slides his hand across the table to find mine. I retreat and stare at him." The couples around us are listening.

"Don't be like that." He looks hurt. "It's only been a few months; by now I thought you'd have reconsidered and come back to me."

A flush of anger heats my face. This is the stuff of nightmares. My ex is publicly embarrassing me while my real date, or whatever he is, has done a runner. "Maybe you'll believe me if I have you dragged away." Hopefully that bluff will work. If not, I'll try to extricate myself from this chair and leave.

"Hey, babe. I thought you were going to wait for me at the bar," a honeyed voice asks. She raises an eyebrow when she sees me. "Oh, hello," the woman tosses her long blonde locks back, then extends her hand to me. "I'm Candy, Tim's girlfriend."

"Sweetheart," Tim says. "I didn't see you come in." He turns to take in the room. "I got here early. I was at the bar talking to Jerry, that new bartender, when I see my old recruiter sitting alone," Tim replies with an overlay of charm. "This is Kellis, she's the one that got me the job at Variance."

He's given too much emphasis to the word old. Candy is only a few years younger than me. "Nice to meet you," I say with a fake smile. At least he didn't claim I was his last girlfriend.

I look at her more closely. Her pretty features look familiar. This woman isn't his usual type. He likes them conservative on the outside, wild on the inside. At least that's what I thought. Looking at her, I think maybe he doesn't have a type.

"Candy is a chef," his arm snakes around her waist. "You might have seen her show *Candy's Kitchen*?"

Now I remember. She has a cooking show on a local cable channel that's only seen in Santa Clara county. I've seen an article about her in the *Metro*. Her show is campy, like Betty Paige meets Betty Crocker. She dresses provocatively while she cooks in a sexy, girly kitchen and gives health and exercise tips.

"Sorry, Sugar," Tim gives her a squeeze.

He used to call me 'Sugar' when we were together. You'd think he'd have found a different pet name for her. "Could you find the hostess and tell her we're ready to be seated?" His arm falls away from her waist and she gives him a pouty frown. "Please, Sugar, Kellis wants to tell me about a new opportunity and I don't want to bore you. I'll only be a few minutes, then I'll give you my full attention."

She smiles wide enough to brighten the room. "It's great meeting you," she coos at me. "If you ever want to see a taping of *Candy's Kitchen*, email me through the website. I'll give you the VIP treatment since you worked for Tim." She waves before weaving her way around tables to find the hostess. Tim watches her backside with interest.

"Now will you leave?" I hiss. As soon as he leaves, I'm going to bolt for the exit and Uber back to my car.

He turns his attention to me. "The word on the street is that you're the recruiter for Drachen?"

What fresh hell... I give an exasperated, "Yes, that's right."

He traces the condensation on my water glass. "I know you were bummed when you closed your business. Seriously, I'm glad you went back to doing what you love." There's a faint note of sincerity in his voice. This is a glimpse of the old Tim, the one I dated in the early weeks of our budding relationship. Sweet, supportive, and he listened to me occasionally. "I like Variance, but I've always wanted to work for Drachen. If you come across something you think I might be a fit for, let me know."

My recruiting brain kicks in. I like finding perfect talent for the right company and Tim is a talented software engineer. A Texas A & M grad, from Texas and a talker, unusual for an engineer. That's why companies wanted him for technical sales or marketing positions. After I'd placed him with Variance, he was my gateway to more staffing assignments for the company. The windfall of fees was unbelievable that year. All that time working with him, we'd gotten close. The night I took him out to celebrate his new job, we tumbled into bed at the end of the evening and stayed together for two years. If Tim working for Drachen ever became a reality, I didn't know how I would handle seeing my ex frequently. Maybe he would consider another site outside of California?

"Kellis? You haven't said anything."

49

"I'll think about it," I say grudgingly.

Tim leans onto his elbows. "That's all I ask. And Kellis…" The way he says my name gives me pause. "I've missed you. Earlier was my hurt ego talking; I want you back."

This is too much personal stuff floating out about me in the ether. We're providing too much entertainment for my fellow diners. He needs to be gone and me shortly after. "You should leave. I'm waiting for…"

"No one," that lazy smirk returns. "Or is it a taciturn engineer you're trying to convince to take an offer?"

He's right. I've been abandoned; no one is coming.

I'm watching Candy in an animated conversation with the hostess. "What about your date?"

"She's nice, but she's not you." He leans in closer. "Let's talk about this later…"

"You're sitting in my seat," rumbles an irritated voice. The hum of conversation stops.

Tim doesn't take his gaze from me. "Give me a minute, buddy, this is a private conversation. The lady wants me here." I look up and shake my head and mouth "no."

"If you don't get up, I'm going to haul your ass out of that chair."

No response from Tim. He catches my hand and holds it. I try to tug it away.

"This is Matt Westmore, my date." I emphasize the word 'date.' I'll deal with Matt's reaction to that later. "He's the CEO of Dark Star."

Tim releases my hand and looks up. Our industry is too small for him not to know who Matt is. "Aw…Matt…right," he says recovering quickly. "We met a few years ago at a conference in Vegas."

Matt doesn't respond.

"Kellis and I go way back. I dropped by to talk to an old friend."

The busser arrives with the second place setting. Matt says

nothing, continuing to glare down at him.

It dawns on Tim that this line of conversation isn't fruitful. He glances over his shoulder. "I've got to get back to Candy. I see she's already at our table." He scrambles to his feet and extends a hand. "I'm Tim Cortez; maybe the three of us could meet for a drink and talk shop?"

Matt shakes his hand. "Have a good evening."

Tim nods, then throws an unfazed glance in my direction. "Kellis, nice seeing you. We'll talk soon. Enjoy your evening."

Matt slips into the seat. The busser swiftly arranges his placement. Tim has seated himself a few tables away in my line of vision, but Matt's back is to him. Is this episode too much drama for the low-key Matty Ice? I keep hearing Nina in my head, 'As long as you keep it low-key, you'll be fine.'

"The waitress will be with you shortly," says the busser and leaves.

"I apologize for the long wait." His face is unreadable. "Another call slipped in after the first and that was a bigger crisis. Do you really know that guy? The hostess said you might need saving."

I hesitate. He's searching my face. Best to tell the truth. "I placed him at Variance a while ago in sales." He turns around. Tim nods at him. How did he know Tim was watching us?

"Is he an engineer?"

"Yes, he is. Software, Texas A & M."

Matt grunts. I'm not sure if it's his phone call or Tim that has him in a mood.

"You know we can do this another time," I offer. "If you need to take care of something…" I wasn't sure, but I didn't think he planned to work during dinner. But if he's monitoring a crisis, at least I can give him the option and let him choose.

"No, I'd like to have dinner but not here. I'm guessing one of your previous hires is going to stare at you through our meal. Let's get out of here and find another place to eat." He produces a wallet and places a couple of bills on the table. The waitress arrives. We remove ourselves from the confining spaces. "Sorry," Matt says, "but we've changed our mind." Matt cups my elbow and keeps his body between me and the diners. I can't see Tim or Candy as we walk between the tables.

We're full of falafels and banana shakes, from the Falafel Drive-in. Even after professing our love for a good falafel, and recalling how we each found this place, it feels like we're back to square one of getting to know each other.

Matt suggests we stroll through Santana Row, an upscale shopping district that looks like somewhere in Europe. There's outdoor music tonight, something soft and jazzy. They've begun decorating for the holidays, garland mixed with holiday sales posters in the windows.

The lights from the stores and restaurant emit a soft, romantic glow. All this ambiance is wasted on two young, healthy people who aren't in love or on a date.

"I want to get to know you," Matt says, motioning to a bench. We sit, keeping a little distance. I'd feel safer if there was a desk between us. Then I'd have protection from his blue eyes or the smell of him that distracts me when he's near.

He places his arm on the back of the bench. "Maybe I should go first. I promise no cheesy lines." His smile is warm, the kind that invites a kiss. I can't even blame my thoughts on a drunken haze. I catch my braid to pull it to my front. His attention is on my hand. "Your hair is very long... have you always worn it like this?"

He's fascinated. I've seen the look before. The urge to unravel my hair or unravel me. His eyes follow my fingers as I stroke my braid. I do this to calm myself, like a security blanket. "My mother kept my hair short when I was a kid. It's thick so it's easier to manage it short.

When I was old enough to do my own hair, I let it grow. I'd be tripping on it if I allow it to grow past my waist."

His gaze is unfocused like he's thinking about something else. "I bet you look like a dark-haired Lady Godiva." He stiffens, realizing what he said. "Sorry if I've overstepped."

He's picturing me naked on a white horse riding through the streets of Coventry. "No, you haven't overstepped. I'll let you know when that happens. And, for the record, I've been told that before." not hiding my amusement.

He coughs. "Good to know. Maybe we should talk about something else? Did your mom stay home or did she work like her daughter?"

How to explain my mom? "She stayed home with my brother and two sisters until my parents divorced, when I was thirteen. She went back to school after the break-up to get a doctorate in Philosophy."

"Did she open up a little philosophy shop after she graduated?"

"No," I giggle.

He's about to laugh at my reaction. I fight the urge to touch him; the light falls softly on his face, eyes teasing. He looks at me a little too long then looks away, shaking his head.

"She writes books," I chide, needing to steer the conversation away from Reny Ivarsson; professionally she uses her birth name Renee Exton or Dr. Exton. The clients think it's more legitimate to get a Tarot reading from a doctor. "I thought you were going to tell me about yourself?"

"You're right. I did… what do you want to know?"

I watch couples strolling down the sidewalk, wondering how their first date had come about. Then I think this might be the perfect opportunity to change things up a bit. "We could drone on all night about our relatives and where we went to school, but I want to know the real you."

"Sounds intriguing," he says, but there's no denying his slight reluctance. "What do you suggest?"

"I'll ask you three questions and you have to answer them truthfully without hesitation."

"You mean truth or dare."

"Please," I say, waving a dismissive hand, "we're not sixteen. More like an association test. The key is not to censor your responses. Say the first thing that comes to mind."

"Okay, I'll agree to play."

I narrow my eyes at him. "This isn't a bogus party game; I'm conducting a serious experiment."

He surrenders, throwing up his hands. "Okay, I mean participate," he corrects, still with a wisp of a grin on his face. "Only if you answer the same questions too. That's fair, right?"

"Deal." I'm anxious to loosen up Mr. No Drama. "The topic is guilty pleasures."

"Stuff you don't admit to?"

"Yes."

"Okay," he stares at me.

"Food."

"Spam."

"You mean compressed pig meat?"

He rubs his chin, like I've presented him with new and puzzling information. "It doesn't sound appetizing when you put it like that." He shrugs. "I like a slab of fried Spam, mayo, on white bread. It reminds me of my childhood. I grew up on a farm in Vermont. My tastes are simple. Now you."

"Potato chips," I half whisper. "Anything with a potato."

"Why wouldn't you admit to that?"

"They're a banned substance in my house. I would probably mainline potatoes if I could." I lower my head, ashamed of my lack of control where spuds are concerned. "I'll admit it, I'm a potato junkie."

"Have you seen someone for that?"

I look up in horror. "Potatoes Anonymous?" I suggest.

He's pleading with the heavens. "Next question."

"Okay, second guilty pleasure. Movie or TV show."

"That's easy. *Keeping up with the Kardashians*."

I can't decide if he's teasing. His face is an innocent deadpan. "You're kidding...right?"

"What? Those women are hot and misunderstood."

He's about to say 'your turn,' but I beat him to it. *Taken, Love Actually* or anything with Liam Neeson. I imagine he's my dad and he's coming to kick ass to rescue me or give me advice."

His laugh is loud. "Have daddy issues?"

"Maybe, more like daddy please stay."

His face softens. "I forgot your parents are divorced...sorry. What's the last question?"

"It's not a guilty pleasure. It's a skill question. What are you the best at?"

"Sex," he says, without hesitation.

I open my mouth, but say nothing.

"What?" he says, surprised that I'm still staring at him. "You asked for the first thing that came to mind."

I bark out a surprised laugh. "I'm not comfortable exploring that answer."

He gives a halfhearted shrug. "It's up to you. I'm happy to help with your social experiment. I can give details if you need them."

I shove my hands in my pockets and try to figure out if he's serious or if he's just teasing. No matter, I think I might have seen some of the real Mr. Westmore. I'd never guess this Vermont farm boy would have a wild side. "I don't think I want to go wandering around your psyche any further. I declare my social experiment well and truly over...for now."

He grins. "Are you sure? It was getting interesting." He looks over his shoulder. "Would you like a coffee? I think Cocola is still open;

we can slip in and have dessert."

"Would you mind if we end the evening now?" wishing I could spend more time with him. "I have a 6:30 a.m. interview scheduled with Munich."

The Dark Star parking lot is deserted. Matt pulls up alongside my car. He climbs out, slams the door, and jogs around to my side. Before I touch the door handle, he pulls it open. "I wouldn't be a gentleman if I didn't walk you to your car." I stand, but Matt doesn't move. He's looking down at me with a look on his face that guys get at the end of an evening. He shouldn't kiss me, he shouldn't want to, but it seems like he might try.

I step to the side offering my hand. "I want to thank you for a nice evening," He looks at my outstretched palm and a grin is about to cross his face until he catches that I'm serious. This is not a date; this is two colleagues having dinner.

His hand is big and warm as he shakes. "Thank you for the hard work, Kellis. Dark Star appreciates it."

"You and Dark Star are welcome." Then I head for my car to avoid any more awkwardness.

"Would you think it was weird if I asked you to dinner again? If it had nothing to do with Dark Star or Drachen?" he calls after me.

He says this casually, but tingling bells are going off in my head.

Matt's leaning against his car, pinning me with a frank gaze. "I like you and I'm not afraid to be upfront. I don't have many friends for a lot of reasons, but I thought we connected when we worked on the night crew hiring." His eyes spark and I'm treated to his boyish grin. "I'd like to hang out with you. But, if you don't mind, I'd like to keep us a secret for now."

I can see his point. There's nothing to talk about. Why be the subject of rumors?

"Nina mentioned you like sports. How about we catch a Sharks game? You like hockey?"

I grab for my door handle. Despite all the warnings in my head, I say, "Yeah, I'd like that." I climb into my vehicle. I don't want to think about what it means that Matt asked to see me outside of work.

"Kellis, you didn't answer the last question."

I couldn't think what he was talking about. "What question?"

"When we were at Santana Row. The last getting to know you question. What are you the best at?"

I close the door and placed the key in the ignition. I smile up at him. "That's easy. Kissing." I shout it out of the window.

Chloe's door is closed when I walk by, and the soft snoring means she's in deep slumber and won't wake easily. My phone zips. I pull the cell out of my bag while I push the door closed to my room. I squint at the message.

Godiva, I liked that you told Tim at the restaurant I was your date. Thanks for an interesting evening. Good night, Matt.

CHAPTER 8

Hail to the Chief

I come up from the dungeon a little past 1 p.m. and the main floor is a flurry of activity. Haley finds me entering the long hallway and keeps pace alongside. "I've been meaning to call you." She's breathy with excitement. "Word is that they're calling an all-hands meeting in thirty minutes. Not just for the Americas headquarters but all the sites."

"Did they say what it's about?" I ask as we pass Nina's office and head through the cubes.

"No, just that everyone has to be on their best behavior and that all our desks should be cleared of personal items. We'll be meeting downstairs in the lower level. Didn't you see the crew setting up when you were down there?"

"I did see about four or five people wheeling equipment at the far end of the floor, but the space is so huge I didn't pay attention to what they're doing. I must've left just as they started to set up the seating and video equipment for the meeting."

We halt outside my cube. There's the ever-present tapping of keyboards with an overlay of low conversations. Haley pulls off an old sign-up sheet for a steps competition that was pinned to the outside of my cubicle. She hands it to me. "Allison actually walked down here from her office and stood where you're standing and did a small impromptu announcement,"

Riku, the cute HR analyst that looks like a K-pop star, scoots his chair to the entrance of his workstation. "You should've been here. She was tightlipped about why the meeting was being called." He brushes artfully cut bangs out of his eyes. "I think it's killing her not to tell us what's happening,"

I hope for Haley's sake that her short intake of breath at Riku's unconscious gesture was only audible to me, but maybe Riku did hear and ignored it. He's startlingly beautiful in an unaffected way. I had the same reaction to him when I first met him, but we've been working with him for a while and you'd think she would've gotten over it by now.

Haley pulls her gaze away from Riku's grinning face and moves her concentration back to me. "Allison's been in the CEO's office all morning and just came out for about ten minutes to give us the news. All the heads did a short meeting with their departments."

"Something this big must be an announcement," I say. "I've been working on a proposal with Dark Star for a new government contract, helping them with staffing estimates. I'm betting that we got the contract and this is a celebration."

Riku joins us, resting his arm on top of my cube wall. "Maybe you're right about Dark Star, but I think they've bought a new company." His presence is affecting Haley. She's shifting her weight and avoiding his gaze. My poor coordinator has it bad for this very sweet guy. I wonder if he's even noticed.

I sit at my desk, still looking up at Haley and Riku. "The proposal packet was submitted to the government weeks ago and we're just waiting," I say to a skeptical Riku. "This will be huge for Drachen. It'd be worth a celebration. Just about every site in the Americas would have a responsibility to help fulfill the contract." After the announcement, I'd have to text Matt and congratulate him. I didn't think he would come to the main headquarters to receive his accolades. He'd prefer to stay at the Dark Star facility and celebrate with his employees.

I quickly grab something to eat before the meeting, which makes me one of the last people to find a seat among the sea of employees. HR is seated a few rows back from the dais. Normally everyone sits with their departments, but I've worked with many of these people during the hiring process and I take a seat with Accounting. I'm chatting with Emily, a new hire in the tax department, when I sense eyes on me. I glance toward the stage and see Allison glaring at me. She looks down at the HR team sitting together. Obviously, she doesn't like that I'm several rows away with the accounting department. Later, I'll hear a snide remark about my seating choice.

Two screens stand next to the podium in front of the room. The setup crew have been busy. Not only did they arrange the chairs and set up the equipment, but there's a large table alongside one wall. A sheet cake in Drachen colors of yellow, red, and black sits in the center of the table. Nothing is written on the cake and there's no banner that indicates what we're celebrating. The leadership team is keeping whatever they're going to announce under wraps. I'm excited about the announcement because no one brings a cake to a layoff.

Richard Longborn, the CEO of Drachen Americas, takes the podium. He's a fit 47, a transplant from Denmark that's been leading the division for five years. His image is projected on one screen while the other screen has several split images of other sites. Richard is dressed in slacks and a dress shirt instead of his usual jeans/shirt combination, another sign that something important is occurring. The leadership team is seated in the first row, confidently waiting for information they already know. Top 40 music is playing in the background, which underscores the animated conversations in the room. The music is cut abruptly and Richard begins to address the crowd.

"I want to thank all of you who're able to attend the all-hands meeting today. We're a busy group and many of the employees are on travel, but at least the people who're here will be taking part in a historic day. Drachen technology is a strong leader in its sector. We've made significant strides due to our careful management of resources and our striving for excellence and innovation. But our real strength is monitoring trends to identify emerging industries that will become important in the future. For that reason, the global headquarters has assigned Kurt Heinrich to be the head of our R&D division. He has been an executive manager of R&D in Munich for the past five years. We are fortunate that he is taking the reins in the Americas and will be a strong advocate for our division. I'd like to introduce Kurt Heinrich."

My stomach does a slow roll then tightens into a knot. Kurt wasn't scheduled to be in the US for another week. We had a meeting yesterday and he didn't mention he'd be here the next day. He bursts through the side hallway, moving with agile, measured strides, then breaks into an almost jog when the assembly begins clapping. He grips the sides of the podium and searches the assembly. Short, cropped blond hair, lean, strong body, his movements are compact confidence. I can finally see what the fuss is about. I never thought of him as anything more than an irritating, high-profile hiring manager. I was too busy trying to stay one step ahead of that steel intellect. But now he's more real standing at the podium than he was when he sat in a darkened conference room talking to me through a video feed.

Emily leans into me, her shoulder brushing mine. "Why didn't you tell me he was so good-looking?" she whispers in my ear. "Trying to keep him all to yourself?" she's playfully jabbing an elbow in my

Hail to the Chief

side. I can see him through her eyes, how he appears as a conquering hero from Europe, but it doesn't matter... they don't know him yet. All I know is that he's the bane of my existence.

He addresses the crowd easily with some obligatory platitudes, that he's humbled by this experience, then he goes into some self-deprecating small talk that has the crowd laughing. He ends with a he's glad to be here and is looking forward to working with everyone. I only half listen. I'm thinking about how to slip out of the room without being noticed. Richard takes the microphone for the final remarks and invites everyone for cake at the buffet table. Several employees crowd around Kurt, including Allison. She must've met him earlier when she was in the CEO's office. There're enough people between Kurt and I that he probably doesn't see me. I start walking backwards and of course bump into Nate, one of my hiring managers from accounting.

"Whoa, you're going the wrong way, Missy. The cake is in the other direction," he says with a wide grin. "And I think you should be going up to the dais to meet our new leader."

I'm trying to think of a plausible explanation so I can get out of here, but Nate's big body is blocking the exit. "I have to prepare for an interview," giving a quick glance over my shoulder. "I've got to leave now. I can say hello to Kurt, I mean Mr. Heinrich, later when he's less busy. I really don't need any cake." I smile up at him. "I can't afford the sugar rush this late in the afternoon."

Nate's broad face turns quizzical, but he steps aside to let me pass when I hear Allison's voice sail over the crowd. "Kellis," the voice is too strong and honeyed to ignore. I turn to see Allison heading towards me. Nina is standing near the group surrounding Kurt. She shrugs, giving me a *there's nothing I can do look*. When Allison reaches me, she begins talking in an angry whisper. "Where are you going?" her cheeks are flushed crimson. "The rest of HR is meeting Mr. Heinrich and you're trying to head out."

Her anger is ready to explode. I've work with Kurt for the past few weeks. I'm really the only person he knows out of this group. I hate to admit it, but she's right; it doesn't look good that I haven't said hello before leaving. I thought with all the adulation from the other employees that he wouldn't remember me.

"I have a candidate arriving soon," I whisper back. "I have to prepare for the interview. I thought I would say hello to Mr. Heinrich later when he has less people around." Her eyes flash disbelief. It's a lie, I know, but plausible. She would have to check my schedule to see if I'm telling the truth, but I don't think she'll go that far.

Allison looks back at the large group surrounding Kurt. He's still in the middle of introductions. "I suggest you let me introduce you," she says, not taking her eyes off him. "He's been asking about you since he arrived earlier today. We told him you were busy with interviews and that you would meet him during this announcement meeting. He knows you're busy, but you still need to say hello."

I follow Allison as she parts the press of people. Kurt looks over at her when she approaches. She steps to the side, revealing an uncomfortable smiling me.

He's seated and in conversation with Richard when he catches sight of me. "They said you were busy with interviews today," he says, standing. He extends his hand toward me. I step closer, clasping it. "I'm glad that you took the time to greet me." The corner of his mouth quirks up. I've never noticed that his eyes are ice blue. The camera, in our meetings, must have muted his features. He releases my palm before it becomes awkward. "I hope you'll have time to attend a meeting later. Allison says you should be free at the end of the day."

I flash a look at Allison, whose intense gaze is still on Kurt. This is something new. I had her pegged as having no room for other people in her life. But now I think this cold-hearted witch is smitten by our savior from Munich. It might be that he's rumored to be the next CEO of the company that has her looking at him like a plate of cheesy nachos. I stop wondering about her motives and focus on his statement. Why would we be meeting with him? My last session with Kurt was my final wrap-up on the candidates he was considering before the executive search firm, Exigent, takes over the project. "Yes, welcome to America, Mr. Heinrich," with as much sincerity as I can muster. "I'm looking forward to the meeting later."

"I see you're still using Munich's honorific." In a voice loud enough for everyone to hear. He passes his gaze over the people still near us. "But I'm in America now," as if I'm the only one who didn't get the memo. "Please call me Kurt, and may I call you Kellis?"

Jeez, these people are a minefield. I throw a look at Allison for confirmation. She gives me a slight nod. "Yes, that would be fine," hoping the bewilderment is out of my voice. But I understand. He's in a new environment and we're not as formal here in the Americas; it would be best for him to adopt our protocols. He would be meeting with clients and even government officials and no one uses surnames.

He grins, registering something in his calculating brain. Probably trying to figure out how best to make my life more difficult.

I arrive at Nina's office and catch her hanging up her phone. I'd ushered my last candidate of the day to the lobby. I have thirty minutes before my meeting with Kurt in Allison's office. "Do you have some time to speak with me?"

Nina sweeps her hand towards the chair in front of her desk. "Sit. Tell me what's on your mind."

I shift into the seat. "I'm not sure if you heard, but when I met Kurt this afternoon at the party, he said he wants to meet today. Has Allison mentioned anything to you?"

She shakes her head and relaxes back in her chair. It squeaks slightly as she rotates back and forth, thinking. "No. Allison hasn't said anything. As far as I know, Exigent has been working on the search for Kurt's second-in-command. She hasn't shared any updates with me. She's managing the process on her own. I'd bet Allison either has a candidate in mind or a colleague has suggested someone for that position."

I hadn't thought about that. Placing a personal pick as second-in-command to a VP who might be the CEO of the company would be a coup. Corporate intrigue and power struggles were something I'd never had to deal with when I managed my own firm. "Have you been invited to the meeting?"

"No…not sure why since I'm your manager. But I'll hear about it later."

I pull out my phone and glance at the time. "I'll know soon enough. I've got to go. I'll give you my update tomorrow. I'm heading home after the meeting."

Kurt's standing outside Allison's office, checking his phone. He pulls his gaze away from the screen. I can't be sure, but it looks like he's waiting for me. He's almost at attention when I come near. Grabbing the door handle, he opens it for me with a flourish. Allison's already seated at a small round table, talking with a man.

Allison looks over as we enter. "We're all here… we can start the meeting," she says. "I want to introduce you both to Steve Dunning. He is our representative from Exigent." The man's slick demeanor screams salesman. "Steve, this is Kellis Ivarsson, our recruiter, and Kurt Heinrich, the VP of R&D." He inclines his head at each introduction. I still can't figure out why I'm here to listen to a report from Exigent.

"I'd like to hear your latest update," Kurt says. "We spoke last week about candidates you had suggested I meet."

The man looks directly at Allison. Something passes between them before he addresses Kurt. "Yes, we have performed preliminary interviews and have selected two new candidates we think would be a fit. I emailed the resumes to Allison yesterday. Have you had a chance to review them?"

Allison breaks in. "I asked Steve to send me the candidates first. I knew you were in transit and I wanted to get a jump on reviewing them for you. You were copied."

Kurt gives Allison a slight nod. "I looked them over last night. They were unsuitable." He turns his attention to Steve. "They don't have the background I'm looking for." The temperature in the room drops a few degrees. "They shouldn't have been presented. I've seen these resumes earlier in our search when Kellis performed the recruiting. We had decided to reject them. Do you have any other candidates you wish me to review?"

Steve shifts nervously, looking to Allison for help, but she remains silent. "I would have to discuss this with our recruiters," he says smoothly. "I wasn't aware there was a list of candidates that you had rejected..."

"There must've been a miscommunication when we gave our original information to your company," Allison says, her gaze drifting to me.

She's floundering, trying to figure out how to placate a pissed-off Kurt. It looks like they're going to blame this fiasco on me.

I break into the conversation. "I emailed everything to Exigent and copied Haley. I included a list of candidates that we had already reviewed, as well as candidates I had identified as potentials, but had not gone through a first-round review."

"You've had this assignment for three weeks and you haven't produced a viable candidate," Kurt says with bored coldness.

Steve is unruffled. "Searches like this take time. We're dealing with high-level candidates that need more than a phone call to get their interest. We have a few of our best recruiters working on this and I'm confident that we'll find a candidate that's suitable. I'll review this with the team and let you know when you can expect resumes to review."

"Allison's voice cuts through the tension. "Why don't we take a step back. Exigent is a highly successful firm and we shouldn't rush the process. Let's give them a week and see what they can produce in that amount of time. Is that agreeable with all parties?"

"I don't think we need to take any more of Mr. Dunning's time," Kurt says, the meaning clear to everyone.

Steve stands, his composure still intact. "Then I'll be in touch." He nods to Allison then strides out the door.

Kurt turns his attention to a guarded Allison. "We don't have the luxury of time. I was sent here to expand the R&D team and I need a second-in-command."

Both men are looking to her. I'm curious to see how she will resolve this growing tension. Allison, carefully laces her fingers together; her response is like a soothing balm. "Exigent has been highly recommended. But if you're not happy, we can contact another firm to handle the hiring."

Kurt stares back unaffected, leaning on the arm of the chair. "I agree. I think we need to cut our losses and place Kellis back in charge of the recruiting effort."

What? No, no. I shout in my head. I don't want to be on the project again. Allison was right for once. Neither is paying attention to me. Both are locked in a stare down.

Allison breaks the standoff with a challenge. "Kellis doesn't have the experience to recruit for executive-level candidates."

"This isn't an executive hire and she was doing an excellent job. I know you're the head of human resources, but I wasn't consulted about hiring an outside firm or removing Kellis from the project. I've given your decision a fair amount of time and now I wish to work with Kellis again."

Both are Silent.

I'm witnessing an old-fashioned power struggle. Both are VPs of their own divisions. The only person who could settle this dispute would be Richard Longborn, the CEO, and I don't think they would involve him in such a small matter. I'm betting that Kurt will have his way. He's been tasked to revamp the R&D division and if rumors are correct, he might be the next CEO of Drachen. Allison is doing the calculations in her head. If I've realized she has a weak hand, then it must be obvious to her. She has to be thinking about her future with the company.

"I'll agree to Kellis working on the project again," Allison concedes. "As you say, time is short. But if she's not able to find a candidate and hire them within a month, then we'll contact another agency."

I find myself outside Allison's office looking into Kurt's smug face. "I think that went well." He says. "I got your job back."

Yeah, thanks for absolutely nothing. You've landed me back in hell with a more pissed-off Allison. I try not to roll my eyes. "What time tomorrow should we meet to discuss the project?" Eager to end this conversation and go home.

"7 a.m. And do you have a car?"

"Yes, why?"

"Because I need a ride to my hotel."

It's an uncomfortable forty-minute drive in unusually heavy traffic. I have to take side streets to avoid an accident on 237. Luckily his hotel is only five minutes from my house. I pull up at the entrance to the Marriott. "Thank you for the ride." He gives me a genuine smile." Now I feel bad for trying to figure out ways to push him out of the car as we drove.

"You're welcome," I say, meaning it. "I'll see you at seven."

He slides out and slams the door. He lowers himself, leaning against the window, forearms extended into the vehicle. "I'll see you at six," he corrects in a clipped tone.

69

"But you said our meeting is at seven, or did I--"

"You're correct, the meeting is at seven, but you should pick me up at six. Five, if you want to join me for a jog. Again, the smile.

"Six then."

I swear under my breath as the sliding glass doors close behind him.

CHAPTER 9

Spin Me Right Round

The next morning Kurt's standing outside the hotel as I drive up. It's early and a reverse commute, so it doesn't take us long to arrive at Drachen. After entering the building, I head downstairs. Dark Star is expecting me about 8:30 a.m. I'm going to leave Matt a phone message to tell him I'll be late. I'm sorely in need of a coffee. I pinch the bridge of my nose as I listen to Matt's direction to leave a message when I hear, "Hello."

The cell nearly slips from my grasp. I wasn't prepared to talk with him, not without coffee. "You're up early. I didn't think you would pick up." dropping into my seat. Hearing his sexy voice is a great way to start the day.

"I got into the office early. I'd normally let it go into voice mail, but when I saw it was from you, I decided to take the call."

I can imagine him smiling, tiny lines crinkling around his eyes full of mischief. "Well, that's good to know."

"It must be serious if you're calling this early. Has something happened? How are you feeling?"

An unexpected warmth blossoms through me at his concern. "I'm fine. I've got a meeting here at 7 o'clock and I don't know how long it will last. I'm meeting with Kurt Heinrich to talk about hiring his second-in-command."

"I heard he came in yesterday. I was out with a client when they called the meeting. This is actually going to be a boon for the Americas. If they're sending Kurt, that means they see potential and that means real growth for the division."

My phone is giving me a fifteen-minute warning for my next appointment. I want to talk more, but I'm running out of time. "I'll let you know when I'm finished with the meeting and ready to head out."

"Don't worry about checking in. I know the second-in-command is priority."

"Alright, see you then."

"Kellis?"

"Yes?"

"When you get here, I want to talk about a Sharks game."

Matt's words that *the second-in-command is priority* gives me a stab of cold fear. I only have a month to prove that I can find and hire a candidate. Allison didn't say it directly, but her meaning was clear: if I can't produce, I'll be replaced. Right now, I'm worrying about how I'm going to find candidates. Exigent had several recruiters working on the project for weeks. They've got more contacts and resources than I do. It's possible they've already worked all the available leads. I have to come up with something fast or I'll have both Allison and Kurt screaming for my blood.

Elbows on his desk, Kurt studies an orange he's carefully peeling. Even performing such a mundane task, he manages to look like he's posing for a photo shoot. His clothes, movements, even his expressions are camera ready. It's disconcerting to be this close to him, like a movie come to life. Better to think of him as a cat toying with a mouse.

I pick my way through the maze of boxes that has yet to be unpacked. I sit and place my laptop on the edge of his desk. He offers me a section of orange. I shake my head no. He shrugs, then pops it into his mouth. "I don't have anything to report," I say, searching emails I'd checked five minutes ago. "I'll need to get Exigent's files before I can give you an assessment. I need to know who they've contacted so I don't duplicate their efforts."

He briskly rubs his hands, and the friction from his palms releases the scent of orange into the space. "It might take time for you to get their files." He pushes a flash drive toward me. "I have a copy of what they've sent to me. We can work from the files and my notes. I was talking to a colleague last week who told me about a candidate that'll be on the market shortly." He stops for effect to whisk the bright orange peels into the trash. It sends another wave of orange scent wafting. "Okobi is not happy at Endeavor."

I tried not to gape or salivate.

"The company has lost funding on a pet project that he's working on. He's looking for another home to do his research."

I'd met Kyle Okobi years ago before he started at Endeavor. Brilliant is just one of the adjectives to describe him, and that would be the least you could say about him. "Are you sure Kyle is ready to move? He's been courted by several companies and each one has failed to recruit him away from Endeavor."

"I've been told that he's interested in working in the R&D division at Drachen. Several years ago, we talked to him about coming to work in Munich. At that time, he'd just completed his master's and was looking for a company to work with that would align with his PhD thesis."

"Endeavor is headquartered in Arizona. It's much cheaper to

live in Tempe than Silicon Valley and I hear he has a family now; it might be a difficult sell."

"But the weather is better here. His wife is from Southern California. I hear she doesn't like the Arizona heat."

I tap the keyboard, searching my contacts. Several phone numbers come up for Okobi, but I haven't talked to him for a while. If the numbers aren't good, I have several phone numbers of Endeavor employees. A couple of them owe me. Getting Kyle's number would be worth calling in a favor. "I'll give him a call to see if he'd like to talk with us."

Kurt pushes away from the desk, moving around toward the window. He did this often during our meetings, needing to be in motion as he worked out his ideas. "That bit of information about him leaving Endeavor is not public knowledge. He confided in my colleague and I was told to keep it quiet. But I've an idea how we can contact him. In two weeks, there's going to be an R&D conference, the Associated Semiconductor Consortium (ASC) is meeting in Las Vegas this year. Several companies will be there, and he'll be attending from Endeavor."

An in-person meeting with a candidate is always better than a cold call, and meeting at a social event even better. "Do you plan to approach him at the conference?" If he can convince him to come to Drachen, this could be a slam dunk. I couldn't take direct credit for this candidate, but Kurt would hand him off to me and I'd keep Okobi warm and toasty through the hiring process until he signed his offer letter. I'm too excited to keep silent while he thinks it through. "I could coach you," I offer. "Give you some suggestions on how to approach him and how to open up a conversation about considering a move to Drachen."

"No, I don't plan to talk with him at the conference. I don't want my colleague to think I've betrayed her trust. I want you to approach him."

There's a tightness in my throat that makes it difficult to respond. He studies me, enjoying my shock. Recruiters never go on field trips. Maybe they did, but not contractors and not with a VP.

"I would like you to accompany me to the conference," he's selling the idea. "It would be good for you to attend some of the seminars and meet the engineers who'll be there. I can also introduce you to my contacts, which will help your recruiting. I want you to pay particular attention to Okobi. He's been known to like the women."

I do an awkward glance at my laptop to avoid eye contact. Did he want me to recruit or use me as bait? In my early days of recruiting, I worked for an agency where I'd accompany the manager to visit clients, even to companies I wasn't assigned to work with. I'd also attend client parties with him. He was an effective marketer and taught me a lot about marketing clients to get the sale. I was excited about his mentoring until another recruiter told me that he'd heard the manager boasting that I was his eye candy and the best little marketing tool he had. I don't want to be used.

"Kellis, why are you hesitating? I'm not suggesting anything tawdry, or maybe the word dirty is a better choice. But you get my meaning. I think you would have a better chance of getting his ear. You will know what to say. We're just fortunate that you're a beautiful woman. If he agrees to talk with us, then I'll speak to him away from the conference."

The silence between us lengthens as I try to figure out how to respond. He leans next to the window, wondering what he's just said. He's forgotten that our communication rules are stricter in the US. I've gone over it with him a few times on what he can say to candidates, but he must think it doesn't apply to employees. I open my mouth to speak, but now I'm having a problem squaring that he thinks I'm beautiful. "Thank you, but don't say that out loud to an employee."

He cocks his head, skepticism pulling down the corner of his mouth. "It's true, you're beautiful. I'd have been more diplomatic if I thought you weren't."

"Gee thanks, I appreciate your thoughtfulness." It's obvious the irony is lost on him. "Remember the dos and don'ts of interviewing in America?"

He nods.

"It applies to the workplace too."

"Yes, I see. I heard about this, but I didn't think it was true. I'll remember."

Doubt is creeping into my mind. This man is savvy. Is he serious or having a tease at my expense?

"What do you say?" As if everything has been resolved and it's only my decision preventing his plan from moving forward. "Will you go to the conference...it's in Vegas?" he teases.

That R&D conference in Vegas is a big yearly event. All the heavy hitters in the sector will be there. I'll have a treasure trove of contacts by the end of the conference. "I don't think Allison will approve. She'll have several reasons to deny my request."

"I've already spoken to Richard. The CEO thinks it's a great idea and the cost will come out of R&D's budget."

"Then, I'm in."

He flashes a smile. My breath hitches as the room brightens, then I realize it's only the sun shining through the window.

Kurt strides out of the building like he's on a mission as I roll the car to a stop. He opens the back door and slides his briefcase in. Settling into the front seat, he buckles his seatbelt then turns to me. "You're late."

And good afternoon to you, Herr Heinrich, I refrain from saying. He's unapologetic and I have to squash an urge to floor it before he pulls the door closed.

The traffic is moving along without a slowdown. I drive past our usual exit and take Alpine Road off. "Where are we going? This is not our exit."

I slide my gaze over to him, enjoying his unease. "I'm doing a five-minute detour," turning onto the street. "Your hotel is close to where I live. I'm meeting my mother for dinner. But I have to go by my house to pick up her birthday present. She wasn't here on her birthday and I want to take her my gift now. Your hotel is close to the freeway. After I drop you off, I can take it to the restaurant." He says nothing. I pull up in front of the house and turn off the ignition. "I'll be back in a couple of minutes." Before he can respond or ask a question, I slide out of the driver's seat, edging around the car, and bounce up the steps. Chloe is in the kitchen looking out through the curtains. I walk past her. "Did you move Mom's present? I left it in the foyer."

"Who's that?" She points to the window. "Is he coming inside because he just got out of the car and is walking down the street."

I join her at the window and gingerly pull the curtain aside just enough to see outside. I crane my neck to see which way Kurt has gone. He's moving at a clip around the court. "That's Kurt Heinrich. That's the VP from Munich I told you about."

Chloe's eyebrows creep up. "I remember you talked about a grumpy VP from Munich, but you never said he looked like that."

Kurt finally comes into view, slipping something into the breast pocket of his jacket, and climbs back into the car. "Maybe he decided against hiking back to his hotel," I say to myself. I frown at my sister. "Come away from that window, Chloe. Where's the birthday present?"

"I put it in your bedroom," looking out of the window distractedly. "Where it belongs." She flings a hand in an unspecified direction. "You scatter everything around the house and forget that every item has a place. If it needs a temporary home, then it goes on your desk in your bedroom. You're welcome, by the way." Chloe is trying to get a better look at Kurt. "Are you going to ask him inside? It's rude to leave him in the car. Isn't he your boss?" Her voice booms at my back as I walk away.

I scoop up the gift and return to the kitchen. Chloe is still trying to find the right angle to look out of the window. "First off, he's not my boss. He's the VP of R&D, not human resources."

"Then if he's not your boss, why are you driving him around?"

"That's a good question," I mumble. This is the second day of driving him. "I don't have time now to discuss it. If Mom calls, tell her I'm on my way to the restaurant. But she's a psychic, so she should know that."

"Nice house," he says as I place the present in the backseat. "Do you like this neighborhood?"

"Yes, actually I do like living here," The neat ranch-style houses are typical, built in mid-century when the city was filled with orchards. "It reminds me of the house I grew up in. That house was located on a court as well. I'm lucky that I have great neighbors." I pull the car out into the road. "I saw you walking down the street--"

His attention is focused on the landscape, but he's quick to answer. "I wanted to stretch my legs a bit. I didn't know how long you would be. I have a hard time sitting in one place for too long. I also wanted to see the neighborhood."

I pull up in front of his hotel and before he opens the door I blurt out, "Kurt, do you drive?" He isn't surprised at my strident question.

He meets my gaze amused and unfazed. "I don't drive. The transit system in Munich is excellent or I hire a car."

"But don't you think that--"

"I don't know anyone here. I'm enjoying this time with you. I didn't go on any of the goodwill junkets to America that Munich offered as a way for some in leadership to get to know this division. Socializing with colleagues is different when you're in management."

Now I was feeling uncaring. I never imagined he might be lonely.

"Thank you for offering to drive me. Your rides are helping me with the transition. I hope you will continue, and I want to do my part and pay you for sharing the ride."

The money was not the point. He probably comes from a rich family and expects to be driven. I'm weighing the advantages. Matt said I need allies to survive. Kurt has already proven effective with Allison and, on the plus side, half my gas would be paid.

"Yeah, sure why not?"

He's looking more like Kurt the nice guy than the evil Herr Heinrich. Although there hasn't been much evil coming from him since he arrived, only glimpses.

"Let me know what an appropriate amount is that I should pay you each month. I'll add it as one of my work expenses. I'm looking forward to seeing you tomorrow at the same time." He pushes out of the car, retrieves his case from the back seat, and is gone before I can say goodbye.

Mom stands as I walk to the table. I move into her outstretched arms. "Kellis, honey, I'm glad to see you. The book tour went long, but I'm happy to be back home. You look well. How are you?"

My mom is smaller than me. I'm bending down and she's on her tip toes to hug me. I breathe in her Chanel No. 5 through her apricot cashmere sweater and her bracelets tinkle as her arms slip from my neck. She runs her hands down her trim waist, which is a result of yoga and hikes in the hills near her center. Her long dark hair floats just past her shoulders in loose waves, courtesy of Gerald, her stylist in Saratoga. She's kind, unforgettable, and has been mistaken to be my sibling more than my parent.

"I'm fine, Mom. Don't fuss." I smile so she knows I'm teasing. "Things are working out at Drachen."

She touches my hair, deft fingers smoothing my bangs. "I see for the most part it's working out. But I sense that there's still some uneasiness and challenges you think you might not overcome."

My mother appears otherworldly when she throws out a psychic

79

tease. I never can decide if she really has a gift or if she just knows me so well. It's possible that it's both.

"Well, if it ever becomes too much for you, there's a place at Madre Luna. I always hoped that one of you kids would work with me and eventually take over the company. I've always envisioned us as a family enterprise."

It's not that I wouldn't enjoy working for my mom — I'd be expected to work as hard as any of her employees — I just see it as settling. My mom was able to make her dream happen. I want to have the same chance to be successful at what I choose. Maybe, eventually, down the line I'll work at her company, but I want it to be my choice, not that I had to.

"What do you see for me?" I say it without explanation. She nods, knowing what I want answered. A faint smile crosses her lips then she transforms into Dr. Renee Exton. Even in this crowded restaurant, she draws inside herself. Her eyes flutter close as she takes a breath. "The love of your life is a handsome blue-eyed man."

Joy floods my body like a warm gentle wave. Matt Westmore has blue eyes.

CHAPTER 10

Jump the Shark

Saturday morning and no Kurt for two days. Yes, I'm doing a happy dance in my PJs. I refuse to feel guilty. I'm sure he'll find something to do for the weekend. Me, I'm going to a Sharks game with Matt later. My first date with him and I'm excited, nervous, and can't wait.

Chloe left early to attend an opening of a food pantry with her boss and the mayor. The house is quiet and mine for a few hours. I pour a mug of coffee Chloe brewed earlier. Poking my head into the refrigerator, I add cream to my mug. A quick check of the egg carton reveals two left for an omelet. Sliding onto a stool at the counter, I flip open my tablet to the sports scores when a truck rumbles down the street, stopping at the house next door. My curiosity nudges me off the stool to see who would be so industrious on a Saturday morning. I covertly push the kitchen curtains aside. The realtor is pulling up the 'for lease' sign, the kind that had a box for flyers attached. Two strapping men walk around to the back of the vehicle as a third man pulls the heavy truck door open. Steel tracks unfurl from the opening. The usual couch, chairs, and dining room set are eased down the tracks. Christmas decorations, tree, toys, and bedroom furniture make their way down the makeshift ramp. I hope this family is as nice as the last. Chloe and I will walk over with flowers or something to welcome them after they settle in. I ask the virtual assistant to turn on music to drown out the moving sounds and return to my stool. Aw, the joys of a wired home.

The glare of headlights beams from an unending line of vehicles three deep loading passengers in front of the SAP center, nicknamed 'the Tank' to Shark fans. We move in step among a subdued crowd away from the Tank, traveling down the street toward the city center. The crowd would've been livelier if the Sharks had won this close-fought game.

"Do you believe it? That last shot should've gone in," Matt says, his shoulder brushing mine as we walk. The accidental contacts are sending little shock waves through me. Not like the electric jolt I experienced when we shook hands the first time, but close. I want to take his hand or have his arm around me as we walk. But we're in first date territory. Every moment is a minefield of not crossing some invisible line too early. I need to be careful I don't do something that will scare him off and have him screaming for the hills. I have to act like this touching is not torturous.

Matt glances at me after the last accidental contact, not fazed. "It's lucky this loss doesn't hurt their chances. They're still going to the Cup finals. This might be the year we win this thing," Matt says, winking at me.

"I'm not as optimistic as you," I say, nearly bumping into the man ahead of me who stopped at the corner for a red light. More people are catching up with us, lingering while we wait for the light to change. "They usually make it into the finals." I sigh, making my old argument. "They've broken my heart so many times, that once they're in the playoffs, I don't want to hear anything about them until they've raised that Stanley Cup trophy over their heads."

Matt gives a short laugh. "That seems harsh. Are you a fair-weather fan? Only like your team when they win?" he teases. We're both decked out in Shark jerseys and baseball caps. We look like superfans who've been attending the games for years. Matt's in a vintage Sharks jersey. His teal cap, that's turned backward, has seen better days. Two minutes after we entered the SAP center, he hauled me to the Sharks' store and bought me a team jersey and cap. I drew the line at an orange foam finger he was eyeing.

He looks off into the distance, gaging traffic flow. Some people have already crossed against the light. "Does that mean you won't go with me if I get tickets to the finals?"

"I didn't say that. I'll go and scream my head off for them, but I won't get my hopes up."

"Good to know that you'll go out with me again if they reach the finals," he mumbles.

I laugh. The light changes and we enter the crosswalk. I stop after a few steps. "Look at me," I say, taking a twirl in the middle of the street, while annoyed fans sidestep me. "Would this pass up a ticket to the finals?"

He shakes his head and slips his hand to my back to urge me along. "Come on. You've made your point; let's keep walking before we get hit by a bus."

We're mostly silent as we walk through the cold clear night. The crowd begins to thin the closer we move toward downtown. I'm anticipating another five blocks until we reach the heart of the city. I'm lost in thought listening to the rhythm of our shoes beating the pavement when Matt places a hand on my shoulder, nudging me off the sidewalk. I'm looking up at the Estrela Hotel as people continue to stream along the walkway behind me.

I'm wondering why we're not in the flow of the crowd. I'm about to ask when he pulls me towards the building and we step into a small hidden alcove just off the entrance. Moving an arm around my waist, he draws me to him and I cling to his body. His heat radiates through his clothes like a blanket covering a furnace and I want to burrow inside his coat for his warmth. I should feel safe with his arms about me, but my heart is thumping at a mad pace. We're two shadows in a dark place that can be easily discovered by anyone walking the path to the hotel. I look up into his inky blue eyes that are more intense under the diffused lights of the alcove. Electricity crackles between us as he holds me tighter. How much of an encounter does he want to risk before we stop or are exposed?

Matt gently pulls off my cap, stuffing it inside his jacket. His hand tenderly shifts the bangs from my eyes then follows the curve of my face to brush his thumb over my lips. I kiss his thumb and he gives me a lopsided grin. His fingers travel until he finds my chin to tilt my face up. His lips are warm and attentive. His mouth tastes like roasted maltiness from the Guinness he drank. It's earthy with hints of chocolate and coffee as his tongue probes, and I open my mouth wider to take him in. He groans at my acceptance and his kiss becomes more urgent. He guides me deeper into the shadows until the wall is at my back. We kiss with hungry passion driven by our need to satisfy our cravings in the darkness. My sense of place begins to slip away when he presses against me, his hand at my hip lifting my jacket to touch skin. I can hardly breathe with the pleasure; my hand is pawing at his clothing, wanting to explore his body. We don't notice distant laughter and shouts until they're almost at the hotel entryway. Matt steps back, the flat of his hand on the wall near my face, looking down at me like we've been talking. My arms drop to my sides, attempting to look less guilty, betrayed by my labored breathing, when the intruders arrive at the hotel entrance. Curious glances are briefly directed at us, but it doesn't stop their talk or prevent them from continuing through the doors.

Matt pulls me back into the light to stand closer to the doors. His lips brush my forehead, then he hands me my hat, grinning. I take it, grateful I have something to do. My body is still tingling from the encounter, but I can match his casualness.

I shove the cap in my pocket and adjust my coat.

He pushes my bangs away from my eyes. "I needed to get our first kiss out of the way," he says. "I thought about doing it earlier; the way you looked in that oversized jersey and cap pulled down low, it was difficult not to touch you."

"So, an oversized jersey does it for you?"

He shakes his head no. "You in a Sharks' jersey, that does the trick."

I tilt my head toward the dark corner and smile.

He glances back to the alcove, a grin forming on his lips as he shakes his head. "Let's go inside the hotel before we get arrested for lewd acts." He urges me forward, holding the door open. "They've got music in the lounge," I reach for his hat as I walk past him and manage to get it off. I hand it to him. "I have a pet peeve about men wearing hats indoors unless it's for religious reasons." He smiles and opens his mouth to reply, but I see what's coming. "Don't tell me you worship at the shrine of the Shark."

"I thought it was worth a try." He stuffs his hat inside his jacket.

Matt asks the waitress for another beer and I order a tonic. "How's it going with Allison?"

We're sitting on a love seat, one of many overstuffed pieces that are scattered about the spacious lounge. The place is lightly populated with Shark fans and others who just wandered in to listen to music. There's an enormous stone fireplace with a fire in the grade crackling away at the far end of the space. "I guess I didn't tell you about the meeting with Kurt and Allison." The waitress returns with our drinks. Matt thanks her and she leaves. "Exigent hasn't done a great job on the search for Heinrich's second-in-command. To Allison's dismay, Kurt has requested the assignment be given back to me."

"How'd you feel about that?"

"I was angry when I was taken off the project, but I should have seen it as an act of kindness. Heinrich was a difficult hiring manager at the best of times."

"He's not abusive--"

"No, nothing like that. I'd describe him as direct, doesn't have a working filter, and isn't afraid to let you know how he feels. He's a prick."

Matt barks out a laugh. "Yeah, there's a lot of that going around. Other than that, I can tell you like your job."

I pick up my drink. "With the exception of Allison and Kurt, I'd say it's damn near perfect." I tip my tonic to him and take a sip.

The driver stops in front of my house. Matt shifts to look at the man who picked us up from the hotel. "Will you wait for me while I see her safely inside?"

He nods.

Matt's arm is around me as we walk to the door. My keys jingle too loudly as I nervously open the lock. "Do you mind if I walk around? I want to be sure everything is fine before I leave." I flip on a light. We're close in the semi-darkness, but he doesn't take this opportunity for another kiss. "Do you live here with anyone? Any animals?"

I toss my key on the table. Then I hear Chloe in my head scolding me. I'll pick the keys up later after Matt leaves. "No animals," I say, "I do live here with my sister Chloe, but she's out tonight."

I allow him to walk around but follow him at a distance while he opens doors and checks rooms. No one has ever been this concerned about my well-being. It's warming that he cares, and disconcerting that no one has done this before. He steps inside my bedroom. I wish I had made my bed and tidied the room before leaving.

He looks around. "Messy. This must be your room?"

"How do you know that? It could be my sister's."

He chucks his chin toward the wall. "The pictures of you and friends or maybe relatives on the corkboard." He moves closer to look at the display, placing a finger on Chloe's face. "This must be your sister. She's as cute as you."

"Yes, that's her. It was taken at a family BBQ a few months ago." At least I took Tim's pictures down. That might have been awkward to explain why a client was pinned to my memory board.

He stands in the living room taking a last look around. "I'm convinced it's all clear,"

"If you wanted a tour, all you needed to do was ask."

"Come here, Ms. Smart Ass, and let me say good night." I move into his outstretched arms that envelop me into a big bear hug. "I had fun. Don't make me wait until the finals for another date."

"I won't. I promise."

"Let me know what you want to do for our second date."

"I'll be at Dark Star on Wednesday, we can decide then." He gives me a sweet kiss that has me thinking it might be nice for him to stay longer. We reluctantly part and I walk him to the door. I wave at the red tail lights leaving the court.

The new neighbors next door seem to be settling in. The porch light is shining on a large Christmas wreath. Maybe they're starting their decorating early. They probably have kids. That'll be fun as long as there're no yappy dogs. A curtain flutters and a shadow moves away. Chloe and I will go over there tomorrow to welcome them to the neighborhood.

Chloe still isn't back when I settle into bed. My phone zips as I'm setting the alarm.

Good night Ms. Smart Ass. BTW, you're a good kisser. Matt

After deleting several clever remarks, memes, and emojis, I send a smiley face to Matt in reply to his message and go to bed with a smile on my face.

CHAPTER 11

Monday, Bloody Monday

$\mathcal{S}$unday is mostly a blur. Chloe and I try a few times to visit our new neighbors but they're never around. Monday morning arrives quicker than I expect. I wake to the smell of cinnamon and coffee. I'm a little slow moving this morning but I manage to shower, apply makeup, and walk to the kitchen in my robe. Chloe sits at the counter reading a magazine while Kurt Heinrich stands at the stove flipping slices of bread.

Chloe looks at me with a self-satisfied grin on her face. "Well, it's about time you got up."

I'm horrified, staring at the man's back. He's moving about the kitchen like he's at home. Kurt turns, giving me a critical eye. He's in a full-length navy striped apron that I've never seen before. It's tied at the waist, covering a blue slim-fit dress shirt and jeans. The sleeves of his shirt are neatly cuffed to reveal a tattooed forearm. "There's orange juice on the counter," he points at me with a spatula. "Do you want one or two slices of French toast?"

"Why are you here in my kitchen?" I demand, after realizing I'm living one of my nightmares.

Kurt looks at me as though I've come from an altered universe. "You've been late the last two days to pick me up. I thought if you started your day with a good breakfast, it would hurry you along." He checks the bread on the sizzling griddle. "I could help you set up a routine. You might consider jogging as part of your morning ritual. It keeps the body fit and senses sharp." He slides a slice of bread onto a plate and places it in my hands. "Sit and have some toast. You should eat it while it's hot." He returns his attention to the stove.

I slip onto the stool, lean across the counter and whisper to Chloe, "Why did you let him in the house?"

She folds a corner back on the magazine she's reading, places it next to her plate and glances over at Kurt. "Meet our new neighbor. Kurt is leasing the house next door. He moved in this weekend."

That doesn't make sense. I saw the moving van. A family was moving in. "Chloe and I went next door a few times with flowers. Where were you?"

He turns with a plate in his hand. "I saw the flowers on the doorstep. They look great in the living room. You should stop by soon to see them."

Chloe chuckles. "He was in and out all weekend mostly talking to the good people at Home Depot so he could repair some minor problems in the house. That's why we didn't catch him at home on Sunday."

He sets his plate down next to me and reaches across for the syrup. "Eat," he instructs. "We have a meeting in an hour, and you don't want brain fog." Kurt holds the syrup bottle over his plate, He covers most of his breakfast with a river of dark liquid, but he's waiting for the last of it to drip onto the toast. He flips it up, peering into the opening to see if there's any more to be had. "I've decided to walk over every morning, to save you the trouble of honking when you're ready to leave. We don't want to disturb our neighbors this early. I think Mrs. Gupta has a heart condition."

He's already met the neighbors?

He puts the empty syrup bottle down, then looks seriously at me. "Don't expect me to make breakfast for you every morning. I've talked to Chloe and we agreed that we should all take turns."

Chloe smirks and claps her hands. She's enjoying this way too much. "I think that's a wonderful idea, but Kellis will probably do toaster pastry when it's her turn to make breakfast. If your stomach can handle that, then we have a deal." She looks up at the kitchen clock. "I've got to get going. I have some early meetings as well. Thank you for breakfast, Kurt, and it's nice to finally meet you. I'll see you tomorrow." She walks out of the room humming.

Kurt leans toward me conspiratorially. "I've a few breakfast recipes that you can prepare the night before. It can be part of your routine. Does your oven have a timer?"

"Yes."

"Good, I'll email them to you today. They're my favorites." He pops a neatly cut square of bread drenched in syrup into his mouth and chews. He points his fork at me and swallows. "I forgot to mention, I've also ordered the morning paper for you. Don't worry, I'll pick it up on my way over."

There's a loaf of French bread on the counter that he must have brought with him this morning. He's been slicing bread and mixing the batter.

"How can I eat this? There's no syrup left," wondering how he's able to insinuate himself into my life even further.

"I know. You should put that on your shopping list." He gets up and moves to the refrigerator, rummages around inside, and produces a year-old jar of pepper jelly. "Here, this should go well with your toast."

I glance at my plate. He's given me the butt end of the bread, which is my least favorite part of the loaf. Year-old pepper jelly and the butt end of cinnamon French toast, this proves he hates me.

Kurt's animated as we ride to work this morning. We discuss the upcoming conference in Las Vegas and Allison's reluctance to allow me to attend. He's unconcerned and chalks it up to his superior negotiation skills that she finally approved my travel. I'm not sure if it's actually his bargaining techniques that won her over, more likely, she's reluctant to go against our CEO's enthusiasm for the project.

I head for my office in the dungeon. I have no interviews today, so I'll be working on searches and contacting potential candidates. I also want the alone time to think. I've never been happy and frustrated at the same time. I want to continue seeing Matt. When my mind wanders, it's to his big open grin and the kiss in the alcove that still gets me. On the other hand, Kurt irritates the hell out of me. He's not malicious; it's his way of communicating that I find annoying.

Sending off a batch of emails is my least favorite activity. I'm more than ready to stop when tapping at the door interrupts my concentration. Riku's tall, lean frame is backed against the door jamb. "So, this is your home away from home," grinning like he's caught me doing something embarrassing. I like him. He's one of the few people who welcomed me when I was first hired. He's a techie genius and has enough lovesick fan girl connections around here to get anything done. I've caught more than one female leaving offerings of food or notes for him on his desk, hoping he'll go to coffee with her, and he does, but never anything more. At least he hasn't said anything to me.

"I've been meaning to come down here to visit you." He looks around, taking in the small office. "This is pretty cool. I'm going to ask Nina if she'll let me have an office down here too. Hey, we could be neighbors. I'll snag the office next door."

"Good luck with that. I had a hard time convincing her to let me have privacy. I had to point out that people were listening to me when I gave offers to candidates."

"Yeah, I remember listening to you. Everyone went silent waiting for you to say" *Drachen is pleased to offer...*"

"I know. She didn't believe me at first until someone asked her if what I offered to a candidate was what we're paying our admins. That day I was escorted down here and told that I'll give my offers in this room."

He holds up his hands. "Whoa, you don't have to convince me. I just thought it would be a nice place to hide when it got to be too much upstairs. But I'm getting off track. Allison came by and wanted to know where you were."

"Did she seem like she was in a good mood?" I ask hopefully.

He folds his arms about his chest and gives me that K-pop look that starts everyone's heart fluttering. I'm not immune to his charm, but he's younger than me and reminds me of my little brother.

"We're talking about Allison Mackey, right? When is that woman ever in a good mood?"

"I see your point. Did she say what she wanted?"

"Yeah, she wants to see you in her office when you get in. I don't think she realizes that you're in the office two hours before her. I decided not to point this out. Anyway, she's waiting for you. I suggest you visit her now and get whatever this is out of the way."

"Any clue to what she might want?"

"Nope."

"Just give me a minute. I'll walk upstairs with you."

"Enter." Comes the answer to my knock on her door. Allison is at her desk studying something on her computer.

"Riku says you wanted to see me?"

She doesn't look away from the screen but motions me into the room. I sit in front of her desk, wondering if this's going to be my last day because something I hadn't anticipated or knew about has just hit the fan.

She settles her gaze on me. "I had an interesting conversation with Kurt Heinrich about you yesterday. He has this wild notion that you would be the best person to speak with Kyle Okobi at the semiconductor R&D conference in Las Vegas."

I shift in my seat under her scrutiny. I thought this was settled after my conversation with Kurt today. Apparently, Allison has something new to add.

"I agreed on giving you a month to find and hire a candidate. I didn't envision that you'd be going on a trip with the VP of R&D to a conference for three days. I pointed out that there's liability because you're a contractor. However, Kurt wouldn't listen to reason and decided that he'd discuss his idea with our CEO, who, by the way thinks it's brilliant. I have my reservations."

She always thinks I have a hidden motive. More than likely, she's projecting. "I didn't suggest going to Las Vegas. When Kurt proposed the idea, I suggested coaching him on how to approach Okobi. For his own reasons, he says he doesn't want to reach out to Kyle and thinks it would be a better idea if I handled the contact. I'm accustomed to approaching potential candidates. I agree with you. I told him it isn't a good idea for those reasons you just outlined."

Her nails tap the desk while she thinks. "You're telling me this is not your brainchild?"

I shake my head vigorously. "No, I tried to discourage the plan."

I'm not quite certain if she believes me. Giving someone the benefit of the doubt isn't in her nature. She might be thinking of the possibilities of this going very badly or of it going quite well. Kyle Okobi's defection from Endeavor would be a coup for any company. There's also the possibility that she couldn't take credit for this since it's not her idea. If we're successful in hiring Okobi, this would not be one of her picks for the position, and she'd lose any leverage she was planning.

Allison forms her fingers in a tense steeple. The stress must be killing her. She doesn't even have her green alien doll on her desk for comfort. "I regret that we didn't talk after our meeting with Kurt and Exigent. But I'm sure that you understand my position. This is a critical job that must be filled quickly and with the best talent. You have one month to find and hire a candidate for Kurt's second-in-command position. If you fail, you'll be let go. Do I make myself clear?"

I was right. That one-month allowance she had given me when I received the project back was an ultimatum. I'm not an employee. I'm a contractor and work at their pleasure. If they aren't pleased with my performance, they could let me go at any time, without notice, and without explanation. "Very clear," I say.

"Good," she says and gives a deep sigh, knowing that in all likelihood I will finally be gone in a few weeks. She's betting I'll fail, and there won't be anyone that can stop her when she lets me go. "Then we're on the same page. Please be sure that Nina is updated on your progress."

CHAPTER 12

Missed You

Haley and I walk back from the Grilled Cheese Rebellion. She surprised me by texting that my favorite food truck would be in the employee parking lot today. Her bubbly personality and nonstop chatter seem a bit subdued, but our short jaunt helps take my mind off the conversation I had with Allison earlier.

We've got identical brown paper sacks with an Italian Uprising, my favorite food in the world. The smell of cheese, three salamis, and herbs is enough to make me want to drop where I am and tear into the sandwich, but I refrain. Instead I listen to Haley talk about a couple we met in line. I think they said their names were Emma and Austin, a nice enough couple. The guy was wearing a black T-shirt that said Do it all day at Georgia's in pink letters across his back. It was hard not to notice him or an advertisement from my favorite day spa.

Microwave doors slamming and the aroma of heated frozen food is pervasive in the lunch room. We arrive with our sandwiches and snag a middle table. The employees around us are discussing the cute guy in a Georgia's day spa T-shirt, who looked like a wrestler. During my spa visit next week, I'm going to ask Mary, their receptionist, if he's doing marketing for them.

We've been chatting all through lunch, but it seems there is something on Haley's mind. Most of the other employees have left the small break room. I gather up the remains of our lunch and deposit it in the trash. "You're not at your usual level of banter today. Is something going on I don't know about?"

She looks up at me with genuine discomfort. "There's always something going on in this place."

"I get that," sliding back into my seat, "But this time it looks like something's bothering you."

"Hey, why didn't anyone tell me the Grilled Cheese Rebellion was here?" Riku says.

Haley nearly jumps as Riku walks up behind her.

He saunters around her chair, drops his bag on the table next to her, and sprawls into a seat. He smiles at me and nods at Haley, who's looking down. "Wanta eat with me?" he says to me, but is looking at Haley, who still hasn't glanced up. "I was finishing up a report and it ran long. I think I got the last sandwich off the truck. Good thing because I wasn't about to get into my car and drive for fast food. I don't think I can take one more day of vendor machine food for lunch either."

"We have a meeting with Nina in a few minutes. We have to be going," she says, getting to her feet.

We have about fifteen more minutes until we meet with Nina. I'm not sure why she's in a hurry to leave but I get up anyway. "We can have lunch tomorrow," I say to Riku, "if you want to hang out. Just let me know."

He smiles. "Sure, there's a new burger place in the mall down the street; maybe we can go try that. Want to come too, Haley?"

"I'm kind of busy. I've got a report that's due tomorrow. Maybe another time."

Riku's bemused gaze follows us as we shuffle past him and disappear around the corner. We walk a few steps into the hall, then I stop and turn to her. "What was that all about? You haven't said more than two words to him since I've joined our team. Do you have a problem with him?"

"No, no problem. I just have a lot of work."

"You know you're talking to me. The person who assigns your work. Tell me what's going on. I see the way you look at him."

She stops, leans against the wall and wraps her arms about herself. "It's difficult to work around him," She confesses. "I'm attracted to him."

"Okay, that's not uncommon. People are attracted to each other all the time in the workplace. If you think about it, we spend more time at work than at home…less chance to meet outsiders."

She still holds on to a troubled frown while she waits for two employees to walk by us before she responds. "You don't understand," she says in a whispered wail of pain. I'm surprised that she's getting emotional. I look around for a place to talk. I grab her arm and pull her into the mother's room. Haley plops down in a chair. "I dream about him. I think about him all the time. At night, I replay what passes for our interactions during the day in my mind. When I'm near him, I can barely speak or function. I feel like an idiot."

"Yeah, you and the whole female population around here that's under 60 feels the same way."

"I don't want to be one of those fembot fan girls that hang around him. You have to help me. I've been meaning to talk to you about it, but I know you're going through a lot."

"That doesn't matter; tell me about it."

"You know this is my first job. I don't want to screw it up. You're older. What do you do when you are attracted to someone at your job?"

I grimace recalling my relationship with Matt. Oh, I don't know, maybe have a couple of make-out sessions with him. Then plan to jump his bones as soon as possible. But still wait an appropriate amount of time so he doesn't think I'm a slut for wanting to play hide the sausage with him. Somehow, I didn't think that would be the right advice here. Lines crease her forehead while she waits for an answer that can make this right. "Has he shown any interest in you?" I ask.

"I avoid him. I can't trust myself to have an adult conversation, especially when he gives me that look." Yeah, everyone knew the look. The one that says *you're the only one I see in this whole God damn world*. She throws her hands up in exasperation. "I swear, I've never crushed this hard on anybody."

At first, I think this misery is just dramatics because her personality is wired that way — she has a double degree in dance and human resources – but no, she's really in pain. "Haley," I say, trying to talk her through the problem, "The way I see it, you have two choices: either continue to ignore him and hopefully this will pass, or try to suck it up and get to know him. It might not be what you want, but you'll find out pretty fast if he's interested in you or if he just sees you as a coworker."

She slumps back in the chair, thinking. "Okay, I see what you mean. If I don't resolve this, it'll get worse." She turns to me, face hopeful. "You've got to be my wingman, right? I mean wingwoman. I can't do this alone."

"Yeah, sure, no problem," trying to calm her, but I'm curious about what she wants me to do to help.

"Let's take a walk," Nina suggests. "I need the air and I don't want to be disturbed while we talk." Haley and I are standing inside her office about to sit down. "Go put on your sneakers; I'll meet you both in the back of the building in ten minutes."

The company's been promoting exercise during work hours with a friendly steps competition. Walking meetings were becoming the norm for the departments. This isn't our regularly scheduled meeting. With the Las Vegas conference looming, Haley and I are scrambling to schedule as many interviews with candidates as possible for the other sites. I'll only be gone for three days, but that means Haley would have to handle everything on her own. I assumed when Nina asked us to meet, we would discuss how my brief absence would be handled.

We reach the industrial park's common picnic area. The benches we settle on are dry and warm from the sun. Haley's frowning and I can't help feeling uneasy. Nina sighs. "I called this meeting to discuss the new direction for staffing. Allison asked me not to say anything, but I disagree with her. Nothing I'm about to say is a secret."

She turns her concerned gaze to me. "The last two weeks you must have noticed that your caseload has been lighter."

Staffing levels fluctuate all the time, but to call attention to it in a meeting is not good.

I sit straighter. "Yes, I've wondered about that. I'd heard rumors about a freeze and thought that might be the cause."

Nina shakes her head no. "It's true this company is always talking about a freeze on hiring, but that's not the case. Allison has asked me to assign all new openings to Haley."

The shock has me twisting in my seat. "And why are you giving Haley my work?" an uncomfortable hard knot of anger and fear roils in my gut.

Nina and Haley exchange a glance, but it's Nina who responds. "To be completely honest, Allison says you won't be with us by the end of the month. She's preparing Haley to be the next recruiter. We're already interviewing coordinators to take her place."

"If this is her intention, why not let me go now?"

Nina lets out a breath. "She's being pressured to allow you to go to the Las Vegas conference. You have powerful friends who have confidence in you. She thinks the confidence is misplaced and wants to hedge her bet. She needs someone in place that knows the hiring managers and the positions."

Haley speaks up. "I've been wanting to tell you this for a long time. I discussed this with Nina, and she thought that we should talk to you together. Allison has been meeting with me nearly every day since she's been on board."

I shake my head, trying to absorb the intrigue. Matt was right, corporate culture is like surviving on an island. "I'm angry," I admit, "but I don't have a right to be. Haley, you're an employee and I'm essentially temporary help. Allison can use my talents any way she feels will help her division."

Nina is kneading her fingers, trying to contain her emotions. I can see she thinks this is unfair. We're friends, but she's also my manager and she's risking a lot. "The truth is Allison is uncomfortable with your expertise in talent acquisition. Although she's a very good HR administrator, she has little experience and a lot of misconceptions about staffing."

Great, I'm dealing with a VP's humongous ego. No surprise. But you'd think she'd want someone who has experience to help her in an area where she's deficient.

Nina anxiously watches me while I try to process this information. "I know it's a lot to take in, but since you joined us, the staffing program has been successful and the hiring managers have nothing but praise for you. Allison is more comfortable with Haley because she's not threatening and won't know to contradict her when she wants to implement something that won't work."

If she really doesn't want me on her team, then attempting to recruit Okobi might not be worth the effort. I look off into the distance, considering this option. "It might be easier if I cut my losses and leave now."

"Kellis! Don't you dare let her push you out," Nina warns. "Myself and a few other people in this company want you here. We'll do everything we can to support you. You'll have a lighter case load thanks to Allison, so concentrate on Kyle Okobi. If you're able to bring him to Drachen, Allison can't end your contract."

I stay later than normal at my desk in the dungeon, mostly staring at my laptop and trying to formulate a plan. The pressure is mounting, and I've got nothing at the moment. Kurt called earlier to let me know he was going to a dinner meeting and wouldn't need a ride home. He also reminded me that it was my turn to fix breakfast tomorrow. I'm relieved I don't have to endure a ride home with him while I listen to his questions or suggestions.

It's too quiet. There're normally a few people milling around on this floor during the day, but it's late and I hear no one. The light from my office is the only one that spills out into the dim hallway. I decide to pack up my laptop and head home. Maybe tomorrow will bring a different perspective.

"I hoped I'd find you down here."

I look up to see Matt's concerned face, his presence filling the small office. He steps inside and closes the door.

"Hi you," I say, glad to see him.

"I tried to call a few times, but it went to voicemail. Are you okay?"

I frown at my turned-off phone sitting on the desk. "Sorry, rough day." Slipping my phone and laptop into my case I find my purse in a drawer. I adjust it on my shoulder and face him. "Did you have a meeting with Richard? Is that why you're here?"

"I did see Richard. I spoke with him briefly. But that's not why I'm here." He places a hand on my arm and his touch sends tiny little pulses through my arm. "I can't wait until Wednesday. I'm here to see you." Before I can ask more questions, he gathers me in his arms. My bags slide to the floor and I move into to the hardness of his body. I want nothing more than to stay here with him and be comforted. I sigh, breathing him in while his lips brush my forehead. "I guess you did have a bad day." He draws me tighter. "Why don't you come over to my place and I'll make you dinner? You can tell me all about it."

I'm surprised at the offer. It feels like it's too soon to go over to his house. But suddenly it's all I want to do. "Yes, I'd like that. I need to go home first and change. Give me your address and I'll meet you there."

The shower steams the bathroom quickly. It's the first thing I do when I get home. It's a long, hot, soapy affair to wash away some of the day's tension. Still warm from the water, I towel off, blow my hair nearly dry and slip into a shirt and a pair of jeans. Chloe is not at home. I text her and she says she's leaving work now. I tell her I'm going out with some coworkers tonight and will be back late. I get a smiley emoji back. I don't want to tell her about Matt. Not just yet. It's still too early to talk about him. I want to see where this leads. Talking to Chloe is like talking to my mom. If one knows, they both know.

The hall closet has somehow swallowed my coat. I'm swiping garments I haven't seen in years to the right when a car pulls up outside. The light in the kitchen is off. I walk to the window and part the curtains enough to see out. A black BMW is parked next door. Two people get out of the vehicle, talking too loudly, like they've been drinking a little too much. One is Kurt and the other is a tall blonde. I can see from here she's a beautiful model type. They're laughing. That's surprising, because I've never seen Kurt laugh. The most I ever got from him was a disapproving smile. They seem awfully chummy. I thought he said he didn't know anyone here. They link their arms and weave up the path to his house. They stop briefly on the porch and she kisses him, until Kurt breaks the contact, opens the door, and ushers her inside. "Dinner meeting, my freaking ass," I shout at the window. I stomp back to the closet and yank a jacket out. I find my keys and head for the garage.

CHAPTER 13

Winner Sausage Dinner

The car lights in front of me suddenly flash red. I'm too close and brake hard while I pull the wheel to the right. I'm angry driving, which is stupid. I take a deep breath and resume driving with more attention to the road. Instead of thinking about my dinner with Matt, my mind wanders to Kurt and his friend. "Kurt doesn't have to tell you where and who he goes out with," I mumble to myself. "He's never shown any interest in you other than being annoying as hell. What if he made a move?" That was interesting. Where was I going with this line of reasoning? I make an exasperated sigh. I'm sure the pressure at work is finally getting to me. I don't answer the annoying question. The GPS on my phone announces I've arrived at my destination. I pull into Matt's driveway. It's a ranch-style like mine in taupe and white.

Matt's already in the doorway in a T-shirt and jeans. Light streaming from behind makes him an imposing shadow. He walks down the path and over to my car. We stroll back to the house with his arm around my shoulders. He takes my coat and disappears around the corner. I hear him come back but he makes a detour through the kitchen. When he reappears, he has two drinks. He hands me one. "Didn't ask if you like white wine. I figure you being a girl and all that white wine would be fine."

I take the drink. I can tell him later that I would've preferred a beer. But it's a sweet gesture, and I'll let him take care of me. There's tension along his jawline. The implacable Matty Ice appears a bit anxious. I smile at him to ease his nerves, then take a sip. "This's really good, thank you." There's a bike wheel leaning against the wall and a chain on a side table. Thanks to my brother, I know something about the sport. "I like your home."

He looks around, maybe really seeing what it looks like to an outsider. "I've been here a long time — maybe it's time to update the furniture — but it suits me."

The house has a lived-in family feel to it. I can picture him here working on his bike in the living room.

"Would you like to sit in here or in the kitchen? I know I promised to make you dinner, but I like you too much to expose you to my cooking, so I picked up Chinese food."

"We can eat and talk on your comfy couch," I'm already walking toward the aroma of food. A half dozen small paper containers litter the kitchen counter. I'm excited and start opening them, appreciating the rich aromas that tickle my nose. Matt is leaning back against the counter watching me, delight lifting the corner of his mouth. I stop opening a container and place my arms around his neck, leaning against his body. I kiss him and his arms go around my waist. His wine-soaked tongue is probing and mine tangles with his. I liked the first kiss we had in a dark alcove. That had the danger of discovery, but this is nice too. He could feel like home if I let this happen. He holds me tighter, lips hungry, wanting more. I slide my hand down, rubbing his hip, then slip my hand into his back pocket. He pulls away. The way he looks, handsome and sexy, I want to continue kissing. I pull on his shirt to lower his lips, but he resists and searches my face. "What do you want?" he asks, his voice husky.

He's letting me choose to take this further. "I could you eat you," I say, my fingers tracing his jaw, "but then there'd be a chunk out of your pretty face." I separate from him and grab a plate from the counter. "Here, fill this." He reluctantly takes the plate. I finish opening the remaining containers. We spoon several portions on our plates.

I'm about to grab a fork when Matt holds out a pair of chopsticks. Not the unfinished wooden kind that comes with the meal, but a beautiful polished ebony. "Is this from a set?" I take the pair from him.

"It was a wedding present. I got it in the settlement."

I knew about his marriage, but it's the first time he's mentioned it. This might be the house where he lived with Jena, although I can't imagine that posh supermodel living in suburbia.

I follow him back into the living room. We kick off our shoes and sit cross-legged on the couch. I'm rusty with the chopsticks but it always comes back to me when I'm starving.

"Want to tell me about your day?" he says, shoveling a large portion of rice into his mouth.

I've just finished biting into a pot sticker. I chew for a bit, swallow, and chase it down with a sip of wine. "Oh, you know, it's the pressure of finding and hiring candidates for managers that have been requesting approval on additional staff for months. When they finally get it, I'm to produce the candidate overnight."

"Is it different from when you were running your company?" He seems interested, munching away.

"The basic work is the same, but I made the decisions. If I got overwhelmed, I hired someone to help me. I didn't have to clear it with seven other people."

"What you're trying to say is that you need a vacation?"

I laugh. "I haven't been at Drachen long enough to get time off.

Although, taking off to an exotic island sounds really good right now."

He points his chopsticks at me. "Everyone needs a break. I think you need a weekend away," he grins. "How about us going away for a couple of days? We can go wine tasting in Sonoma, skiing in Tahoe, or we can always go to the beach and hang out. We can go this weekend." He says this like it just occurred to him, but I suspect he might have thought about going away together before this conversation.

I'm picturing us together in a ski lodge or a beach bungalow. I almost say yes until I realize that would be the weekend after the Vegas conference. I'll probably be working the whole weekend to catch up. If I'm successful with Okobi, I'll need to be available to him before he signs his offer letter. A myriad of problems always arises with high-profile candidates. "That's not a good weekend. I'll be going to the R&D conference in Las Vegas this week."

"You should be back on Friday or Saturday the latest. We can head out after that."

"Aren't you going to the conference?"

"That's for R&D. I work in manufacturing. How did you get approval to attend?"

"Kurt Heinrich. There's a candidate that he wants me to approach while at the conference. His name is Kyle Okobi."

"You'll be there alone, representing Drachen?"

"No, Kurt and I are going together."

He stiffens and reaches for his glass.

"Have you met Kurt?"

"No, I only know him by reputation. We haven't had the chance to meet yet."

"I have an idea," I say. "Why don't we make plans to go away for a weekend after Kurt's second-in-command is hired? It has to be completed by the end of the month."

Something is still bothering him. "Okay," he says reluctantly, putting his drink down, then shovels food into his mouth.

We finish our meal, fat, happy and a little buzzed from the wine. I'm prone on the couch, my head on the armrest, enjoying the eating afterglow. Matt pulls my feet onto his lap and massages my foot, using his thumb to gently knead my arch. His touch is soothing and sensual as his hands work their magic. I close my eyes, basking in the attention. I know he's watching me, gaging my reaction. But I don't care. I sigh and relax; it feels too good to say no. My right foot tingles, the warmth gone when he turns his attention to the left foot. He takes time, working silently like he did with the first. I purr and mumble to myself, sinking deeper into the pleasure, tension draining from the rest of my body. When the pressure ceases and the tiredness is gone from my feet, he waits a few moments, idly stroking my ankle. Then he slips over to my side of the couch and moves his body beside me, one arm stretches out to a box on the side table. He taps it and music fills the room with something soft. He changes his position to move his heavy body on top, sinking me deeper into the recesses of the couch. "Tell me if you don't want this," he says, then places a kiss on my forehead.

There's so much right about him, it's me who's afraid to accept that he wants me. "Tell me why," I ask, but he doesn't need to. I can feel the physical proof growing against my thigh.

"Tell you why?" he repeats, pulling my braid. "Do you want poetry?"

I touch his face. He grabs my fingers and kisses them. I've thought about him, us, together. His face is the last image I see before I fall asleep. But my father's warning floats to the surface, pushing in like an unwanted guest at a dinner. 'Kellis, don't get your honey...' I drown it out. It's not fair, he seems perfect, or close enough. Or is it my mother's warning about a woman and two men that will destroy my life? There're too many people in my head. I push it all away and concentrate on what's in front of me.

"I like you," he says and kisses my open palm. "I want to know you." Another kiss. "I want to be someone important in your life." His lips land softly on mine, but it doesn't take long for the intensity of our need to return. "Not here," he whispers in my mouth, "not for our first time."

He stands, extending his hand to me. I'm barely on my feet when my legs are swept from me and I find myself in his arms, moving deeper into the house. There's music here too. The bedroom is large with nothing to break up the grey-blue walls except for the white doors and ceiling. It's a spartan existence with only a bed and a side table.

Matt settles me on the bed, touches my face, then moves away. I watch him bathed in soft half shadow from the lamp. He holds my gaze while his hand moves slowly, easing the black cotton up to expose taut abs. The tease is only for seconds, but I want to tear the fabric from his hot body. I'm denied my fantasy when he pulls it over his head. Seeing him half naked is like a shot of caffeine that sends my pulse racing. He takes his time to release his jeans button and slides the zipper open. The outline of his sizable bulge is visible through the fabric of his shorts. The sexy show continues until his clothes are discarded at his feet. He stands with feet apart, displaying the lean hard muscles of a cyclist. I reach out, mesmerized by his broad shoulders, to run my hand over the smooth, well-defined power of his deltoids. He tugs at my shirt. "This is the part where you get undressed," fingers reaching for my top button. "Let me help."

I let his fingers brush my skin as he slowly releases each button. I'm shivering, wanting him to be less considerate of my clothing. His hand slips the fabric off my shoulders. He gazes at my almost nakedness, a glint playing in his inky blue eyes. His touch lingers on my skin as he pushes the straps off my shoulders. "I like you pink and lacey," his voice wolfish. "I'll remember you like this when you visit me at work." His hand reaches around to release my bra hooks. The support for my breasts falls away to the floor. The coolness of the room reaches me, but I don't think about it when he unzips my pants, his big hands moving over my ass to push the jeans down. I step out of them and they join the rest of my clothes.

He pulls me to him, his grip firm at my waist. I relax into his chest, breathing him in and listening to his heartbeat. His hand catches my braid, threading it through his hand until it reaches the end. He winds the thick plait around his fist. My breath catches when he tugs my hair back, tilting my chin up to look at him. He stares at me with wicked, bright eyes that invite me to play. Then he kisses me hard, holding my hair taut. I respond to his lust and the strength of him holding me captive. I move seductively against his body, his cock insistent at my hip, my pussy wet with wanting him. I pull my lips away. "Take me to your bed," I breathe, wanting us in a mindless hot frenzy making love.

He loosens his hold, turning his attention to the length of hair in his hand. "This is the first thing I noticed about you when you walked past me that day," he muses. "That sexy braid swaying with your hips like a come fuck me invitation." His interested gaze comes back to me. "Tell me, Ms. Ivarsson, is that what you were doing? Because you got my attention."

I smile up at him. "I'm sure it was some cosmic force that brought me to the building, so I could wiggle a proposition at you."

Unexpected laughter bubbles up. "Something out of our control is conspiring to put us together?" He gives me a disbelieving shake of his head. "I'm glad we got that straightened out, and here I thought it was because you had a cute butt." He releases my hair, letting it fall to my back.

I rock up on my toes to brush his lips to tempt him. "This is the part where you take me to bed and fuck me senseless."

His lips drop to my ear. "On the bed and sit back on your knees. I want to see my Godiva unbind her hair for me."

I try to keep my knees together kneeling on the bed. He's a few feet away from me as I finger the band at the end of my plait and begin to unweave its length. I perform this slowly as he watches with hooded eyes. His cock twitches with anticipation until my coffee-colored locks fall to my waist. I lift my hands, my posture abandon, raking my fingers through my hair to tease it into fullness.

He returns to tower over me, sweeping the hair away from my shoulder, his lips brushing lightly. He urges me onto my back, pinning me with his heaviness, his mouth kissing, nibbling at my neck while his hand urges my legs open.

His big hand is at my mound rubbing slowly, teasing at my slit, my body squirming at his touch until his finger invades me, pushing deep inside my pussy. I gasp, aware of how wet I am as his finger moves. His thumb brushes my clit and I moan. The heat of his breath tickles my ear. "Would you like more, Godiva?" his voice a husky tease.

I arch my back moaning.

"You need to say it."

I close my eyes. "More," I breathe. "I want more, I want your cock."

"Not until I know you're ready." He kisses me and slips another finger inside.

My hips follow his fingers moving in and out. He's watching, varying the movement, prolonging my pleasure. I let him explore me, run his hand over my contours, enjoying his mouth trailing where he touches. I pull my hand down to reach for his cock. It pulses inside my palm, thick and hard. I curl my fingers around its head. I have his attention while I move my hips down enough for the top of his cock to meet my entrance, using its head to rub my clit, tempting him to push his hardness inside me. He draws my hands away, placing them over my head. He holds them there with one hand and guides himself inside me. I welcome the pressure. He moves inside me slowly, lazily, continuing to tease. "I'm ready," I moan.

He responds with a grind of his hips. The action sends me into shivers, but it's only enough to torment. "You're sexy as fuck with your hair all around you looking like a wild, deflowered nymph. He makes another slow grind. I clench his cock and he moans.

"I'm more like a fairy captured by a horny god who decided he wanted a plaything." He chuckles and hits my sweet spot.

"You don't look real, Godiva, but you feel real enough. Don't disappear before we finish; you've already bewitched me."

I'm crazy. Ready for my release. I can't believe his control. He looks like he can do this all night. He did say that he was the best at sex, but I thought he was just flirting that night. "Matt, let's do this." I want to come so badly that I'm considering satisfying myself.

"I want you to come when I say." His lips are on mine, stopping my protest. I writhe under him, wanting to touch myself, but his hold is firm. "I'll release you, if that's what you want, but if you trust me and do it my way, your orgasm will be intense." He smiles. "And when you've come harder than you ever have and think it can't get any better, we'll do it again."

I'm on the edge; my body is aching with want. I'm looking into the face of my own cocky porn star that's promising to take me to orgasmic paradise several times. "Your way," I breathe.

His hard cock and his sexy whispered words take me to the edge several times. I respond to each movement, every dirty suggestion until I almost beg him for my release. I hold on to his strong body like I'm suspended on a ledge about to drop to my death. I'm unable to sustain the wanting any longer. I dig my nails deep into the flesh of his back. He twists to release my painful hold but doesn't protest. Eyes dark with lust, he peers down, fixated on me. "Now," I whisper a demand. "I want it now."

His kiss is hungry as his hips grind. I hold his face in my hands when I catch the beginnings of my surrender. I lift my hips to meet his thrust, and the contact ignites me. I cry out when my climax explodes, as it fires pleasure through my body. Matt swears with his last deep drive, his warm fluid spilling into me. I'm heady with the thick, heavy musk from our bodies. His slick frame stretched out on top of me, unmoving. I'm still tingling when he rolls away and gathers me in his arms. I say nothing, content that he's holding me. He kisses my hair. I close my eyes and bask in his arms.

"Don't fall asleep," he whispers, "we're not done."

Matt's curled around a pillow asleep when I slip from his bed. The music is still playing. I gather my clothes, putting them on in the living room. I tap the black box on the side table. The quiet is almost eerie.

It's late when I pull into my driveway. The car idles as the garage door makes its slow ascent. The black BMW is still parked outside and there are no lights on in Kurt's house. My annoyance with him reasserts itself. Why am I so irritated with him? Why shouldn't I be? He's inserted himself in my life and there's no way to ignore him until after the Vegas trip is over. Then I'll have a talk with him about finding his own way to work. But he did give me a chance at the biggest candidate prize of the millennium. I should remember that and turn my attention to Matt when I have an urge to strangle Kurt. I smile. Matt's scent lingers on my skin, and it conjures up a sexy montage of us together in his bed. I can't wait for this hire to be done so we can play the weekend away.

CHAPTER 14

Transformation

I drag myself into the kitchen at about 5:30 in the morning, tired from lack of sleep. It's my turn to cook and since I'm banned from heating toaster pastry, I've figured out how to save myself from ridicule. It's a stroke of genius that I made a breakfast casserole during the weekend and all I have to do is warm it in the oven. Kurt walks into the kitchen with an unfamiliar thirty-watt grin on his face. It's a change from his normal bad-boy brooding presence. He takes his place at the counter and unfurls a newspaper. "Did you have a good dinner meeting yesterday?" curious at what he'll say.

His grin goes up a few more watts into toothpaste commercial territory. "Yes, thanks for asking." He says this like he doesn't have a sex kitten stashed in his house. "My meeting was very productive, but we weren't able to finish our discussion. We've decided to meet again tonight. I'll find a ride home after my meeting."

Why can't he say he's met someone? I shove the utensil drawer a little too hard after retrieving a spatula. He swings his gaze over to me. I ignore his unasked questions of why I'm banging around the kitchen and continue working. Kurt pulls the napkin from his plate and places it on his lap. That's another condition he insisted on when he proposed this breakfast club: formal dishes and cloth napkins. I covertly look out the window. Sure enough, the black BMW is still there. Looks like Sleeping Beauty needs her rest. The timer goes off. I put on my oven mitts.

"Good morning," says Chloe. She stops to peek at what I'm pulling out of the oven. "Smells good. Did everyone sleep well?" she beams.

I side-step her to place the casserole on the counter. "Actually, pretty freaking great," I mumble.

"Excellent," he says, throwing a sideways glance at me.

Chloe opens the refrigerator door and pours herself a glass of orange juice, then brings the pitcher to the counter. "When are you two leaving for Las Vegas? Is it this week or next?"

Kurt looks up from his plate. "We leave in two days. That reminds me. They've sent me our travel agenda. I'll send you the email. It'll be easier to hire a car to go to the airport. Would you like to book the car, or should I do it?"

"I'll book the car," I say.

He reaches for the spatula and digs out a wedge of casserole. "We won't have to worry about transportation while in Las Vegas. We'll have the use of a car service." He glances over at me with a spark of excitement lighting his face. "I've never been…is it as sinful as they say?"

I take the seat next to him and move my napkin to my lap. Now he wants to know what kind of mischief to get into in Las Vegas. "I've been to Vegas," I say casually. "It can be anything you want it to be."

Kurt raises an eyebrow. "That's interesting. Was it for work or pleasure?"

"Kellis had a..." Chloe stops herself before she completes the sentence. She looks over at me, then begins again. "Kellis was there often visiting a friend."

I'd been to Las Vegas many times to visit my concierge boyfriend who worked for one of the big hotels on the Strip. He was well connected and I met a lot of wonderful people through him.

Kurt leans toward me with an unmistakable glint in his eyes. "You'll have to show me around when we're there."

He's probably feeling frisky after his night with his mystery woman. I shrug, not willing to participate in his excitement. My job is on the line. Okobi is my only concern, not playing tour guide to this privileged VP. "I thought this was strictly a business trip...or am I missing something?" It was meant to be playful, but it comes out sarcastic. I didn't mean to express what I was feeling, but it hits him like cold water.

Disbelief widens Kurt's eyes. I've never seen him at a loss for words. He drops his gaze and stabs at his plate. "You're right. Let's concentrate on Okobi," he says, getting back to business.

I look over at Chloe, who gives me a disapproving stare that makes me wish I was somewhere else.

Kurt pours orange juice in his glass. He offers to pour for me, but I shake my head no. "The attendance will be light on the first day of the conference," he sets down the pitcher. "People are coming in from all over and checking in at different times. There'll be some workshops to attend in the afternoon, but the big event of that day will be a cocktail party. There might be a possibility to talk to Okobi at that function. You said you knew him?"

I use my napkin before I answer. Kurt appears to be past my unfortunate buzz kill. "I was one of many recruiters that tried to place him at a company before he graduated from college. It's unusual for an outside recruiter to contact a college student with no experience. I did it as a favor to a hiring manager. We spoke several times and kept in touch over the years."

"Good, then this won't be a cold contact. Make a point of talking to him briefly at the cocktail party to catch up on the first night. I know he'll be attending the dinner party on the second day. At that function there'll be a chance for a more in-depth conversation with him. You'll need to be laser focused on him during the dinner party."

I nod, feeling better that we have a game plan.

Kurt pushes his plate away and turns to me. "There won't be a chance to speak with him on Friday, the last day of the conference. There's a golfing event planned for that day. I know Okobi isn't a golfer. He'll probably fly out early. You only have two days. We need a commitment from him by Thursday, no later than Friday."

My stomach tightens into a knot, and that quickly I'm not hungry.

"I'm sure Kellis will get the candidate to commit." My big sister comes to my defense. She reinforces the statement with a look that's reminiscent of our mother. Kurt nods, but he's worried.

Kurt picks up his plate, rinses it in the sink, and places it in the dishwasher. We follow his lead and do the same. In a few minutes, the kitchen is spotless.

"Kellis, I need to speak to you about Mom."

Kurt gets the hint. "I'll wait outside. We need to be on the road in ten minutes."

Chloe starts talking when we hear the front door close. "I want you to come home as soon as possible after work."

"Why, does Mom want to see us?"

"Mom always wants to see us. I said that so Kurt would leave the room. You're stressing about this trip to Las Vegas."

"I'm okay. I can handle this. "Approaching candidates is nothing new."

"I didn't say you couldn't. I have an idea. Hear me out before you say no."

She looks too serious. I agree to listen to the suggestion she thinks will help.

"Why don't we do a spa visit and some clothes shopping for your trip this afternoon? Tomorrow we can visit the hairstylist. It might give you the boost you need when you're in Vegas."

Allison's no confidence in me was making me doubt myself. If I was going to have any chance of getting Okobi to Drachen, I'd have to be at the top of my game. Something new to wear might be what I need. I hug my sister. "Great idea. I'll leave work at noon."

I pick up my bag and my phone zips.

Godiva, Thank you for a great evening. I missed you this morning. Dinner tonight? Matt

A repeat of last night is tempting, but I can't have any distractions. I'll text him back with a soft no. It's only a few days more. We'll pick up where we left off when I come back from Vegas.

We're in a boutique in Santana Row trying on dresses. The saleswoman and Chloe stand in the entryway to the dressing room looking at me. I've lost weight and all the dresses look like sacks on me. "I'll get a size smaller in all these dresses," says the saleswoman. "I'll be right back."

Chloe watches me through the changing room mirror. "Cheer up, most women would kill to lose weight, and you did it unintentionally."

We do another round of trying on dresses. This time the dresses fit but Chloe isn't satisfied. "If you're trying to get the attention of a man, any man, these dresses aren't going to do it."

I run my hands over the front of the dress. Turning to the side, I check the fit in the mirror. "This is a business function. I can't hang out of my dress. Do you want them to call me the slut of Drachen?"

A 'ha' explodes from Chloe. "You don't need to expose your girls. You can be conservative and sexy. Give me a few minutes and let me find something."

Chloe returns with an armful of dresses, frocks that I would never have chosen. The fabrics are clingy and do a good job of covering me, but they also show off my waist and hug my breasts.

I'm staring at my finished weekly staffing report. I have little to do today and my mind is wandering more since my workload is shrinking. I'm thinking about my new wardrobe I bought yesterday for Vegas. It's only 9:00 am and I'm looking forward to being pampered at the hairstylist today.

Haley's frequent trips to Nina's office for advice is wearing down the carpeting. She's frantic with her increased responsibilities. I suggested she talk to Allison about hiring a coordinator as quickly as possible. She tells me that they've narrowed it down to two candidates, but Allison has decided to intervene and wants to do additional interviews with them. Our VP of HR is making it a habit to circumvent Nina's choices when she's hiring for her team. It's unusual for a VP not to trust her manager. Allison is bringing the term micromanaging to another level.

I asked Haley about Riku. She throws me a *please, with all this shit going on?* look. I don't push the point, grateful not to open that Pandora's box of her feelings right now.

Matt was supportive about my reasons not to see him until I return from my trip. Seriously, I'd rather curl up with him on his couch tonight than stress about Las Vegas.

With little work to do, I leave the job at three and arrive at the hairstylist at four o'clock. Chloe is walking up the path when I push my way into the shop.

Jenny, my stylist, appears from the back room and greets me. "It's been a long time since you've been in. Have a seat and let me take a look at you." I'm wearing my hair in a long ponytail instead of my usual braid. She pulls the band from my hair and lets it fall. It looks healthy enough. "What are we doing today, a trim?"

Chloe pushes into the shop and walks toward Jenny's chair.

"Would you like me to fit you in as well?" Jenny says as Chloe approaches. "I had a cancellation, so I have enough time to work on both of you."

"Thanks, but I think we should just concentrate on Kellis."

Jenny talks to me through the mirror while securing a black cape on me. "What would you like to do today?"

Chloe speaks up. "I think she needs a new look."

"What do you say, Kellis?" Jenny asks.

"I don't know, maybe some highlights?" I respond.

"I think you should cut it."

The statement is so surreal we both stare at Chloe.

"My hair has been this long since I was a teenager," I say, still looking for her to say this is a joke.

"Exactly, you're not a teenager anymore. You rarely wear your hair down and it's always in that braid."

I reach for my hair like a security blanket. It's been like this for so long, I won't recognize me. I look up at Chloe. "How short are we talking? Two or three inches?"

"Don't stick your toe in the water, jump in. Commit to it and cut it off at least to your shoulders, maybe a bob." We both look at Jenny.

"You do have the face for it. I think you'll look really cute with the bob. But if you're not--"

"She's ready," Chloe interrupts. "I'd say go shorter like a pixie, but a bob will do the trick."

"I'm not sure." I'm staring at the dark hair in my hand.

Chloe bends at the waist until we're at the same level, both hands on the arm of the chair. "Do you trust me?

I don't answer.

"You want to win at Corporate, then show them you mean

business. Mom told me this is the way to get your power back."

My hesitation falls away when I see the conviction in her eyes. A wave of nervous energy rips through me and I'm ready to do something that I thought I'd lost. I'm ready to fight.

I glance at Jenny in the mirror. "Do it," I say with determination.

She pulls a gleaming pair of shears from the drawer, poised to cut. "Are you sure?"

Chloe nods at me.

I glance at Jenny. "I'm sure. Do it,"

Jenny grabs a length of hair from my right side and cuts from the base of my neck. I cringe at scissors snipping through hair; it sounds like tearing this close to my ear. She lays the length of hair on the table. I grab at the remaining short ends, but a big chunk of me is missing. My eyes are stinging. This was harder than I imagined. I avoid their stares from the mirror to prevent them from seeing the tears threatening to form in my eyes. They'll think it's silly to mourn for your hair.

Jenny turns me away from the mirror so I can't watch her as she works. She continues to rough cut through my hair until she gets it into a manageable length to style.

Jenny places a hand on my shoulder. "Come on. Let's wash and condition." The water is soothing, but I'm still screaming in my head this was a bad decision. When we return to her station, she swivels my chair to avoid the mirror. The rest of the styling takes much less time. What I end up with, when she turns me to face the large mirror at her station, is a messy bob. The wide-eyed girl with her too-long bangs is gone. The style lends me a heavy dose of sophistication. The wisps of hair frame my face and accentuate my large hazel eyes. I stare at the stranger, wondering who's looking back at me.

Jenny pulls the cape from my shoulders. "So, what do you think?

I turn my head to the right to judge my profile. My hair falls forward and I place a lock behind my ear. "It's different," I say.

"It looks perfect," says Chloe.

My head feels cold as we walk to our cars. I can't keep my hand from my hair. I look at myself in shop windows as we pass, trying to reconcile what I just did in the salon.

Chloe stops before we turn the corner to head for the garage. "I've got another surprise for you," she says in a sing-song voice.

I'm too traumatized to think about a surprise. I'd left a big part of my life back at the salon.

"I thought if you agreed to have your hair cut that you'd need one more service."

The shop was a few doors down from the stylist. We meet with a makeup artist and spend a long time with a woman whose makeup seems overdone. I sit having this woman smear color on my face to please my big sister. I leave the shop with a huge bag of makeup and several sheets of paper explaining how to achieve each look.

Chloe is already at home when I roll into the driveway. I pull my bags out of the back seat and close the door with my hip. I glance at Kurt's house. The black BMW is gone.

CHAPTER 15

The Bay of Mandalay

The car is outside waiting to take us to the airport. I slip into my coat and pull on a hat. The sun isn't up yet, but I know there'll be traffic this early. Chloe is holding the door open as I guide the case onto the porch.

"Have a safe trip. Remember to text me when you get there." I lead the bag to the curb, where the driver jumps out of the car to place it in the trunk. There's a light on at Kurt's house, but I don't see him. We need to get moving and on the road. We decided to have breakfast at the airport after going through TSA. "I'll just go and get the second passenger," I say to the driver. "I'll see what's holding him up."

I walk up the stairs and touch the doorbell. The sound rings through the house but nothing else. I wait a bit. When there's no answer, I knock softly, then harder, almost banging. "Kurt, the car is here we have to go," I shout. No reply. It's cold out here, the wind is whipping at my coat, and the driver is getting impatient. I wave at the driver to reassure him I'm still working on the problem, then try the knob. It's unlocked. I push.

The door opens wide. Stepping inside the foyer, I move further inside, continuing to look around, awestruck. Every inch of the house is decorated for Christmas. Not in a tasteful modern color scheme or traditional red and green, but gaudy dime store stuff, my grandmother would say. The decorations aren't even coordinated. It's like a five-year-old had reign and bought every shiny, tinsely item they could get their tiny little hands on. I pass the living room, where there's a real Douglas fir that's as tall as the ceiling and is packed with ornaments. A strong scent of tree, cinnamon, and apples fill the house. Wrapped gifts of all sizes are strewn around the base like the tree vomited presents. Maybe he's expecting his family to visit?

"Kurt, are you here?" I call, moving further into the house. I peek into the kitchen. Christmas decorations are here too, and the place looks ready for Mrs. Claus to pull out a tray of cookies from the oven. I continue my search. Halfway down the hall I hear Kurt speaking in German mixed with English. "Ja, ja, ich verstehe. Let me know if conditions change. Call me no matter what time. I'll fly back to Germany if I need too. Danke sehr."

"Kurt," I call again.

"Yes, I'm here."

I follow the voice to a room at the end of the hall. He stands near a desk, staring at the phone. He turns red-rimmed eyes towards me, tension creasing his forehead. I'm startled by the transformation. "The door was open," I throw a hand in the direction of the entryway. "The car is here; are you ready?" I want to say more, but I'm not sure how he'd respond to questions.

"Good," he says, distracted. "My bag is in my bedroom. I'll just be a moment. Please wait for me outside."

We're silent during the ride, and only the driver's music, a stream of Bollywood hits, interrupts our quiet. We check our bags at curbside then enter the terminal, moving among a sea of people destined for other locations. After leaving the TSA line, we walk to our gate. I point out a few places on the way where we can eat, but Kurt rejects them all.

"Getting through the TSA line took longer than I anticipated," he says. "I'm sure when we arrive at the gate, they'll be calling passengers to board soon."

He's right. Soon after checking in, the first-class passengers are called to board. Kurt grabs his carry-on and starts to walk towards the boarding gate. I scramble to my feet, following after him. I'm about to remind him that this is not a call for everyone to get on board. When I catch up to him, he's handing over his ticket and passport to the attendant. She glances at the items and nods. "Do you have your ticket?" he says to me. "You'll need to give it to her so we can board."

I don't question him; I just fish in my purse and pull out the ticket and my passport. I know there's a rejection coming but I figure we're already in line and maybe she'll just let it slide. The woman glances at the documents. "Welcome aboard. I hope you have a wonderful flight." Kurt begins walking through the gateway.

Once at the entrance to the plane, another attendant reviews our tickets and gestures us to the right. Kurt nods and walks into first class. "I think our seats are here," he says. "Would you like me to store your things? I hand him the bag and he hoists it into the overhead compartment. I shrug out of my coat and he stows that as well.

"Does Drachen always allow you to go first class?" I'm thinking right now that I'm really enjoying working for a big company.

"Have you ever flown first class before?"

"No, never." I admit.

"Well, first class in an international flight is much better. Asian and Arabic airlines are much more luxurious. Unfortunately, this is a short flight. Although you'll be comfortable, you won't have much time to enjoy it. Would you like the aisle or window?"

I take the window and savor my surroundings. I don't care. I'm flying first class to Vegas. Kurt is cordial, talking about work, but he never says anything about the phone call at his house, and I don't ask him why he seems tired and distracted.

We roll into the lobby of Mandalay Bay. We hadn't requested early check-in, so the hotel offers to store our luggage until our rooms are ready. We walk over to the meeting area and find the conference. We check in and are given a badge and a schedule of workshops. I note the cocktail party will be at 5 o'clock. There're a couple of seminars I might attend, but I'll leave early from the conference to get ready for the party.

Kurt scans the schedule. "I see that Ichabod Johnson is speaking. That seminar has already begun." He glances toward the meeting rooms. "Is there anything you need before I leave?"

"No, I'll be fine. Have a good time."

"Then I'll see you at the cocktail party." He walks toward the meeting rooms. He passes several people and nods at a few as he continues to stroll.

"Kellis?" A distinctive Nigerian voice sails across the room. I look into the crowd to see Kyle Okobi walking towards me. I pull off my cap and run my fingers through my hair. I had hoped our first meeting would be at the party tonight.

"Kellis, it's you. It's been too long."

"Kyle," I push out my hand and he shakes it in a warm greeting. "I was told you might be here. Have you just arrived?"

"Yes, yes. I've just arrived. The other members of the Endeavor team will be here shortly. I hear you're working for Drachen? Is that correct?"

"I have for a few months now. It's a good company." Before I can continue, we're overtaken by other members of the Endeavor party. I'm introduced to a woman and two males, all engineers. I make my apologies to leave and ask him if he will be at the cocktail party this evening.

"Yes, we all will. I hope to see you. We can catch up later."

It's nearly time. I'm in front of the mirror trying to fasten my earrings. My nerves are causing my fingers to seem fat and bumbling. You'd think I'd never done this before. When I finally get them in place, I step back to check the black sleeveless cocktail dress that clings to my body and the red heels. The woman staring back at me is confident. I smile. I think I'll throw a little caution to the wind and be the woman in the mirror tonight.

I enter the ballroom to a mixed bag of suits, business casual, and a few women in cocktail dresses. Neither Kurt nor Okobi are here. I walk to the bar and order a tonic and lime from an efficient bartender. I'll stay sober while my companions get ripped. Drunk engineers. Not a pretty sight.

I walk around, not seeing anyone I know. I'm reluctant to insert myself into a conversation, so I find a seat at a café table and people watch. I've been out of the business for a long time. In the old days I could walk into a room like this and know everyone here. I'll remedy that soon. I'll engage Okobi, but if Kurt arrives first, I'll ask him to introduce me to some of his contacts so I can start the evening out right.

I slip my phone out of my bag to check messages.

"Kellis, I can't believe it. I see you twice in a couple weeks. I almost didn't recognize you. When I saw those long legs and you staring down at your phone, I said to myself *fresh meat*. I had to come over to introduce myself. When lo and behold, it's you."

I glance around to see who's noticing this conversation, then turn my attention to him. "Why are you bothering me, Tim? Go away." He's right; I go for months without seeing my ex-boyfriend and now he's popping up again.

"I'm going to ignore that." He looks around at the crowd. "I don't see your new boyfriend. Is he here?"

"What new boy... Oh, you mean Matt. No, he'll probably show up at the manufacturing conference next month. Where's Candy?" His new girlfriend is nowhere in sight. The question doesn't even register a blip on his radar.

He shrugs. "I don't know. Taping her show maybe? Candy is not in the same business, but you are. How about taking me up on my offer? It's still open. We could celebrate getting back together again and consummate it as well. Dump Matt, I used to be married to a supermodel, Westmore. That guy isn't right for you. He's too, too Vermont for you."

"What do you mean by that? Never mind." I throw a dismissive hand at him. If I keep walking into his verbal traps, we'll be here all night. "Are we going to have the same conversation that we had in the restaurant, the last time I saw you--?"

"Still testy, I see. Is it because of your new hair?" He leans in. "I like it, by the way. You look pretty damn sexy tonight. Why don't I give you my hotel key?"

I pull back from him. I'm thinking about throwing a perfectly good drink at him when Okobi enters the room with the Endeavor team. Kurt arrives too in the opposite direction. Tim catches me looking at the new arrivals.

"That's Kurt Heinrich, the new VP of R&D at Drachen in the US. I heard he's looking for a second-in-command to help him whip that division into shape." He shakes his head and looks at me accusingly. "Kellis, I'm disappointed in you. You promised you'd contact me if there was a job that would fit my skills."

"I don't have time for this. You need to leave."

"You don't have time for this because I see whiz kid Kyle Okobi walking in as well. I know what's going on. You're here trying to get Okobi away from Endeavor. Why else would a recruiter be attending an R&D conference for her company?"

I stand up and swipe my purse off the table. "I'll let you ponder that one on your own. I'm busy. I would like to say it's been a pleasure, but it hasn't." I hear that stupid chuckle as I walk away. I spare a glance in Kurt's direction. He's watching me with narrowed eyes and a frown of disapproval. That's no surprise. He's probably thinking I'm trying to pick up another man.

I wave at Okobi as I approach him. He tilts his head up in acknowledgment. When I reach him, I greet the members of his team, but they quickly move away to talk to other people at the party.

"Kellis, can I get you a drink?" Okobi says. I smile up at him, and he responds with a wide grin.

"Yes please, I'd like that." We stroll over to the bar.

He turns to me. "What will you have?"

I'm glad it's the same bartender who made my first drink. "Would you like the same drink, miss?" the bartender asks.

I almost sigh in relief. "Yes, that'll be fine."

Okobi orders a whiskey neat and we find seats at a table.

Okobi raises his glass. "To old friends."

"And to new adventures." I add touching my glass to his.

His eyes spark. "Could you be speaking about your job at Drachen or is there another adventure you have in mind?"

"Every day is a new adventure. I think you told me that once."

"I probably did, because this is very true. You've landed on your feet." He tilts his drink towards me in appreciation. "I was sorry to hear when your business closed. But look at you now. Prosperous and as beautiful as ever."

I flash him a smile, then take a sip of my drink. Okobi is the product of a Nigerian father and a French mother, educated in South Africa, England, and the US. The interesting mix of genes produced an off-the-chart intelligence, confidence, and a damn sexy man. He was about to finish graduate school when we met. Sparks flew at our first lunch meeting. Unfortunately for me, he was dating his then gorgeous girlfriend, his now wife.

After several meetings and long phone conversations over the years, we've settled into a flirtatious friendship. He makes me laugh and is someone I can debate the philosophical points of life. Lovers I have, but good friends like him are few. "Thank you, Kyle. How're Gracie and the kids?"

"My children are growing like wild weeds. Gracie. Well, she misses California."

"How do you like Arizona?"

"Me, I like the hot weather, so I'm very content in this. But as they say, happy wife, happy life."

"Does this mean it's time to make a change?"

"I would say..." he hesitates for a bit. He's not someone who plays coy when it's important. "It might be time to consider it..." his gaze drifts to his colleagues across the room.

"How's your project at Endeavor?"

Slight tension frames his face as his attention trails back to me. "It's no secret that my project is being curtailed in favor of a more lucrative contract with the government."

Time to press the pain point. "Are they talking about you taking over the new project?"

"They have. We've had several meetings on the subject, but it's not something I'm interested in. You know me, Kellis. I must be passionate about what I do or there's no point in the work."

My finger traces the rim of my glass. I meet his expectant gaze. "I do know you're a passionate man," I say with a dash of flirtation.

He laughs. "I never tire of this little game we play, but do you seriously have something in mind?"

I don't want to present my proposal too early, but I have to give enough to pique his interest. "Kurt Heinrich needs a second-in-command and I think you would be perfect for the position. Besides the generous benefits we'd offer, as the second-in-command you would maintain the team and it's expected to grow. You would have your pick of projects." Out of the corner of my eye, I see the Endeavor team paying more attention to our meeting. I sigh. "I'll need to leave you soon. Your colleagues think I'm monopolizing your time. We don't want them to get the wrong impression."

He looks at me like my leaving is a blow to his ego. "Will you be attending the dinner tomorrow?" I say.

"Yes, I'll be there." He stands and extends his hand. I rise and shake his palm. I lean toward him and whisper. "Think about what I've said. If you're interested, we can speak more about the opportunity. Privately, of course. If not, we can continue catching up. I know you have a ton of pictures of the kids I haven't seen."

"I'll think about your proposal very seriously," eyes bright with mischief. "I look forward to seeing you tomorrow."

Kurt and I don't speak during the remainder of the cocktail party. More people arrive and there're some I know. I spend the time catching up with old friends but I'm always aware of Kurt's eyes on me. And I'd also bet that my ex Tim is watching me like a hawk. The cocktail party is winding down and people are discussing where they're going for dinner. I receive a couple of offers, but I decline in favor of a bath and ordering room service.

My key lands on the side table beside the bed. I pull off my shoes. These new red heels make my calves look great, but they're just a little too high. I'm pleased with my meeting with Okobi. I have more hope now than I did when the idea was proposed. If my luck holds, I could close this deal tomorrow and we could have free champagne on the plane to celebrate on the way home.

I'm about to limp into the bathroom to turn on the water when my phone rings. It's Kurt. "Hello?"

There's a moment's hesitation. "Yes, Kellis. I want to invite you to dinner. I'd like to do a debrief to discuss your conversation with

Kyle. Is this acceptable?"

I really want to take a bubble bath, rub my feet, and binge watch something on TV. But we're here for business. There's too much riding on this gamble not to debrief and form a plan for tomorrow. I have to get Okobi's commitment by Friday or sooner. "Yes, that's acceptable. What kind of restaurant are we going to? Should I throw on a pair jeans?"

"No, I don't have time for you to change. What you're wearing is fine. Meet me in the lobby in about 5 minutes." He clicks off.

CHAPTER 16

Fly High

The driver opens the door for me. This is not an Uber ride. This is a small limo. When we're both inside the car, Kurt slides the window separating us from the driver and gives him the address to Cosette's. I'm glad I didn't throw on a pair of jeans. Cosette's is a high-end French restaurant off the strip. I've heard the restaurant is exclusive. You need to secure reservations months in advance like the French laundry in Napa.

Kurt shifts in his seat. His shoulders are tense under his expensive suit. He has difficulty making eye contact with me. What is not right in his world this time?

"Who was the man you were speaking with when I arrived?" he says, not in a nice way, before I have a chance to lock my seatbelt.

I snap the belt closed and twist my body to look at him. "He's someone I placed at Variance. I'm not sure why my conversation with him has anything to do with the Okobi debrief."

"I just want to make sure you're staying focused on the target.

That you don't become sidetracked."

We were starting the evening off with a fight. Better to soothe the waters or this will be a long night. "He approached me," I say evenly. "I was waiting for Okobi and in the meantime, Tim shows up. If you were watching me, then you know as soon as Okobi arrived, I spoke to him."

"Tim who?" he says, very close to demanding.

Tim, it's none of your fucking business. Instead I huff out. "Tim Cortez."

He slides his attention out the window. "He looked very relaxed speaking with you. I thought it was a personal relationship."

"He's in sales and marketing with an engineering background. They're all like that."

We were thankfully silent for about fifteen minutes into the ride. I want to eat at Cosette's but I'm not looking forward to dining at a quiet restaurant with a bunch of stuck-up rich people. I'm back in Las Vegas. The city vibrates with life and I feel a familiar pull to be out in the streets. I turn to Kurt, who looks like he needs a good time as much as I do. "You said that you wanted me to show you Las Vegas." Kurt looks over at me, surprised I'd spoken.

"Yes, but I thought you might like dining at Cosette's."

"Normally I would. But I think if we do that tonight we're going to get on each other's nerves. I think if we go out onto the strip and to some other places I know, maybe it will loosen you up a bit."

"Who says I need to be loosened up?"

"I do. Ever since I've met you, you mostly have that frown of disapproval when I'm talking to you. I'm not sure if you can't stand me or if this is the way you treat all women. I sigh. "If we're going to work together, you've got to get to a place where you can at least tolerate me."

"Is that what you think of me?" he says, bewildered.

I just stare at him.

He stares back at me, but the man is no match and gives in. "All right, I'll let you plan the evening."

"Then I suggest you call Cosette's and cancel our reservations." He doesn't look happy when he punches in the number.

Kurt informs me we have the limo for the entire night. I ask the driver to drop us off at Banger Brewing in downtown. The place is packed with raucous patrons and music that's close to concert level. I park Kurt at a table and order two Red Dead ales and bacon popcorn at the bar. I throw a coaster down in front of him and place the beer on top. "I've ordered appetizers. They're coming."

Kurt looks down at his beer suspiciously.

"You're meant to drink that," I say, slipping into my chair. I take a sip and relax back in my seat. "Lord, that's good," I mumble to myself. Kurt is still staring at his drink. "If you don't like it, we can find you something else on the menu. It's interesting what they're doing with beers these days; it's on a par with wine. Some of the beers are fruit-infused. I'm more of a traditionalist but some of them are pretty good."

His brows furrow in an almost comedic gesture. "You skipped Cosette's for this?"

"I thought it was a better atmosphere to get to know each other." I raise my glass. "Think of this as a team building exercise."

He takes a sip, then a gulp. "I think it's a good plan," he says to his beer. "Do I tell you stories about my childhood or my philosophy on managing a division?"

"Let's start small," glancing around the room for inspiration. We've never relaxed together. I drove him to and from work and there were meetings in between. We never chatted. I want to ask him about the phone call he had before we went to the airport. That's a subject that needs working up to. "What's your middle name?" It's an easy place to begin.

Kurt stops drinking long enough to answer. "Dieter. Do you have a middle name?"

Why am I not surprised? He could be the poster boy for Germany with that blond hair and crystal blue eyes. "Rhiannon," I say.

He smiles. "Like the singer? *Umbrella*?"

I grimace picturing *Umbrella* sung in German. How does he know about Rihanna? There's a slight grin on his face like he's scored a point. "No, Rhiannon," I breathe out. "Like the song. My mother is a Stevie Nicks fan, and she has a habit of naming her kids after things she likes. Chloe is named after a perfume. Rhiannon is actually my first name but when I was five years old, I announced to my family that everyone must call me Kellis. What do you think of the beer?"

He picks up the half-full glass to inspect it. "Different...I like it." His gaze travels to me. "You were headstrong even when you were a child?"

"I like to think I was decisive."

"Hey Kel. I thought it was you. Kick ass hair, by the way. Who's your friend?"

Jerry's imposing bodybuilder presence is looking down at me with his bar bouncer face.

"Hey Jerry. It's been awhile."

"Yeah, it has. You missed our last new beer release party."

"Stuff happens, you know that." I give him a pleading smile. "I promise to make the next one."

"I'll text you the date."

"Jerry is the manager here," I say to Kurt.

The two men nod a greeting.

"Kurt and I work together. He's never been to Vegas. We're attending an R&D conference at Mandalay Bay."

Jerry gives a nod of approval.

I raise my glass to Kurt. "I thought I'd take him to the best brewpub in Vegas. But they were closed, so I brought him here."

Jerry lets out a roar of laughter. "You had me going there for a minute." He shakes his head. "This being your first time here, I'll set up a tasting. Have you decided what food you want to order?"

"We'll have two of my usual with just crispy fries."

"Just to be clear, you're ordering two smoked bangers in a bun with a side of just crispy fries."

"Two orders of the fries. Jerry, you know I do not share."

Jerry laughs as he walks back to the kitchen.

"How'd you do that?"

"Do what?"

"He chucks his chin towards Jerry. How are you able to talk to people so easily?"

"Recruiters don't have a problem talking to anyone." I shrug. "I've always been like this."

He looks like he might say more but decides against it, then he puts on his business face. "What happened with Okobi?"

"Your colleague was right," I slide into work mode. "He isn't happy at Endeavor and his wife is pressing him to go back to California. I hadn't planned on talking about our proposal this early, but I did tell him about the second-in-command opening."

"Was he receptive?"

"I gave him the bare bones of the position and told him if he's interested that we would meet privately to discuss it. And yes, I think he's receptive."

Relief floods his face. "This is good. Promising. This is more than I hoped for. You've made a good start. You seem to be handling the candidate well on your own. I have no advice to offer."

"Is the debrief done?" I'm eyeing my beer.

"Yes, for today," and he takes a long drag of his drink.

I had no idea Kurt was a lightweight. Jerry is moving around the table removing the remains of our bratwurst and fries. Four trays of beer samples sit between us, and much of it contains empty glasses. I wouldn't say Kurt looks bleary-eyed, but he's on the way. He long ago removed his jacket that is now sitting on the back of his chair. He's rolled up his sleeves, revealing a wolf tattoo I wasn't able to see earlier. A loosened collar has him looking more casual than I've ever seen him. We're a few hours into the night, not quite talking like old friends, but I noticed fewer flareups are happening between us. He does have a grin plastered on his face.

"I'm guessing here. But I don't think you go out beer drinking much," I say.

He peers around the glass he's holding up. "No, I did more of that when I was in college. Once I started working for Drachen right out of school, I stopped that. Can I call you Rhiannon?"

"No, my name is Kellis. Did you forget that?"

He points a finger at me. "I distinctly remember you told me your name is Rhiannon. Your mother named you Rhiannon."

Yep, he's drunk, but at least he's a happy one. "Okay, buddy, maybe it's time to end the evening early and get you back to the hotel."

He looks askance at me. "You promised to show me Las Vegas. Now you're going back on your promise." Before I can convince him he should go back to the hotel to get his beauty rest, his phone rings. He looks around to see where the sound is coming from. I bite my lip not to laugh out loud at his confusion. He finally realizes the sound is in his jacket. He fishes around in the pocket, pulls it out, and gives a myopic look at the phone, then pushes the button to answer the call. He begins speaking in German to a person on the other end. He stands, holding up a finger to me to say he'll be right back, then walks to the back of the pub near the beer tanks. His demeanor changes as the conversation goes on. The grin disappears and is replaced by worry. He ends the call and sways a bit as he maneuvers back to the table. He falls back into his seat, staring somewhere past me. "I'm not in the mood to go back to my room," he announces to no one. "I'd like to see Las Vegas."

I'm concerned about his call. Was that the update he'd been waiting for? Whatever the news, he looks miserable. Guilt tugs at me. So he's a little drunk...sometimes that's the best way to see Vegas. Screw it. A promise is a promise. I excuse myself to go to the restroom and on the way pull Jerry into a conversation. "Does Bob still sell half price tickets to the locals if he can't find enough people to fill the tour?"

"Yeah, you know, that's funny, he just called here about 20 minutes ago to ask if I knew anybody. Let me give him a call and find out if he still has those two slots available."

"I'll check with you on my way back. If he still has those seats, tell him I'll take them."

"Are you sure? We're talking the deluxe tour; it's going to cost you even with 50% off."

I glance back at Kurt, who smiles and waves at me. "Don't worry, he can afford it."

When I return, Jerry's beaming. "He says he still has them, but you need to be at the airstrip in about fifteen minutes. Do you need a ride?"

"No, we have a car outside."

"Have a good time," Jerry says, looking at Kurt, concerned. "Let me know if you need help with Mr. Suit."

"Kurt," I say as I grab his jacket and hold it out to him. "Put this on, we're going on a tour. I'll let the driver know where we're going." He regains that stupid grin on his face, nods, and complies with my instructions. He's steady enough, but I slip my arm around his waist anyway to prevent him from kissing the pavement and scratching that pretty face of his. The driver helps him into the back seat and the car pulls smoothly into the traffic. I lower my window to let in the cool air. It's stuffy, but it's more to help soften the buzz Kurt has going. I reach across to Kurt's side to hit the button. While the window makes its descent, Kurt's nose grazes the top of my head. "You smell like fruit and flowers." He breathes in deeply. "I bet you taste good too."

I move back to my side and avoid looking at his bewildered face. Kurt is almost likable. Maybe I should slip something into his orange juice in the mornings? Everyone at work would thank me.

We make it with a few minutes to spare, but Bob says the pilot is in the helicopter doing final checks. He tells us we have a little time and offers us a glass of preflight champagne. I try to refuse it, but Kurt insists. We down it like two people dying of thirst, then head out to the airfield.

We jog across the pad. Kurt no longer needs my help. It's a cold, clear night and I can't help but marvel at the scattering of stars and the slender sliver of moon in the sky. The sky at night in Vegas always takes my breath away. I board first and pull Kurt inside with me. There's another couple seated further back, giggling and cooing. They're having a hard time sitting still. From the looks of them, they're probably on their honeymoon.

"Welcome aboard, folks, to Las Vegas at night. I'm Tony, your pilot and guide for this tour. You're about to experience the best way to view our world-renowned city. Sit back, relax, and be dazzled by the city of lights or what most people call us... Sin City."

The bird lifts off. The familiar excitement builds inside me as we soar into the darkness approaching the distant lights. Kurt is wide-eyed as we near the Mandalay Bay hotel that marks the beginning of the strip. He twists his body several times to find the best vantage point to see the sights. He finally settles against me in this close seating and places his arm around the back of my seat, eyes bright as he gazes toward the view. I don't mind the invasion of personal space; in this tight area it's unavoidable. I'm glad the tour I've chosen appears to delight my caustic companion. He draws even closer for a better view, the scent of champagne and faint aftershave clinging to him. I've never been close enough to know he wore aftershave or to see the beginnings of blond stubble along his jawline. He turns his head and I'm staring into his crystal blue eyes, mesmerized by a deep stirring of attraction and an overwhelming longing to touch him. I pull my gaze away from him, embarrassed, hoping that he didn't see what's so obvious to me.

I look out at the strip below, glad to re-focus. I've been on this tour a million times with friends and family, but with Kurt's childlike eagerness, I try to imagine the glittery sites through his eyes. The helicopter rounds the Stratosphere Tower. The top spins as red lights on the tower wink at our passing. Kurt's body adjusts slightly, his face in shadow, and the stubble of his chin brushes my cheek. He is closer than he needs to be and I can't help but respond to his nearness. Without warning, a surge of energy whips through me when his hot whispered voice lingers at my ear, his lips brushing me lightly. "This is exactly what I needed, being here with you. Thank you for this." I suck in a tiny intake of breath as the words send my senses whirling. But he's not finished. His finger finds my chin, guiding me to see the seriousness in his eyes. His kiss is inviting as I melt into him, forgetting where we are while Vegas moves underneath us. The voices of the pilot and the couple are in the distance like noise drifting from another room. It's background for this moment until the pilot's voice reasserts itself and we pull apart.

"You two on your honeymoon?" Tony asks, probably used to keeping his guests from climbing all over each other.

Kurt doesn't answer; he continues to keep his gaze on me. He grins. "Yes, we are," comes his hoarse response. My eyes widen, my heart thumping at his answer. He takes my hand and squeezes it.

"Bob said you guys were locals. Did you meet here?"

"Yes," I say, still distracted by Kurt's response.

"Why isn't she wearing a ring?" Tony says.

Kurt continues to keep my gaze. He responds in the character of a newlywed smitten by his wife. "She took off the cheap costume one when she showered today. Kellis isn't used to a ring on that finger. Kurt slips a signet ring off his pinky. He takes my hand and pushes the bulky piece of gold on my left ring finger; it's a snug fit. "Try not to lose this until I get you a wedding ring. I want everyone to know you're mine."

"Don't let her go, mate," says the pilot, "She's a keeper."

CHAPTER 17

Venice at Night

The deluxe tour consists of rooftop stops at three hotel/casinos. They treat us to tours of the high-roller accommodations, exclusive club access, and all the while they ply us with more food and champagne. At the last casino, we're given a private lesson on how to play baccarat in a high-roller room.

We have fun thanks to Tony, our entertaining pilot, and Kaylee and Wyatt, the couple who share our tour. They're trust fund kids from Texas, just married five days ago, and are about to go on a year's travel wandering the world. They're a lively couple and the four of us have a blast together. The tour postpones the awkward discussion of Kurt's kiss. I've already begun to rationalize it as a product of his inebriated state and, like Cinderella, fun-loving Kurt will be gone by the end of the night. I watch him out of the corner of my eye while Kaylee is telling me how her husband proposed. Kurt's throwing up his hands to emphasize a point or impart some great truth to Wyatt, who appears engrossed in the conversation. It's good he's enjoying himself. Then it

147

occurs to me that I could use this Vegas trip as leverage to remind him how unKurt he was. You never know, it might be useful one day.

Kurt continues to act like we're newlyweds. We all take lots of pictures on our camera phones and the staff is nice enough to oblige when we ask them to take pictures of us. Kurt appears to be having fun with the deception. I don't see any harm, so I play along as well. The extent of being his wife is hand holding, walking with his arm around me, and a few sweet kisses. We even made up a story about our crazy Vegas chapel wedding to entertain Kaylee and Wyatt. I think this pretense might give him a slight respite. He was so down after his phone call, maybe this will help him cope with whatever problems might be troubling him.

At the end of the tour, our driver picks us up at the airport. Our hotel is close, and it won't take long to return. Tomorrow we'll attend the R&D dinner at the hotel. Depending on what happens during the dinner, it would be wise not to plan anything until I'm sure about the evening. I'll invite Okobi and a few other engineers out for after dinner entertainment to make it look like it's just a few old friends getting together. I've already sent texts to some of my contacts in the city in case I need tickets to a show or other attractions they might find interesting.

The driver pulls out into traffic. I suggest to a distracted Kurt that instead of returning to the hotel we should drive the strip and continue on to the Fremont Experience, where the original Las Vegas casinos were built. He's seen the strip by air, but to appreciate it fully, you must experience it at street level. I know it will take a while for us to traverse the whole strip, especially at this time of night, but no one should go home without seeing the city up close. He likes the idea and seems to relax watching the sights.

More than halfway down the street, I spot Treasure Island on the left. It looks like they're about to start the pirate show on the big galleon out front. I'm about to suggest we get out to see the show when

Kurt asks the driver to slow down. "Is that the Venetian?" he says.

I crane my neck to see and, sure enough, the hotel is up ahead. "Yes," I say. "It's beautiful, we should go inside and look around."

Kurt tells the driver that he'll call him in a couple of hours. He's welcome to find another fare while we're gone. He grabs my hand and pulls me out of the car to join a multitude of people pouring into the Venetian. The grandeur is overwhelming as we arrive at St. Mark's Square, their interpretation of San Marco Square in Venice. The time here is always twilight. The soft lighting and the painted vaulted ceiling are meant to mimic the sky in early evening. "I've heard that they have gondola rides," he says, looking around for evidence. "I'd like to take a ride."

"It's up a little further." I pull on his sleeve and point in the direction. He retakes my hand and we walk to the landing. By now I realize that since the tour began, he has held my hand or his arm has been around me holding me to him. We have no audience to entertain, but he keeps up the pretense like we're on a date. I'm getting used to this attention. I know I'll remember this moment when we're back at Drachen and I'm looking at his disapproving face. I push it out of my mind. I decide to live in the moment.

Kurt helps me into the boat. We nestle beside each other and he puts his arm around my shoulders, my body resting against him. The boat pushes off to glide down the make-believe Venice grand canal. The gondolier places the large pole in the clear blue water to propel us forward as he sings softly.

"Las Vegas is many things," I say. "What did you expect to see on a tour?" The boat is gliding lazily through the water. We pass other boats, but they are too engrossed in their own experience to notice us. Kurt angles his head toward me. "I'm serious," I say, so I don't smile. "I really want to know."

"Maybe what everyone else thinks about this place. That I'd see bare-breasted showgirls and mobsters?"

A laugh escapes me. "If that's what you wanted, I could have arranged for you to see a vintage Las Vegas show." I think there might be some time to catch a show off the strip, but I realize this isn't a vacation, so I don't make the offer. "And as for mobsters, there's a museum."

"A mobster museum? I didn't know there was mobster art!" He feigns surprise.

I start to giggle at his dry humor. We've had no alcohol for a few hours. He's keeping up the pretense of my handsome, attentive husband. "No, silly, it's not that kind of museum. You must know that this city was founded by mobsters, at least the gambling."

"I remember reading something about that." He squeezes my shoulders. "I know we have to go back to the hotel soon. You have a big day with Okobi tomorrow, but when we get back to the landing there's a shop I saw down that path that I'd like to visit."

We head in the direction of the shop. About six doors down, we enter a Christmas store. Kirk's eyes light up as he walks around the store looking at the ornaments and the assorted holiday paraphernalia. The shop attendants are dressed as Santa's helpers and I wonder how they stay sane with the looped Christmas music.

We're standing in front of a glass display. Some ornaments are arranged on the top, the pricier ones in the case. "I noticed that your house is already decorated for Christmas." His attention is on a large snow globe. "It must have taken a long time to arrange everything," I say evenly.

"Yes, I'm ready for the holiday."

I can't help my curiosity. The decorations in his house are way over the top. There were enough presents under the tree for a large family to exchange. "Is your family coming to visit?"

He places the globe back on the shelf and picks up a small elf ornament. "No, my family won't be visiting me."

I really should shut up, but I can't. I keep pressing. "Friends?"

He turns on me and I see that disapproving frown. "No friends and no family will be visiting me for Christmas. I hope I've made myself clear."

I don't know whether to be angry that he barked at me or sad that he'll be alone on Christmas. He retreats and strides to the back of the shop. I take that as my cue to walk outside to wait for him. I keep an eye on him through the shop window. He's watching an elaborate train set chugging around the base of the tree, then travels to each section of the store. He takes his time inspecting everything in the small shop until he selects a few ornaments. After making his purchases, he joins me outside, holding the handle of a huge bright red bag with white tissue peeking out of the top.

We stroll in silence for a few steps. There aren't many tourists at this time of night. I stop, too irritated with him to continue. "I know I'm too curious for my own good, but we've spent the evening together and I thought that we've, well, gotten closer. You told me in the shop that you decorated an entire house and nobody's coming?"

He takes a deep breath and lets it out slowly. "I apologize for snapping at you. It was inappropriate." He resumes striding toward the exit.

I catch up, halt in front of him, and place a hand on his chest. He's irritated but I don't care. "I didn't say all of those things for an apology," applying a small amount of pressure to his chest to keep his attention. "I genuinely want to know what's going on with you."

He realizes he's not going to bully his way out of answering my question.

I slip my hand down to his palm and entwine our fingers. "What is it, were you a spoiled rich kid and your parents didn't pay enough attention to you?"

"You've got it half right," he admits. "I didn't come from wealth. My father was a baker."

He says this as a matter of fact. I'm a little stunned, but more curious about him. I look around for a place to talk. "Come on." I pull on his hand. "Let's sit for a few minutes and talk. It's too difficult to jog to keep up with you in these heels." He says nothing while I guide him to a bench.

We sit. He places the shopping bag next to him. We probably look odd sitting on the bench with a huge red bag that's as high as his shoulder. He folds his arms like a child who has a timeout. "Do you want to know about my family?" His tone is petulant. "I have two younger siblings. My father barely made a living at his profession and my mother was too ill to contribute to the family's coffers."

It's difficult to believe that this polished, educated, arrogant man didn't come from money. "How were your parents able to afford college…or were you able to get scholarships?"

Kurt leans back, looking off into the distance. "For as long as I can remember, my parents struggled financially. I'd help my father in the shop when I was old enough, but he had other issues that prevented him from moving ahead in life." He stops talking and rubs his jaw. "Are you sure you want to hear this? The story is quite boring."

His clipped tone doesn't fool me. He's making another attempt to put me off. "It can't be boring if it's about you," I say, more interested in his story.

"Alright then, I'll continue. I was about twelve when things changed. I spent as much time as I could at school to avoid going home. Someone working for an ad agency saw me in a school pageant, broadcast by a local television station. He tracked me down and asked my parents if he could hire me to be the kid drinking a can of cola in a print ad. That job started my modeling career."

"I thought you were followed in the press because you're young to be a VP of a major company."

"No, working for Drachen increased the public's interest in me. What do you Americans say? It proved I wasn't just another pretty face." He leans closer to show me his profile. I roll my eyes at the tease.

He gives up and leans back. "A big agency signed me soon after and I was in demand. Overnight I was the breadwinner for the family. More opportunities came my way and it was suggested that I also do commercials and even try for an acting career. My parents couldn't travel with me. My mother was sick and my father wouldn't leave her. They hired a minder and a tutor and sent me off."

I should have paid more attention when he was reluctant to talk about his life. I shift, wondering how I can move the conversation in another direction.

He looks off into the distance. "Before I became the family's sole support, Christmases were sparse. They made no effort to celebrate; it was just two sad people making excuses to their kids why they couldn't have a better Christmas. The rules were simple back then: you were not to ask for anything."

"I didn't mean to stir up sad memories," trying to offer some solace.

He leans toward me. "You wanted to hear this, remember? I'm not finished."

I nod, hoping this is at least cathartic for him.

He settles his arm across the back of the bench and picks up the thread of the story with little effort. "When my bank account continued to expand, my parents bought a house. They became accustomed to living with luxury. There was always a job near the holidays, especially in Asia. My parents encouraged me to work no matter what time of the year. They were finally having a great life, courtesy of me, but without me." He glances over at the bag. "I've been collecting the ornaments you saw in my house for a long time. I bought some of them when I was a kid traveling around. It was hard at first, but I grew used to Christmas on my own. Now it's just something I do."

"But you don't need to work during the holidays. Can't you fly them here or go to Germany?" I was thinking it'd been years since that little boy spent holidays alone.

153

He thinks about this for a moment. "That's the funny thing. All those years I've sent money and wasn't in their lives. So essentially, I'm a stranger. I've missed a lot of milestones in my brother and sister's lives. Now they think of me as a cash cow. When I receive a call or text from my family, it's always for money."

"I'm sorry, I didn't mean to open..." I stop, looking at his passive face. "I thought you were going to tell me about some quaint family tradition. I had no idea." Who knew Mr. Perfect didn't have an idyllic childhood?

"It hasn't been all bad." He gives me a wry grin. "It settles the question of who's going to put the angel on the tree top. What's Christmas like at your house?"

I reach for my braid, something I do to calm myself, and remember it's gone. How can I talk about my family after that story? "Chloe and I put up a tree," I say, pushing a lock of hair behind my ear. "Other than that, there aren't a lot of decorations."

Kurt's eyes narrow. "I'm sure there's more than that. Chloe looks like the kind of person who would get into the holidays. I'm going to guess you all sing carols to the neighbors."

"No," I snort. "None of us can carry a tune, but yeah, Chloe likes the holidays, any holiday." He's waiting for me to describe some family tradition. I guess doing family Tarot readings is out. "We do have one family tradition that we still stick to. My parents are divorced, but they made this pact that no matter who they're dating or married to, that for one day it would only be us together as a family. It's my parents, sisters, and brother having breakfast, decorating a tree, lunch, cooking dinner, and from sunrise to midnight it's just us."

I can't gage his reaction. It can't be easy to hear about another family's holiday, when he has nothing but an empty Christmas house to look forward to. He glances at his watch. "I think I'd better text the driver and let him know we're ready."

We stand, ready to leave. Kurt seems unaffected while he

straightens his jacket and retrieves his shopping bag, like the part of his life he described happened to someone else. He takes my hand — I think he does this now out of habit — and we stroll towards the exit.

We're walking through the hall of the hotel toward my room. Kurt is still holding my hand even when we stop at my door. His room is on the same floor further down the hall. I wait, watching his distracted face. I think he might kiss me again, or does this signal the end to my fake husband? His focus is on me, deciding something. He hugs me, his body stiff during the embrace, like he's hugging his sister. Herr Heinrich has returned. "Thank you for the interesting evening," he says formally. "I'll see you in the morning."

I call out "you're welcome" to him as he moves down the hall, but there's something bothering me. If he's at odds with his family, then who was he concerned about on the phone?

I switch the light on and stumble into my room. It feels like deja vu, only this time I throw the key card on the side table and it slides off and lands on the floor. I'm so tired I fall face down on the bed. Before my face hits the pillows, I register that something seems different in the room. I raise up onto my elbows to see a huge bouquet of flowers; actually, it's closer to a floral explosion. A surge of energy gets me to the desk. I slip the little envelope off the fork-like plastic holder. *I miss you*, it says. I find my phone and scroll through my texts. Matt's been texting me throughout the day and I hadn't returned one of them.

I text back *I miss you too*. Thanks for the flowers.

He texts a smiley face and a snoring emoji. *Sweet dreams.*

CHAPTER 18

Raining Men

I wake up with a slight headache the next morning. Checking my phone, I see that I've slept through breakfast. That's okay, because I plan to go downstairs and find Okobi during the lunch break and ask him and anyone else if they would like to go out with me this evening after the R&D dinner. I'm not too worse for wear when I examine my face in the mirror. At least nothing that some makeup won't correct. I dress quickly and leave the tag on my door for the maid to clean. I just have enough time to catch the elevator and make it downstairs for the first arrivals for lunch. I step into the empty elevator and push the button for the lobby. I'm about 20 floors up and impatient for the elevator to get downstairs. Somewhere around the 10th floor the doors open and Tim walks in.

"Well, well," he says with a smug grin. "What do we have here? If I didn't know better, I would say you're planning these little chance meetings on purpose."

He looks like he's just stepped out of the shower. His dark slicked-back hair is still slightly damp and that beard he's working on is just a bit past the stubble stage. In business casual, the pale lavender slim fit shirt and expensive jeans are tailored to show off that really hot body. I'm not immune to my ex. He's, after all, a gorgeous man, and I can feel sex rolling off him in waves and the familiar pull of his energy that affects me when we're close and alone. But I'm not going down that road again.

I wedge myself into the corner of the elevator and clutch the railing. "Slow your roll, Mister." With Tim you have to be firm and convincing; if you're not, he'll pounce on any sign of weakness, just like a predator. "I'm not following you. We're bound to run into each other because we're attending the same event. So, don't act like this is divine intervention."

The doors open and I moved past him, but before I can clear the elevator he latches onto my arm and walks me over to the side. "Okay, I get that you might not be stalking me," he says unconvincingly.

Jeez, the ego.

"But for old times' sake, I'm asking for a favor. I want you to introduce me to Kurt Heinrich."

I yank my arm away from him. "Why do you want to talk to Kurt?" I demand.

He puts both hands up in surrender. "Woah, I want to talk to him about the second-in-command position. I think I'd be a good fit. You know I have R&D in my background, although I make a ton of money in sales. I want to go back to my roots and really contribute to something that's going to make a difference."

Since when has my ex ever wanted to do anything other than fun? "What's brought about this altruistic point of view? Is it Candy? Has she inspired this change?" People are turning around.

He drops the sales persona and lowers his voice. "I know you never saw me as a serious engineer. Hell, you never saw me as a serious person at all. Anyone can change. Look at you working for one of the biggest companies in the world. You even have a VP for a boyfriend. I can go up the corporate ladder too."

"Since when has this been a competition? And I'm only a lowly recruiter. I'm the lowest of the low on the food chain in that place." Now I get it. He thinks I dumped him for a better model instead of crawling back to him after a few weeks. "And what difference does it make what my boyfriend does for a living?"

"Kellis, you're eons ahead of any recruiter. You've managed a firm for years. Your clients were big companies. For fuck's sake, you can manage a division."

"Thanks for the vote of confidence. But I'm going to give you some advice." He gives me that *you got my attention* face. "Kurt Heinrich is very particular about who he works with. He won't welcome the fact that I'm bringing you in out of the blue to talk to him. Your first assessment was right. He wants me to court Kyle Okobi, and that's why I'm here. He's already seen us talking and wasn't happy that I wasn't concentrating on Okobi. If you're serious about the position, I'll talk to him about you. But not now."

"I can't wait that long. I want him to consider me before you reel in Okobi."

I've never seen him so focused about anything. I can't figure out if he has an agenda or if he's just playing me. It doesn't matter; right now, introducing Tim into this mix wouldn't work in any universe. "I'm sorry, that's all I can offer you right now," I say and leave him standing in the lobby.

I find out which room is set up for the lunch. Several people are already milling around the buffet. I scan the sea of faces. Two of the Endeavor team are talking to other engineers, but Kyle is nowhere in sight. It's possible that someone has stopped him on the way and he should be arriving shortly. I pick up a plate and toss a few items on it as I move through the buffet line. I nod to a few people on my way to a table. I sit and wait for Kyle to arrive.

Tim enters the room and thankfully he's not barreling towards me to resume our conversation. He takes a seat on the opposite side of the room and keeps an eye on me. Okobi enters, laughing with two people. I know one of his companions but not the second person. I decide to say hello and use this opportunity to speak to him for a few minutes. I'm moving towards him.

"Kellis, you've cut your hair."

I turn toward the familiar voice at my back. Matt is standing there looking at me as if he's lost. He reaches out to touch my hair, but I pull away. "What are you doing here?"

"I've missed you. I wanted to surprise you," he says, staring at my hair.

I look back over at Okobi, who is still in conversation. "I missed you too," I say, "but we talked about not seeing each other until I finish with the second-in-command project."

He steps closer and I'm afraid he's going to embrace me. I try to put some space between us. This is a business event and there are colleagues all around us. He seems to forget where we are. I can't afford to exchange anything other than a handshake.

"I know we talked about it. But I got to thinking that I could probably help you with Okobi—"

I don't let him finish his thought. "That's very nice of you. But this is my job. I don't need any help."

"I thought I could take you to dinner tonight. Maybe catch a show, then after—"

I'd like nothing more than to break in my hotel room with a romp session with him, but this project is too important. My job's on the line. If I don't get Okobi's commitment, it's working for Mom's company for sure. "I'm going to take clients out tonight," I say, looking up into his pleading eyes. He's come all this way to surprise me. I'll have to make it up to him when I return.

"As I said, I can help you." He steps forward, hand on my

shoulder.

Okobi is now by the buffet with his companions. They seem to be hesitating about staying. Kurt appears at the entrance. He's searching the room. Tim has gotten up from his seat. He's looking straight at me and mouthing *I'm going to meet him* and points at Kurt. I twist away from Matt and step back. "I'm so sorry," I say, still looking at Tim and Kurt on a collision course. "Something has come up and I have to go. I'll text you when we can talk." Before he can respond, I'm heading towards Kurt, hoping I can get there before Tim reaches him.

Kurt grins when he sees me. I look over my shoulder to see Tim waylaid by another attendee a few steps from us. Kurt reaches for my arm. "Don't you ever answer your texts?" he pulls me out into the hall. "I have to speak with you." He finds my hand and pulls me along down the hall, testing doors until he finds an empty room, and we slip inside. "First I need to know if you've talk to Okobi today."

"I was about to when you showed up. He's at the buffet table with a couple of friends. I'm going to ask him if he'd like to join me after dinner with a few of his colleagues to see a show or whatever they want to do."

"Excellent idea. Let me know how it works out." There's more on his mind. Has he found another candidate to consider?

"Do you want to have a debrief tomorrow morning?"

"I would, but I won't be here. That's part of what I want to talk to you about. I have to fly back to Germany. I was planning to have a long discussion with you today, but that's going to have to wait."

"What is it? Are you having second thoughts about Okobi?"

"No, nothing like that. I want to talk about what happened last night." He hesitates for a bit. "I want to talk about us."

Us? What us? There's no us. He's watching me process what he's said with interest. I'm cycling through the stages of surprise. Last night was a joke, a little fun. It didn't mean anything to him. That night is over, done and a memory. Then I remember his pinky ring is still on

161

my finger. He needs his ring back. I begin to tug on the gold signet ring on my finger. It was a snug fit going on and now I'm not able to pull it off. "Wait, you need your ring back," I say as I redouble my efforts to get it off.

He glances down at me struggling. "Don't worry. I'll wait until you can get that off. You can wear it until I come back." He places a hand on mine to stop me. "Kellis, it's not important now. That's not why I needed to find you." His hand slips away and he moves forward. I move back, unsure what he wants until the wall is at my back. He places his hands above my head, forcing me to gaze up at him. His crystal blue eyes are deciding as they search mine. I breathe in his faint musk, the cotton of his shirt, and I realize he's too close. My body is already responding to whatever is exploding between us. All I want is to touch him, but my arms are heavy, useless by my sides. Kurt draws closer, his warm lips brush mine, unsure at first, then his tongue plays along my lower lip until his kiss is real. A small groan escapes him as his tongue probes, twisting with mine as the kiss becomes more demanding. His fingers are running through my hair. I sigh into his mouth, his hard body presses against me and I melt into him like I did before. I don't know why I'm kissing him, only that I need to. It goes on a little longer as I titter on the edge, engrossed in our own world, until the muffled sounds from next door announce we're still in a public place. I place the flat of my hands on his shoulders, urging him away. We pull apart. His hands fall to my waist to move along my sides, our foreheads touching. "Now I think you understand why I want to talk to you." His voice a hoarse whisper.

I nod. There're too many things whirling around in my head to give him any more of an answer. Then the guilt sets in. Why didn't I tell him that I'm in a relationship with Matt? But is that true? What's wrong with me? My father begins talking in my head. 'Don't get your honey...' I want to scream "shut up" at the steady stream of words. Why is he doing this now when we've been working together for months? I can't deny what just happened or how he made me feel. I let out a frustrated sigh, realizing that I'm screwed. But whose honey do I really want, Matt or Herr Heinrich?

His lips brush my forehead, then he steps away. He observes me while adjusting his shirt. "I wanted to let you know that we should talk, but I've been called back to Germany on a personal matter and I'm leaving in a couple of hours. I'm taking a car to the airport now."

He didn't want to tell me why he's leaving. He refers to it as a personal matter, meaning that he doesn't want to discuss it. "When will you be back?" What if Okobi needs to speak with him?

"I'm not sure. And I don't know how available I'm going to be. I'll text you my personal cell number and you can contact me through that number if you need me. I'll let you know when I'm coming back."

I'm in the hallway a few feet away from the door. I take a deep breath to calm down and realign my thoughts. Before this little episode, I was about to talk with Okobi. A few people are walking down the hallway. Two stroll pass me, and they make eye contact but no nod. Matt is leaning against the wall, arms folded, looking at me with a blank expression. Kurt comes from behind; we exchange a glance and he continues down the hall in the opposite direction. It looks like I need to have a longer talk with Matt to convince him that I don't need his help. "Matt," I say as I draw near. "Really, I need time to work."

He looks past me, interested in something down the hall. When his gaze settles on me anger flashes in his eyes. He pushes away from the wall, looking down at me. "Why do you want me to leave, so you and Kurt Heinrich can be together?"

I blink, afraid to register what he just said. "What are you talking about?"

"I watched you walk down the hall with him and slip into a room. I was here when you finally left."

"Yeah, we didn't want anyone to know we were plotting. We ducked in there to discuss Okobi," I say in a low whisper.

"Really, then you better comb your hair and tuck in your blouse before you speak to him because it looks like Heinrich's had his hands all over you."

I stare at his pissed-off face for a few seconds. There's nothing I can say. I walk past him to find the restroom. The full-length mirror reflects my messy hair and my blouse partially out of its waistband. I don't know what I'm going to say to Matt. I finally come out of the bathroom, but the hall is empty. I figure the best thing to do is to find Okobi. I can deal with Matt later. The lunch room is half full, but there's no Okobi. I realize that the afternoon session has begun and he won't be back. I head for my room, realizing that all I've done is a lot of screwing up today. I have one more chance. I can still talk to Okobi at the dinner and invite him out then.

I have hours to go before dinner. It might be a good idea to go for a run or at least visit the exercise room. Anything to clear my head. I'm dressed in my workout clothes, but I'm not ready to go. I spy my cell on the side table. I'm halfway through punching in the number when I realize how lost I really feel.

"Your mother told me you might be calling."

Leave it to Mom to know when one of her kids is in trouble. "Hi Dad. Where are you on the leader board today?" He's off in December, but I ask him the question no matter what time of the year. "Are you ready for Arlington?" That would be his first stop in January.

"I'm in the top five as always, kitten. Bowling is my superpower, as you kids say. There's been some stiff competition lately. But yeah, I'll be ready."

If I was in a better mood, I would ask about his latest girlfriend. He's only been with her a few months and I can't remember her name. "Did you call Mom or did she call you?"

"Does it matter?"

"No, not in the long scheme of things it doesn't." I just want to think that sometimes he thinks about me. I've always been daddy's girl even when he wasn't here.

"If it'll make you feel better, your mother called me. You know I was never good in that department. Tell me what's wrong."

"Would I sound like I'm fifteen years old if I say 'everything'?" I can't help the slight whine in my voice.

"You'd sound like everyone in the world that feels like that at one time or another. Having problems and feeling down is part of the human experience."

I smile and shake my head. My dad the philosopher.

"I'm thinking that it's man trouble. Am I right?"

"Bingo. I keep hearing you in my head."

His deep chuckle rumbles through the cell, and it's like he sitting next to me. "So, what have I been saying?"

I sigh into the phone. "Don't get your honey where you get your money."

"Ah, an oldie but a goodie. That means the man you're interested in is at work?"

"Correction. The two men I'm interested in are at work."

He doesn't respond right away. "This is going to be one of our long talks, kitten," he says. "You'd better get comfortable."

Talking to my dad was just what I needed. It helped me to get Matt and Kurt into perspective. My dad is a great counselor, but when it comes to strategies about how to convince a candidate to work for a company, he's not the one to talk to.

I'm glad Chloe suggested I get a new wardrobe for this trip. What I'm wearing is conservative but still on the sexy side. I know this because people are actually turning their heads as I walk in to the dining area. The Endeavor team has their own table for the dinner. Since that avenue is closed, I slip into a chair at a table that's not reserved, and I can still keep an eye on him. This time I'm counting on no distractions when I approach Okobi. It takes a long time before I have an opportunity. There's the meal and during that time is the keynote speaker, but finally dinner is over and people are talking in groups. I make a beeline for him.

"Ah, Kellis. There you are," says Okobi as he breaks away from the small group. "I've seen you several times, but then you'd disappear."

"Is it possible to speak for a few minutes?" My voice is pitching higher. I'm nervous, realizing this might be my last chance.

"Yes, of course. There's a small courtyard just over there. I think it will give us enough privacy."

We begin to maneuver across the room to the exit. "Were you able to sit in on any of the seminars?" Okobi says. "I think the conference outdid itself this year."

"I did attend a few and enjoyed the parts of the presentations I could understand."

He laughs. "I always seem to forget that you're not an engineer."

"Sadly, no. I just know enough jargon to get by in a conversation."

He holds the door open and sweeps his hand outward. "After you."

The desert breeze welcomes us to an area designed for group conversations. Oversized greenery arranged near sections of outdoor couches give the illusion of privacy. I drift to the railing, preferring to enjoy the sight of the illuminated pool while we talk. "Have you had time to think about my proposal?"

"Frankly," he sighs. "I've thought of little else. After we spoke at our first meeting, I talked to Gracie that night. She's very excited about the prospect of going to California."

I silently say a prayer. If the spouse is willing, sometimes that's half the battle and because he's considering a move because of Gracie, even better. "Does this mean that you'll take the job?"

"It means I'm willing to discuss it with Kurt Heinrich."

"That can be arranged. Unfortunately, we can't schedule a face-to-face. He's been called back to Germany, but I'm sure that he would talk to you by phone and you can get some of your preliminary questions answered."

He leans against the railing. "That would be fine. Although there something I need to tell you."

My stomach twists, fearing the worse. I take a slow breath, determined not to reflect dread. "The compensation package is very generous. I don't think you're going to have a problem with the offer."

He studies the view with a distracted smile. "I have no doubt I'll be fine with the compensation. What I wanted to say is that I'm also talking to another company."

I open my mouth, but I don't get a chance to respond.

"They contacted me with a similar offer, but I've always wanted to work for Drachen. I don't know if you know this, but I had considered working at the Munich headquarters at one time." His nostalgia fades and he turns his attention back to me. "I want you to understand that the only difference in the offers is the location. The other job is based in Southern California. You know I'm considering this move for my wife."

Relief gives me a plan to solve this problem. I begin working with purpose. "I understand; let me schedule a meeting with Kurt to answer your questions regarding the position. As for the rest of the package, let's discuss some possible solutions for Southern California. Why don't I take you and your colleagues out tonight, and we can finally catch up?" I give him my best smile. "I want to see those photos of the kids on your phone. Let me know where you'd like to go, and I'll arrange tickets for just about anything on the strip. There's a very good show at the MGM..."

He spreads his hands in apology. "I wish you had spoken to me at lunch when I saw you last. Another vendor asked to take us out earlier and we accepted. But I appreciate the offer. I know we would have had a much better time going out with you."

CHAPTER 19

Witch of Drachen

I'm grateful I have an early flight out on Friday. It seems strange getting on the plane without Kurt. He was right. The plane ride from Las Vegas to San Jose was short and it didn't give me enough time to appreciate first class. I haven't heard from Matt. I've stared at the phone several times, wanting to punch in his number, but decided against it. Now is not the right time for us to talk. Not until Okobi has made his decision.

Chloe is not at home when I arrive. She decided to spend the weekend with Mom in Carmel. A visit to a seaside town with great food, shopping, and the beach sounded really good. Without my big sister, I'm left alone for the whole weekend with just my thoughts. I push Kurt out of my mind when a memory of him surfaces. I'll deal with him when he gets back. Matt is another story; he might have left angry, but I know he's hurt. That makes me feel like an awful human being. But I didn't ask him to come to Vegas and I didn't invite that snogging session with Kurt. Dad suggested, after our long talk, to be honest. To let them know how I feel. Great advice, if I knew who I wanted. I'll need to sort out my feelings soon, I have a meeting with Matt on Wednesday to discuss staffing projections for Dark Star.

I was in bed on Sunday night when Chloe came home. I didn't see her until Monday morning when I was in the kitchen about to have breakfast. I made a few attempts to get Kurt's ring off my finger during the weekend. I decide to try one last time before I leave for work. While the toaster pastry is warming, I hit a few pumps of the liquid soap dispenser next to the faucet to ooze the soap between the ring and my finger. I turn on the cool water.

"What are you doing?" Chloe says, entering the kitchen.

She brushes past me, pokes her head into the refrigerator, and pulls out a carton of orange juice.

"I'm trying to get this ring off my finger," I say through gritted teeth.

She leans over to watch me tugging at the metal. "Nice ring." She tilts her head, considering. "It's a bit bulky for my taste but I think you can pull it off. Where did you find it?"

"It's a long story," I huff. Suds from the soap are sliding off into the sink.

"Oh, okay." She looks around the kitchen. "Where's Kurt? I thought it was his turn to make breakfast. I hope you're not planning to serve him toaster pastry. God, we'd never hear the end of that lecture."

"He's not coming," I snort. "He was called back to Germany when we were in Las Vegas. Don't ask me when he's coming back. He didn't say."

She stops filling her glass in mid pour. "Why did he have to go back to Germany?" she says, concerned.

I dry my hands after another failed attempt to get Kurt's brand off me. It's either less salt or I have someone cut it off. "It's another long story and I don't have time to give you the condensed version. I have an early meeting today with Nina to give her the final update on my Vegas trip."

Returning to the dungeon after nearly five days seems strange. I use the early morning hours to go through my emails and make a list of calls that I'll need to return. I receive a text at 9 from Nina inviting me up to her office for a chat.

"It's good to have you back," Nina says, as I take a seat. "Haley did a good job, but she's not you and I had to help her with some of the trickier hires. But we got through it."

"I missed you guys too."

"So, tell me," she says with contained excitement. "How was Vegas?"

"I had a good time," I semi-lie. "The accommodations were wonderful, and I loved going first class. Does everyone go first class or is it just the leadership and their entourage?"

Nina tilts her head. She has a strange look on her face. "First class? I think the only person that would be allowed to go first class would be the CEO of the entire company. Everyone else goes economy, or maybe business class for leadership."

"I didn't deal with the travel department. Kurt made the arrangements." I was trying to remember if I actually looked at the tickets he sent me. "Maybe there was a mix-up?" I suggest. "Because we flew first class and had first-class accommodations at Mandalay Bay."

"Hmm, if I were you, I'd talk to either travel or accounting and find out what happened. Maybe they were able to get a really good rate; it's Vegas after all, and they're always running specials. Anyway, you don't want to be charged the difference between economy and first class." She gives me a wide smile. "I am glad you had a good time. So, Okobi will be giving us his answer no later than Tuesday?"

I nod. "We're competing with a company out of Southern California. At least he told me there was competition. But my gut tells me he'd rather come here. Has Allison said anything?"

She sits back in her seat, contemplating. "She hasn't mentioned you at all. Although I've given her all your updates in our meetings. She and Haley have been huddling a lot together. She's been taking over some of her training."

I cringe before I have a chance to check my reaction. "How do you feel about that?"

"How do I feel about someone who's never been a recruiter or managed a staffing department making ill-informed recommendations to Haley? I'm just fine with that," she says. "I'm glad you're back to help with her training. It will give Haley an opportunity to unlearn everything Allison is teaching her and get a real education." Nina looks at her watch. "Allison should be in the office in about 15 minutes. She called me on my way to work to say she wants to see you as soon as she gets in. Maybe she wants to ask you more questions about Okobi. I suggest you be on your guard."

I'm already loitering in front of her office when Allison arrives. I give her a cheery "good morning."

She nods, suspicion frowning her face. "Good morning. I see Nina gave you my message."

I follow her into her office.

"Please take a seat at the table. Give me a minute. I have a short presentation I want to show you."

"Should I pull the screen down?"

"Yes, that would be helpful."

I deposit my laptop on the table and move to the far end of the space to pull down a screen. Some of the meetings we have in her office include presentations. Maybe she wants to go over a new staffing matrix. She's been talking about revamping the process. Allison lowers the lights then joins me at the table with her laptop and a folder. She's looking at me speculatively. "You've been working for us for a short time as a contractor. I've been told by your peers and hiring managers that you've been very effective in your role. However, under my management we'll be going in a new direction and I hope you will be open to   the changes."

"Thank you?" Her compliment catches me off guard; she's never been this nice. "I'll do my best to contribute to the team. But I'm curious, before I left, you indicated that if I wasn't able to fill the second-in-command position by the end of the month I would be let go. Have you been told Okobi has accepted the offer?"

Allison opens her laptop and the company intranet splashes across the screen. "I haven't received any new information," she opens to an official looking memo from Munich. Allison scrolls to a blank page before I can scan the document. "As far as I know, he's still reviewing our offer. I've asked you to meet with me to discuss something very different. It's a delicate matter, but there are guidelines set down by the company that we'll follow."

She's not making eye contact; what could she be talking about? "I don't understand."

"I've received this information yesterday from Munich. They've asked me to go over it with you," she pushes the button on her laptop. A picture blossoms across the screen of me, Kurt, Kaylee, and Wyatt holding up glasses for a toast. It looks like it was taken toward the end of our Vegas night tour. We look like old friends having a good time. What was the big deal? I take clients out all the time. Even if Kurt is my hiring manager, there's nothing wrong with going out for an evening with other people.

In the next photo my face is turned away, like I'm listening to someone off camera. I have a drink in my hand, ready to take a sip. I'm leaning back against Kurt, his arm around my shoulder keeping me close to his chest. His lopsided grin is looking straight into the camera. I don't even remember this shot, I was that distracted. Kurt's holding up my left hand showing off his ring on my finger and looking happier than I've ever seen him. I take a closer look at the image. It's a Facebook post. From what I can see in the caption it's about two newlywed couples on their honeymoons. I glance over at Allison, "Who gave you these photos?"

"Kurt Heinrich is a celebrity in Germany. Apparently, this couple — Kaylee and Wyatt? — posted a series of photos on their Facebook page and a couple of other social media platforms. Both of you were tagged in the pictures. It came to the attention of Drachen."

She's gaging my reaction to the photos. "We're not married, if that's what you think." Allison arches an eyebrow while she looks down at the ring on my finger. I stupidly place my hand on my lap. "Are you going to fire me over a couple of photos on someone's Facebook page?"

She hits a button on the laptop and the photo disappears. "You're a contractor. I can let you go for any reason, but no, we're not terminating your contract. There're more photos and descriptions. The captions say you were married in Las Vegas. We checked and there was no record of a marriage in Nevada or California. Since it's apparent that you're in a relationship with a high-profile VP of this company, we would like you to sign an agreement."

I can't hide my surprise or embarrassment. "What kind of agreement?"

Allison opens the folder and pushes a small stack of papers across the table. "This is the agreement. I think the slang for this document is love contract. It stipulates that you're in a relationship with Kurt Heinrich, that it's consensual, and the relationship, no matter how it ends, will not have a negative impact on the workplace. That's only a basic overview of the agreement. There're more stipulations in the contract. Of course, we are an equal opportunity workplace and will not tolerate any violation of our employees or contractors' rights."

I glance at the paper. "You checked to see if we're married? It's that important to this company?"

She shrugs. "A marriage certificate is a public document. Yes, this is important to the company. There's potential liability if not addressed. They're protecting their interests." She extracts another form from her folder. "Read the papers over carefully. I also suggest that you have an attorney look over the agreement. You have 48 hours to return the signed agreement to me. Are there any questions?"

I stare at the contract and shake my head.

"Good. If you will sign this paper acknowledging that you received this agreement." She hands me a pen.

I scribble my name and the date on the paper. I realize there's something I need to ask. "Wait, I do have a question. Will Kurt have to sign an agreement?"

Allison retrieves the pen. She's dying to ask me questions. I know she's going to stick to HR protocols as she should and say nothing, but she surprises me again. "It's only you and me in this office." She places the pen carefully next to the folder. "I'm going to be candid with you."

This development has me reevaluating her again. If nothing else, I'm curious to hear what she thinks.

She takes a breath like she'll need all of it to get her point out. "I don't know how you managed to snag Kurt. After working with both of you all these months, I thought the two of you were more oil and water. Frankly, it was a surprise when Munich discussed this with me. If I were to bet, I'd have put my money on Matt Westmore. But Kurt is a bigger prize. He wields a lot of power, but he'll have even more once he takes over Drachen." She sits back and gives me a smile that doesn't reach her eyes. "You'll still need to hire a candidate by the end of the month, but if you fail, your contract won't end as a consequence. The project will be reassigned and your reputation will take a hit, but it doesn't matter. Your relationship with Heinrich will help you weather any storm at Drachen. It's a brilliant move."

So, the wicked witch of Drachen Americas thinks I set out to snare Kurt to climb the corporate ladder. If Chloe were here, she'd pee herself from laughing so hard. I need to get away from this insanity now, before I slap that you're just a ruthless manipulating bitch like me, welcome to the club smile off her face. "I think I need time to look over this paperwork," I say with more civility than I feel. "I'd like the rest of the day off to decide."

"I understand, there's a lot to think about. To answer your question, yes, Kurt will have to sign a similar agreement." She closes her laptop. "I'll leave it up to you when you want to announce your relationship to the team. I wouldn't wait. Although Kurt is not a celebrity here, news will get back to us. I need to warn you that it won't be easy to work in the same company with him. Even if you don't report directly to Heinrich, some will think you slept your way to any position you might be promoted to. With your new power, the game has changed. You might be feared, respected, or even loathed."

I head for the door, my body tight with rage.

Allison stands and walks to the light switch. She's near me as I exit. "Sorry, I forgot. Congratulations on your..."

I don't hear the rest of it. I'm doing a speed walk through the cubes. I find an empty one and slide into the chair. I pull out my phone and accept Kaylee's friend request. I swipe frantically through Hawaiian travel photos of them until the pictures from the helicopter tour appear. The whole lie we told about how Kurt and I met and that stupid wedding chapel story is all there in captions with a photo montage. I need to go downstairs to my office to get my stuff before I leave. I'm calling Kurt when I get there. I don't care what time it is in Munich or what personal shit he's taking care of, he's going to talk to me. I round the corner, practically jogging past Nina's door.

I hear my name sail out of her office. I stop. I can't ignore her; she'll just hunt me down. Anger and embarrassment are ready to spill out of me. I'm in no mood for a chat. Nina's walking alongside me. I keep moving to avoid any more attention. "Let me take you out for coffee," she says quietly.

"No, sorry, I can't," I croak out.

"Then, let's go downstairs and you can tell me why you're upset."

We're the only ones in the dungeon. The lights are turned off on this floor, and only the light from my space shines out into the darkness. I tell her an acceptable version of the truth, but I also include Matt in my account. All through my story, Nina's mouth gapes open while she's either looking at me or the love contract sitting on the desk.

"I had no idea," she says. "I thought the two of you barely tolerated each other. I'm not surprised about Matt; he would be a better fit for you."

"Can they force me to sign?" I blurt out, unable to reconcile any of this.

Nina is working her bottom lip, and if she isn't careful, she's going to draw blood. "No, no they can't force you to sign that document." She emphasizes the word force. "But your position might be at risk if you refuse. You'd be seen as a liability. Signing that document says to the company you have no intention of involving them in your relationship. It will give them some cover if you decide to claim sexual harassment."

"But there's no relationship," I protest, throwing up my hands, frustrated that my night in Vegas just blew up in my face. "I get it. I understand their position, but there's nothing between us. I shouldn't sign this document. I'd be admitting to something that doesn't exist." Nina is quiet, letting me vent. "What do you suggest?" I say. "What would you do if this happened to you?"

"I'd sign it," she says quietly. "If you want to continue working for Drachen, you should sign the agreement. At least give the company peace of mind. You don't have to announce anything to the team. If there's nothing going on, there's nothing to announce."

I'm not sure. Kurt's insisting we talk about our evening together makes me think he's about to declare his feelings for me. Jeez, this is

Kurt; it's more likely he just wants to hook up. "But there are photos circulating," I point out. "I saw Kaylee and Wyatt's Facebook page. They've chronicled that whole tour with us."

"Then you might send out a joint statement to get ahead of it. I'm not savvy about the press; maybe Drachen's marketing department might help you formulate something." She stands and holds out her arms. "Come on. Let's hug it out," she says. I frown. I'm not a big hugger. I reluctantly go to her. She's a lot shorter than me, but I let her squeeze me. "It will be alright, you'll see," she pats my shoulder. Nina has become a good friend. She releases me. "Go home. You need to talk to Kurt and time is ticking on Matt. Don't let him find out from someone else about this love contract."

I tell my phone to call Kurt while I'm driving. It goes straight to voicemail. When his generic greeting blasts out through the car speakers, I have to stop myself from blathering out a long message. I tell him to call me and that it's about the love contract. It's too early in the day for Chloe to be home from work. I text Matt while I'm walking to my bedroom.

Hi, when can we meet? Is all I type.

Five minutes later I receive a response. I'll be available tomorrow evening. Where would you like to meet? Your house, my house, or neutral place?

I think for a few seconds where the best place would be to meet him. A public venue might be restrictive, especially if it gets ugly. I don't want Chloe walking in on our conversation. He lives alone. I text back: Your place. What time?

Seven.

I'll be there.

There's no funny sign-off or cute emojis.

CHAPTER 20

Wait a Freaking Minute

*I*t's Tuesday, the day I should get my answer from Okobi. I don't expect to hear anything from him when I arrive at work at 6 o'clock. I could have come to work later while Kurt is gone but I'm used to getting up at five in the morning. If the day goes on as planned, I can celebrate, but I still have Matt to face this evening. Throughout the day I keep checking my texts and emails to see if Okobi has sent me anything. It's almost a relief when I receive an email from Nina about a meeting she's calling in an hour.

When I walk into the large conference room, everyone is here except for Allison. That's no surprise; she rarely meets with the whole team, preferring to conference with Nina, Haley, or sometimes myself. Haley's shy smile greets me when I take the seat next to her. I really haven't talked to my coordinator since I've been back. I know she's been spending a lot of time with Allison and I'm wondering if she's having divided loyalties. It's difficult when a powerful person takes an interest and wants to mentor you. I only hope that she can keep her sweet demeanor instead of ending up as an Allison mini me.

"I've called this emergency meeting to talk about the company Christmas party," Nina says to a groaning assembly. "Calm down, calm down. You know we have to do this every year. Haley, would you help me out and take notes?"

Haley nods and pulls out her laptop.

I lean towards Haley. "Why is everyone groaning about a Christmas party?" I whisper.

Haley answers but keeps her eyes on Nina. "Because each department has to do some entertainment for the party. It's normally a disaster. Every year we have to come up with some kind of act. Last year, if they gave a prize for the worse performance, it would have gone to the accounting department singing carols."

"What was wrong with that? Sounds Christmasy?"

"They sang the carols in German. The manager of that department is in ex-pat from Austria. No one else speaks German. It took them a month to learn three songs. It was excruciating. Saying they sang the songs in German would have been generous. They mangled the language so badly the native speakers in the room looked like they wanted to cry."

I start giggling. "What did the HR department do?"

She rolls her eyes. "We did carols as well."

"Did you sing them in German?"

She glares at me. "No, we played kazoos."

I do one of those silent laughs to try to keep it from escaping. My eyes are tearing and I'm ready to fall off my chair.

Nina searches the group. "Does anyone have an idea for this year's Christmas party entertainment?" She looks over at me, puzzled by my strained convulsions. "Kellis, you're new to the team. Do you have any hidden talent or any suggestions?"

I can barely hold it together. I keep imagining German carols accompanied by kazoos. "No, sorry," I choke out. I'm about to excuse myself to have a laugh in the hall when something does occur to me. I cough to regain my composure before another bout of laughter catches me. "Maybe I do have a suggestion." I clear my throat.

Nina's worried face gives way to smiling hope. "Please, come up and tell the group."

I take a few steps and land in front of our team. "How about lip-syncing to a song, with a dance number." More groans. "Wait," I wave them off. "Hear me out before you reject it." I shout over the noise. "You asked me if I had hidden talents. Well, there's someone here who's talented." Nina is expectant. At that moment Riku enters the room, saunters to a chair near the front, and sits. He leans over to the person next to him. "What did I miss?" he says, loudly enough to be heard by everyone.

"You didn't miss anything," says Nina. "Kellis was just about to tell us how HR can entertain everyone at the Christmas party."

Riku smirks up at me. "By any chance can you sing Christmas carols in another language?" There's a ripple of laughter through the room.

"No, I'm monolingual," I say, giving him a warning look not to interrupt me again, and address the room. "I hear the entertainment you provided last year was lovely, but if you don't want to sing or play an instrument, why not choose a song, lip sync, and add some simple choreography."

"Kellis, I think that's a wonderful idea." Nina's voice sounds unusually high. "I'm going to put you in charge of it."

Everyone is looking at me as if I'm their Christmas savior. "I don't mind helping. If that's what you need. But I can't choreograph a routine. But Haley can." Haley's head jerks up above her laptop, displaying a face of pure horror. I shrug, giving her a *better you than me* look. "She has a degree in dance." Stunned faces swing their gazes over at Haley. Riku just shakes his head like he can't believe that little quiet Haley is a dancer.

181

"Would you be willing to do that, Haley?" Nina says.

"I suppose." She draws this out while sending me daggers. "What song would you like to lip-sync to?"

"Something by Megadeth?" Jeff from the back of the room suggests.

"Interesting choice," Nina says, "But we should stick with something that everyone knows. Anyone else have a suggestion?"

"Maybe something seasonal?" A suggestion flies up from the one of the interns.

Riku does a face palm. For someone who is normally way too cool, he sometimes acts like a dork. "We're not going to do more Christmas carols," he groans out his disbelief. "I mean, it's already been done."

"Why not a parody with a twist?" I suggest.

"That's settled, we'll do a song lip-sync," says Nina, resuming her place in front of the room. "We can go back to work. Good meeting, people." We all begin filing out. Nina signals Haley to wait. "Can you have some suggestions ready in two days? We don't have that much time to get ready. Won't we have to coordinate costumes? Get a few of the others to help; I don't want this all on you." Nina turns her attention to the remaining people milling around. "Give Haley your music suggestions. I want everyone to participate, people."

The light from my headlights is shining off the dark, rain-soaked road. I'm only a few blocks from Matt's house when nervous dread twists my stomach. I'm not sure what I'll find when I see him. We never had an argument. I've never seen him angry, but I've seen what hurt looks like on his face. We'd already started something until this craziness in Vegas got in our way. I'm not sure if there's enough between us to salvage what we've begun.

Matt doesn't come out to the driveway to meet me. He greets me at the door barefoot in gray jeans and an old shirt he's still buttoning. He moves aside to let me enter. The strong scent of soap wafts around him. He looks like he hastily showered and dressed. No offer of a hug or kiss as I walk past him into the living room.

"Would you like something to drink?" he says, buttoning the last button. "I have water, juice, or another bottle of that wine we were drinking when you came over for dinner."

I drop my purse on the couch and sit down. "Whatever you're having, I'll have the same."

Matt returns with two beers, hands me a bottle, then sits in a chair opposite me. I take a drink. Him wanting distance is not lost on me. "How shall we do this?" I say to my beer.

He tips his bottle up for a drink then sighs. "I don't know. Maybe you can tell me what the fuck you were doing in that room with Heinrich?"

I perch on the edge of the couch and place the bottle on the table in front of me. "What I told you was true. We went into that room to discuss Okobi. Then things got out of hand."

He glances over at me. "What does out of hand mean exactly? Were you too overcome to say no? Or did he force you?"

I meet the challenge in his gaze. "It means that Kurt had some crazy notion that he might enjoy kissing me. I didn't invite it; it was a surprise. Before I could react or talk with him about what he'd done, he left. I haven't spoken to him since."

"Did you like it?" The question is an accusation, one that will lead to more hurt.

"I don't want to talk about Kurt or Vegas." I'm trying to make him understand I don't want this to end. "I want to talk about us. If there's still an us? Can we do that?"

He's looking past me and balancing the beer on his knee. "I get that we haven't been dating for long, but I missed you. I get this great idea in my head to fly out to Las Vegas and help you with Okobi. I don't know what to think when I see this completely different woman with short hair and sexy clothes. You tell me to leave and run to Heinrich as soon as he walks through the door. Why would I think there's an us?"

I don't answer; he has a right to his anger. I take a big chance and push away from the couch. His eyes follow me as I slip over to stand beside his chair. His free hand is draped indifferently on the chair's arm. I'm unable to resist the opportunity to gently run my fingers over the scraped knuckles, to soothe an injury he sustained during a recent bike spill. Maybe he'll remember how much there is between us or can be. I'm about to tell him I'm the same person who was in his bed when he pulls his hand away.

Cold eyes meet mine. "You wanted to talk." He tilts his head. "This is us talking."

I return to the couch and swipe my beer from the table. I take a long drag of the pale brew that now tastes unappealing. I'm eyeing the exit, but I decide to try again. "I've told you everything."

He doesn't look at me. "You haven't told me anything. I saw Heinrich with that shit-eating grin on his face leaving that hotel room and you wandering down the hall dazed. What happened? Why did it happen? If you're not going to tell me, then why are you here?"

This is karma slapping me in the face for kissing Kurt. I'm angry that he's hurt Matt with his antics, and that I was stupid to allow his interest in me because I felt sorry for whatever bad news he received. Matty Ice is unmoved. He might have decided I'm not worth the trouble. "We didn't have a quickie, if that's what you think. It was a kiss." My irritation is rising. "A stupid, overzealous kiss that was over before it began."

He places his beer on the floor next to him and shifts forward. "Let me tell you why I'm having a problem with this. I don't talk about how my marriage ended. The short of it is this, I thought something was going on with Jena and that asshole photographer she started working with. He promised to take her career into a new direction. She's an international model, but their careers are short. Jena was in a vulnerable place; she'd been losing jobs to younger, hotter models when she met him. She'd told me for months that I was imagining something between them. That I was jealous, that she was getting more attention from the media because of Wes, the asshole photographer. I bought it until I surprised Jena one day and found her face down in the guy's lap, my wife eagerly servicing him. When we finally talked, she tried to convince me that it was my fault and that I drove her to him. The truth is the marriage was a mistake. I thought I had gotten over it until I saw you in Vegas. I'm not doing this with another cheating whore."

That was clear enough to ram a truck through. "Calling me a cheating whore sounds like we're done. Thanks for the beer, I'll be going." I grab my purse from the couch and head for the door. He hasn't moved to walk me out, but I need to say one more thing. I try to muster as much casualness as possible. "And by the way, I can do professional. You don't have to worry about this affecting our working relationship." I continue my trek, surprised at how much this hurts. It didn't hurt this bad when I kicked my ex Tim to the curb.

"I'm establishing the ground rules." His voice booms across the room.

I stop. Is he serious? I spin around to face him.

"I don't know if that's the case here, but if you're playing me, then yeah, you need to leave." He pushes up from the chair. "I asked you for the truth, and you've got to tell me everything. Even the parts I'm not going to like. Let me decide." He takes a few steps toward me, then stops.

We stand there staring, a small distance between us that neither of us is breaching. Hurting over a relationship isn't something I want to do again. Walking away from Matt is the last thing I want. He takes a step. I take one too, not sure what we're doing. He extends his hand. I take it and he pulls me to him.

185

"Let's start over again," he says into my hair. "I'll try to listen while you talk. I've got to get used to you looking like this. It's like Kellis is gone and someone I don't know has taken her place." He strokes my hair. "Why did you cut it?"

I lean into him and place my arms around his waist. My cheek brushes the softness of his shirt. I look into his face. We're not back on the same frequency; he's holding back. "Chloe was with me at the stylist. She convinced me it was time for a change, that it would help my confidence for Vegas. The clothes were her idea; she picked them out."

His arms come around me and I get a warm hug. "I'll have to talk to your sister, if I ever meet her."

"Be careful what you wish for, she can be bossy."

He laughs. "I'll remember that." He walks me back to the couch. We lean back on the sofa, his arm around my shoulders.

I squeeze his hand. "There's been a lot of pressure from Allison to get Okobi on board. I know I've been back for a few days, but I didn't know what to say. I thought you might need some time." I glance down at our hands. "I was afraid when I came here tonight that you would end what we started."

He gives me a slight frown. "I'll admit I'd decided to end this, but when I saw you walk out, I couldn't do it. You look too damn cute stomping out of here." He leans forward and gives me a welcome home kiss. I know him enough to understand it doesn't mean all is forgiven. When he finishes, he tugs my hair. "I can't call you Godiva any longer." We chuckle.

This is the best time to tell him about the love contract. It has to be signed tomorrow. I never heard back from Kurt. It's just like him to cause a shit storm then walk away while it's blowing up. I've decided to take Nina's advice to sign the contract and stay at Drachen. Matt may not like it, and he just might tell me to leave after I tell him the rest of it. If we're going to have a chance at a relationship, I've got to be honest.

I take his hand and look into his concerned face. "Kurt," I breathe out. His eyes go wide and I realize what I just said. He jerks his hand away from me. "I mean Matt, I'm sorry. There's more I need to tell you. It involves Kurt, Vegas, Facebook, and a contract." It comes out in a rush.

He leans away from me, looking like he's waiting for the other shoe to drop. "I thought there was more to this. What is it? Why are you still thinking about Heinrich?"

I'm flustered. I've made a bad start. "I need to talk about the night before you saw me in Vegas." I have his full attention. "You know part of my job is taking out clients. Well, it was when I had my company. I convinced Kurt it would be a good idea if I took Okobi and a few of his colleagues out to see Vegas. I've been there many times and I have connections in entertainment there." I'm rambling like an idiot and avoiding the point. I looked down at my hands. "Maybe I should start further back and talk about when Kurt and I were leaving for the airport. You see, he got some bad news--"

Matt's phone rings. He normally ignores it when we're together but the ring tone is different. He snatches it off the coffee table. "What happened, Celeste?"

He's listening to the response.

"She just left you?"

Silence.

"I haven't heard from her in weeks. I talked to Verity yesterday, but she never mentioned anything about this."

Pause.

"For Christ's sake, where are you now? I trusted you to give me a heads up if something like this happened. The only reason I agreed to this vacation..., because she assured me you would be with her at all times."

He glances at the clock on the mantle. "What time is arrival?

Silence.

"I'm leaving now. I'll meet you in baggage." He cuts the call and tosses it on to the couch. He rakes tense fingers through his hair. "I've got to go," he says to no one.

"What happened?" I say. And who is Celeste? "Is there anything I can do to help?"

He looks over at me distracted. "Thanks, no, I have to go to the airport to pick up my daughter and my ex-mother-in-law."

He's never said anything about Verity? Who never mentions their kid? Maybe he thought it was common knowledge? "I didn't realize you had a daughter?"

"Yes, Verity is my...I mean our daughter. Jena has decided to spend Christmas in the Canary Islands with some new friends she met. A little girl would be too much of a bother. Jena wouldn't let her mother call me to warn me this was happening until she landed here."

Chloe was home when I returned. We had a long talk. She didn't appear to be surprised by any of my story about Kurt, Matt, and the love contract; she just wanted to know when she would meet Matt. I made her swear not to tell Mom, but I know that was an empty promise.

I'm heading off to my room, ready to put this day behind me when I get a text. I glance at the message.

Call me.

CHAPTER 21

Moves Like Jagger

Security lets me know when Allison arrives. It's better to give her the signed contract now before she summons me to her office. She doesn't appear surprised when I tap on her open door. She waves me into her office without a word.

"I assume you have something for me?" she says.

I don't sit. I pull a paper from my folder and place it on her desk."

She leans back in her chair, displaying a disturbing smile. "I've received some interesting information from my Munich connections. They say there's nothing between you and Heinrich. It appears you don't have the protection of the second most powerful man in the company."

"Does this mean you don't need this contract signed?" This is me trying not to relay hope in my voice."

"No, Drachen still wants the contract signed. They want to cover themselves if your story changes. What's important is that my original warning to you still stands. That Kurt's second-in-command must be hired by the end of the month or your contract will be terminated."

"Does the hire need to be Kyle Okobi?"

She considers. "I'm not unreasonable. It doesn't need to be Okobi, but I hear finding someone at that level will take time to find and cultivate. Time you don't have."

It looks like she wants to play cat and mouse, with me as the mouse. This is going to be a longer conversation. I sit, placing the folder on my lap. I think better when I'm at eye level. "I spoke to Kyle last night; he wants the job."

Her face tightens. This is not what she wants to hear. "You said the second company was from Southern California. Why would he take a job here when his wife is from Los Angeles?"

"He said his wife's family is controlling. They want to be close, but not too close to her family. A thirty-minute plane ride away from her parents seems to be a good thing. But there are a couple of caveats to the agreement. He's asking for an increase in the yearly salary and sign-on bonus. He wants the offer to him by next Friday. He has to give his decision to the other company that same day. If we don't agree to his terms, he'll take the second offer even if the location is less than favorable."

"Are you sure he's not using us to get the other company to up their offer?"

It was a possibility. Enough hires have used that tactic to increase their offers. I didn't think Kyle would engineer something similar. "I can't guarantee anything. But I think it's unlikely."

"You've been wrong before," she points out, which irks me, but I keep my composure. "You had a candidate for Dark Star that withdrew from an offer."

I didn't want to beat that dead argument again. "Yes, it happened, but we found a better replacement. I'm more confident with Kyle. I've submitted the paperwork to compensation. They're reviewing the offer now."

"Then I'll review it for final approval when it gets to my desk. Thank you for the signed contract."

Score one for me, I think as I walk towards Nina's office. She already knows about Okobi, I just need to fill her on my meeting with Allison. Haley is standing halfway in the door speaking to Nina.

"We were just talking about you," Haley says. "I've just emailed everyone the rehearsal schedule."

"That was fast," dreading what this means. "What do you need me to do?"

"Haley and Riku have worked out a song to lip sync to," Nina says. "Now they need to decide who can dance."

I look over at Haley. "You mean you've already met with him?"

"Yeah, we had a good hour meeting working out the details."

I guess she doesn't need a wing woman. "I'm not that great of a dancer," I say.

"Don't worry, the choreography will be easy; it's more attitude than movement. I'll rehearse you and Nina until you're perfect."

Nina and I exchange a look, like we just created a monster.

Matt has canceled our appointments and is working from home since his daughter arrived. We have brief conversations, but he sounds harried and it feels like he's avoiding me. I'm not the best with kids, but I assume at some point I'll meet Verity. It would be better if her dad and I had already talked through Las Vegas and Kurt, and we were on solid ground with our relationship. It still bothers me that our conversation was cut short. I've been thinking about writing him, but what we need to discuss should be said in person.

Kurt has begun a one-sided text conversation. I respond, but he never answers my questions. He did say he should be back soon, but when I press him for the date, he talks about the weather, how I should see Munich in the Spring. Most of his messages are just rambling. The funny thing is I miss Herr Heinrich. My rides to work are quiet and a lot less challenging. He's caused me a ton of frustration, but I still wonder what he's doing and why he left suddenly.

The Christmas party is in three days. Times are good at the company. This year they've rented space in a swank hotel downtown. Everyone is buzzing, excited about the party. Even Allison has smiled at me a couple of times. I just chalk it up to the season and stay out of her way.

This is the third and last rehearsal for our entertainment for the party. I should exercise more; every muscle is sore. I'm looking forward to a hot bath and a glass of wine as my reward when I get home. I'm waiting for Haley outside, watching her through the studio's glass window. She's my ride home. The cold air feels good after dancing for almost two hours. She's talking to the last stragglers while she moves around the room locking up. We've been meeting at Miss Lila's Dance Academy where Haley teaches part-time. This is something else I didn't know about my coordinator, that she still dances. One day I'll treat her to a girls' night out and have a long talk. She's been a good friend, and having a long talk is way overdue. Riku is back in his street clothes, his costume zippered in a garment bag over his shoulder. He holds it by the hook with two fingers and hangs back, waiting for her to finish. The last three people leave and it's just them. It's interesting to watch their interaction. She's confident in her practice dance gear. He's a little intimidated by this new version of Haley. I think we all are awed by her.

Riku waves at us as he passes our car and climbs into his own vehicle. "Did he have questions about his part?" I ask, snapping my seatbelt closed.

Haley turns the engine. "If you can believe it, he's getting nervous about his performance."

"Why? The dress rehearsal went perfectly."

Haley looks over at me, on the verge of a grin. "I'm impressed. The five of you who are dancing look pretty professional. I'm lucky that some of you had rhythm. It was obvious the rest of the team were relieved when I asked them to play a crowd watching. Riku thinks he should do more than lip sync, a few steps, and look smug."

"I think he's worried that he hasn't seen you perform your part."

She shrugs, pulling the car into traffic. "It's just me dancing around him. We're taught in performance class how to move around a non-dancer. My part is the least of it. It's all of you in costume dancing in unison that will make it worth watching.

Cars are lined up three-deep in front of the hotel when I pull up to the entrance. I decide to use the valet service instead of lugging my stuff through the parking lot. Nina and a few of the other dancers are just inside the lobby when I enter. Nina has already secured a cart and is helping to pile on our costumes and bags. I don't follow Nina's traveling caravan to a changing room. I move quietly away to stroll down the long, carpeted hallway to find the Drachen party. The hotel is decked out in holiday decorations, even seasonal music is drifting from speakers in the public spaces, but Drachen must have hired a service to do their room. There are giant toys everywhere. The theme is Toy Story, the brainchild of the party committee that decided it would work with our company toy and food drive.

"I thought you'd never get here," Riku calls out, tipping a glass of something toward me.

I move to his side, happy to see a familiar face. "Nina and the rest of the team are storing our costumes. They'll be here soon."

Ice clinks as he takes a sip, then sighs his enjoyment. He catches me watching him. "What can I say? I like alcohol."

I shake my head.

He gestures to the corner. "The bar is that way, if you're wondering."

I glance over in the direction, but I'm more concern with the room. There must be at least 300 people attending. Everyone from headquarters to some of the other sites near us like Dark Star are here. I'm trying to get the lay of the place when I see it. Not sure how I missed that when I walked in. Maybe it was the giant-size Woody and Bo Peep that obscured my view. There's a full stage at the end of the space. I don't know what I expected, but it wasn't that.

Riku moves closer to me. We're both staring at the stage. "Pretty intimidating, right?" he says.

I look up at him. "I think I'm going to need a drink."

"Have several," he laughs, "It's free."

I scan the room again. "Where's Allison?" remembering the wicked witch has got to be around here somewhere. Okobi will be signing his offer letter in a few days. My contract will finally be secure, or maybe Drachen will see my worth and offer me a full-time position as reward for pulling off this hiring coo.

"She's over there in the corner talking to Rogers, the guy she replaced as HR VP."

I note her location and continue searching the crowd. Matt said he might drop by with his daughter. Children are not allowed, but they made an exception for Verity if she only stays during dinner.

The HR team takes up two tables for dinner. Allison is sitting at her own table with Rogers, talking his ear off. I'm at the other table bantering with Riku as the salads are set in front of us. Matt appears in the entry, holding Verity's hand. My breath catches to see how sexy he looks in his dark custom tailored suit. I realize how much I've missed him. My heart tightens. If he can't get past my Vegas trip or the love contract, my replacement is probably in this room. There were more than a few women who noticed Mr. Westmore's arrival.

Verity looks like her mother with pale blond waves to her waist in a soft pink and black frock. There's an older woman with them who has a hand at the girl's back, guiding her between the tables. I assume that's Celeste, the ex-mother-in-law.

Matt's searching the party and finally sees me. There're no empty chairs where I'm seated. The waiter is ushering them to Allison's table. He smiles and nods at me as he pushes the chair in for Verity.

We catch one another's cautious glances throughout the dinner. It isn't likely I'll get a moment alone with him as long as his family is with him. The desserts arrive, and I excuse myself to head for the restroom. What I really need is to be away from the noise and laughter. I throw a look at Matt before I leave, but his attention is on Rogers.

It's when I leave the bathroom that I see Matt, his hands in his pockets, leaning against the wall. A playful grin on his lips as I approach. He checks the deserted hallway, then finds my hand to lead me away from the party. We stop on the other side of the building, near a courtyard.

"I don't think anyone will find us here," he says, anxiously pulling me to him. "I sent Verity home with Celeste; you can meet them another time. I couldn't wait for the party to end, I needed to be alone with you now."

I bury my face in his chest to breathe in his familiar scent. I'm more certain of us as a couple when I'm this close to him.

"Kellis," He exhales my name.

I lift my chin to see the hunger in his gaze. Our lips touch and our passion ignites. We're not backing away from what we want. We kiss like we're drowning in each other. But we can't keep this intensity, I swear there'll be bruises on my lips if I'm not careful. I want him, but this isn't the time for a reunion. "We're in a public place," I say, reluctantly ending our knee trembling kiss.

"I can't help myself." he smirks. "You're a sexy nymph,"

I reach out to wipe pink lip gloss away from the corner of his mouth. He catches my fingers and I shiver a little when he runs them across his lips.

"It's been difficult without you," he says, releasing my hand. "I almost called you several times to ask you to meet me." He tips my face up to him. "What's that old line… If the phone doesn't ring, it's me."

"I wish you had made the call," I whisper, happy that he wasn't avoiding me.

He brushes his hand over my cheek, studying me, turning something over in his mind. "It's like we're always starting over," he muses. "I find out something new about you and then we're back to square one. Are you the same woman I saw barreling down the path to Drachen? Are you the nymph that was in my bed? Is it still you?"

I squeeze him tighter. "It's still me," I breathe, wishing we could leave now. "Let's talk tonight."

"I can be away for a few hours as long as I'm back when Verity wakes up in the morning."

"Yes," I whisper.

"I know it sounds cheesy, but let's get a hotel room. Not here. I'll make a reservation somewhere else. I'll text you where."

We're the last act to be called to the stage. At least there were no Christmas carols sung in German this year, but we did have to endure a troop of mimes. We pile onto the stage to take our places, me pulling down this short dress that barely covers my behind. There are shorts underneath, but it's still shorter than I'm used to. There are two large screens that will transmit our performance. Even the tables in the back will see everything.

The five dancers are dressed alike in a white sleeveless, high collar, A-line dress with white ankle boots. Riku joins us, handing Haley his bow tie to arrange. She's in deep concentration looping the bow, while Riku's lopsided grins looks down at her. They're so cute together. Riku seems interested, but Haley's not paying attention to the signs. More stuff to talk about during our girls' night.

Haley steps away to inspect him. She opens his electric blue tux jacket to find his dark glasses and hands them to him. "I hope everyone remembered to bring their sunglasses." We groan back a yes. Riku puts his on and strikes a pose. The rest of his outfit is channeling '90s prom tux gone wrong with white pleated shirt, black pants, and black and white wingtips. I actually think the shoes are very cool. We're lucky that Haley has contacts at a costume warehouse in San Francisco. We look like a professional dance production.

There's still some time before we begin. Haley's giving us our last directions and walking us through the dance. She'll be coming on after the performance begins.

Fifteen minutes later, we take our places. My adrenaline is so high I might throw up. Before I have a chance to dash off, we hear Richard, the CEO and master of ceremonies, announce us from the other side of the curtain. The curtains part and lights dim, revealing us as a crowd of well-dressed people talking in small groups. A synthesized beat pumps out a steady rhythm and rattles the space. The dancers skip out to assemble in a line. We're bored women looking out at nothing, facing the audience. The music is still driving, pulsating like a club beat. The audience knows the song and is stirring to the sound. Riku breaks from the crowd, swaggering out in front of us, looking like a cocky SOB with his female posse in back of him. The beat pauses enough for Riku to pull his mic. He points at the crowd. "Are you ready to party, Drachen?" The crowd shouts out a collective "Yes!" and Riku delivers the first line of the song. The dancers pivot to the right, drop slightly, head turn, and vogue. The crowd roars.

The song courses through the speakers. Riku strides across the stage lip syncing his story, channeling his inner K-pop star with every nuanced movement of his body. He moves effortlessly in and out of our dance formation as we hit our marks. My nausea is gone, replaced by the exhilaration of the dance and the energy from the crowd as we perform with bored precision.

Haley dances in, unrecognizable in a tight yellow cat suit and a wig of long blond ringlets. The crowd is on their feet moving with us to the beat. Phones are out, capturing the performance, and the flashes from some of the cells are nearly blinding me. I glimpse Matt near the front, his mouth open, mesmerized.

Haley is moving around Riku, tossing her mass of curls and tempting him as she moves seductively around him. He was instructed to ignore her and act like beautiful women dance around him all the time. He continues to lip sync and play to the crowd. Some of the women from the audience rush to the stage. Hands raised, they dance in a tight bunch, calling out his name. They go into a frenzy when he looks their way to sing just to them.

The excitement seems overwhelming, but I press on, relying on the dance to push me through. Haley gives a defiant toss of her head, giving up on Riku's lack of attention, and moves back to stand with the crowd a distance behind us.

Riku dances to center stage, his posse on either side of him. Our small crowd on stage comes to life and takes their places directly behind us. We are a mass facing out at the audience. The large screens in back of us flash a freeze frame of a dance scene from the music video. We're dressed like the people on screen, as if we've just stepped out of the scene.

The music video goes live. All of us on stage go into the dance, matching the movements of the dancers in the video. The room goes ballistic. People are screaming so loudly I can barely hear the music. I want to smile, but Haley warned us under pain of death not to break character. We push hard through the final gyrating moves amid the frenzy in the room until the music halts and the stage goes dark. It's a few moments before the lights go up. We're staring out at the murmuring audience as ourselves. We smile, some laughing, not believing we pulled it off. Haley walks out in front, inserting herself next to Riku and the dancers. We link arms and take a bow over the shouts and cheers, loving the rush, happy it's over.

Some of the audience is coming up to congratulate us. I search the crowd for Matt. He's standing apart, staring in disbelief, rooted in place as people stream past him. I'm not sure what he's registering. Nina touches my arm and I turn away to give her a hug. I look out again and my stomach twists. Kurt's in the entryway doing a slow clap.

CHAPTER 22

Fade to Black

Kurt enters the room trying to telegraph something to me, but I ignore whatever signal he's trying to send. I pull my gaze to Matt, who nods. I nod back and he strolls toward the exit. I'll check my texts later to see where I'll meet him. Kurt looks from me to Matt. They acknowledge each other as Matt walks by him to leave the party.

A hand is on my arm. "Come on, they're taking pictures," Riku says. "They want you to pose with the group."

"Sure, give me a minute."

Riku follows my gaze. "What's that guy doing back here? He's been gone so long, I thought Munich kept him."

I make a move to leave the stage. Maybe if I talk to Kurt, I can get some answers now.

Riku's hand is back on my arm. "Hey, not now," he warns. "Is that guy a vampire or something? Are you enthralled, because that's how you're acting?" He tugs at my arm. "Come on, he can feed on

201

your blood later."

Kurt flashes an *I'm up to no good grin*, then heads out the exit. I get an awful feeling as I join the group.

Riku insists on a series of rock star poses. Haley hangs on him while he looks indifferent. The dancers are draped around him looking at him adoringly. We finally push him out of the way and put on dark glasses to do our bad ass girl poses without him. Riku retreats to the bar, unhappy that he can't take more pictures with us. We're laughing so hard after we finish, I've nearly forgotten about Kurt. The whole impromptu photo session lasted a few minutes; I still might catch Kurt outside.

The maze of hallway is endless. Closer to the entrance, agitated male voices are growing louder. I turn the corner and almost run into Matt and Kurt in a heated exchange.

"My advice is to leave her alone," Kurt says. "I'm back now. I know she can be needy at times, but that's no reason to take advantage. You shouldn't have come to Vegas."

Needy? Is he serious? I step closer.

Neither man sees me; they're too engrossed in the moment like two alley cats protecting territory. Matt tries to walk past, Kurt side steps him, not finished with the conversation.

Matt halts, his body tense. "You're insane," he says. "I know you think you're a big shit in Germany, but we're not in Munich. Kellis wouldn't talk to you if it wasn't her job."

Kurt considers this. "My status in Germany isn't the issue. Kellis and I are..." He pauses for the words, "An item. I think that's correct. You're wrong if you think she's interested in you. We're together." Kurt sees me. Without losing eye contact with Matt, he motions me to come to him. I stop in a neutral place near them, not standing close to either man.

"Kellis, schatz, you've found me."

Schatz? Is that some sort of endearment?

"I'm sorry I didn't let you know I was coming. I wanted to surprise you." Kurt says reaching for me, but Matt blocks him. "Kellis, please tell him, he should know," Kurt says.

I look at Herr Heinrich with a warning. "I don't know what you're talking about..."

"If you won't..." Kurt snatches my hand and holds it up. "This is my signet ring on her finger." I try to pull my hand away, but he keeps it in view. The bulky ring with the letter 'K' carved deep into the gold is close to Matt's face.

Matt shakes his head. "A cheap piece of costume jewelry? Is that supposed to mean something?"

"I gave this to Kellis in Las Vegas with a promise that I would replace it with a wedding ring."

It dawns on Matt this might be true. He swings his gaze to me. "Why are you wearing his ring?"

"I couldn't get it off." It sounds feeble, but it's true.

"Why was it there in the first place?"

I move slightly toward Matt, keeping Kurt at my back, and I drop my voice. "This is what I wanted to discuss with you tonight." I say as if Kurt can't hear me. "It's not what it looks like..." I regret that cliché the moment it leaves my lips.

Matt cuts me off before I can get out an apology. "Are you two fucking?" he demands.

"NO!" I blurt out and free myself from Kurt's grasp.

"Not yet," Kurt says as if this is obvious. "She still has to meet my family."

"Shut up!" Matt and I both scream at Kurt.

He throws up his hands in mock surrender. "I get it...and everyone back at the party did too."

Matt has given up on trying to touch me. "Kellis, I need to understand why this happened. I'm not going to believe anything this jackass has to say."

"Christ, does she need to paint you a picture?" Kurt grumbles.

Matt is trying to keep his emotions in check. Kurt's stupid arrogance could piss off a saint. Even I'm fighting an uncontrollable urge to strangle him lifeless. "We need to talk alone," I say to Matt and throw a glare at Kurt to reinforce what I want. It doesn't faze him; he's enjoying this uncomfortable situation way too much.

"Kellis is reluctant to tell you the truth," Kurt butts in. "Let me help this along. You might have remembered HR introduced new contracts that were put into effect a few years ago to help protect the company from harassment, favoritism, etc.; it's a long list."

This is not registering with Matt. "Get to it," he says, annoyed.

Kurt tries again, leaving some of the snark out of his voice. "The contract is the reason she's not interested in you. Kellis has signed a love contract admitting there is a relationship between us. I signed a similar one in Munich. As far as the company is concerned, we're together. We're a couple. I plan to make an announcement with Kellis when I return on Monday. It's part of the agreement."

There's a knot in my stomach. Somehow, I missed that part of the contract. It would make sense, if we declared ourselves as a couple to the company, that we'd have to announce formally to our co-workers. I thought I could keep it a secret.

Matt takes a few seconds to come to terms with Kurt's statement. He takes my hands in his. "Is this true?"

I force myself to look into his pleading eyes. "I had no choice," I murmur. This is not the way I wanted him to find out. If I had more time, I could make him understand.

Matt's fingers tighten around my ring finger. I can't look away from his hurt accusing eyes. They say I'm just another cheating whore, like Jena. He tugs at the signet ring, and it slips off easily. He holds my hand between us and places it in my palm, closing my fingers around the metal. He turns away. Leaving me broken.

"Good man. I knew we would get there eventually," Kurt grins.

Rage stiffens Matt's body. His anger is directed at Kurt, who appears unaffected by a large, sullen man staring at him. I think Matt's going to say something before he walks away. He takes a step back. I move forward, trying one more time to convince him to leave with me. His movements are too quick, and I don't have time to register when his fist flies out at Kurt's face. Kurt's reflexes are just as fast and he jerks back, just avoiding the blow. Matt is off balance with the momentum of the missed punch. The last thing I hear is Riku's alarm of, "Oh, shit." And then I descend into darkness.

CHAPTER 23

No Joke

Chloe stands over me, relief flooding her worried features. "Why are you looking at me like that? Did I oversleep?" I rub the back of my head. It seems tender and I have a wicked headache. "Is Kurt in the kitchen demanding his breakfast?" I finally notice this is not my bed or my room.

A man that seems too young and studious appears from behind Chloe. "Hello, I'm Dr. Tavera. Do you know who you are?"

Chloe nods at me.

Dr. Tavera pushes his glasses further up his nose, waiting for a response.

I play along. "Good to meet you Dr. Tavera. My name is Rhiannon Kellis Ivarsson."

"Good, do you know who the president is...?"

I answer a few more simple questions. "I assume I'm in the hospital." I gesture to my surroundings. "Why am I here?"

"Do you remember anything?" the doctor asks, taking a seat near the bed. I'm in a curtained-off section, with monitors and equipment, an urgent care. "I remember the party, dancing..." I stop for a moment while the rest of it comes creeping back. "I remember talking to Kurt and Matt."

"Anything after that?" he prompts.

It seems to be on the edge of my memory, but I can't grasp it. I shake my head, then regret the movement. My face feels hot and tender. "Not yet. Maybe you can tell me?"

"Let me examine you before we talk." He takes some time to check me out, asking questions about my health. I'm anxious until he hangs up the stethoscope. "It looks good so far. You're healthy other than the bruising to your face. Rest for now and we'd like..."

I look at him expectantly.

His brows go up. "Right, you want to know what happened. You were struck by one of the men. His fist made contact with the side of your face. You're lucky the blow didn't hit you full force or we might be talking about reconstructive surgery. But the impact was enough to cause a black eye and bruising along the side of the face. You fell back and hit your head. You lost consciousness for a bit, and they called the ambulance that brought you here. We'd like to do some tests?"

"Yes, that's fine, if it will get me out of here."

"Great, I'll put in the orders for the tests and the nurse will come in to escort you." He stands. "I'll be back once I've reviewed the results." He leaves, with Chloe close behind him. They have a whispered conversation on the other side of the curtain.

My sister returns with a weak smile. "The doctor says you can have visitors. Are you up for it?"

I push myself up to a seated position. Mom must be here. Chloe is the calm one; she's probably in the waiting room. "Why not?" I say. "I'm not going anywhere."

"I'll be back."

When Chloe returns, I'll ask her for a mirror. I know Mom has one in her bag. The curtains swish open and Matt steps reluctantly to the bed. He grimaces, and I realize my face is worse than I expected. "Kellis, I'm sorry." He looks awful, hair disheveled and blood on his shirt. I don't see an injury; it must be my blood or maybe he took a swing at Kurt. "You know I'd never hurt you."

So, he's the one that hit me. It still seems fuzzy. I do remember we broke up before this happened. Now regret and embarrassment is setting in for everything that happened. Funny, that we're finally alone, but I don't have the strength to lobby for us again. "I know it was an accident. I've thought about taking a swing at Kurt myself." I try to smile, but it hurts.

He sits at the foot of my bed. "There's no excuse. You wouldn't be in here if I hadn't lost my temper and tried to take a shot at Heinrich. I missed and you got hurt."

There's movement just beyond the small split in the curtain. A tall blond man walks by and glances in briefly. He steps away from the curtain, but I know he hasn't left. Matt takes my hand and my attention drifts back to him. "You scared me when you were lying there helpless. They wouldn't let me near you until now. I don't want to feel that way again."

I start crying, wondering why I'm emotional. It's got to be the bump on my head that's started these tears. "This is not how I wanted it to be between us," I sniff. "I screwed up, but not for the reasons you think."

Matt's sigh is deep. "Verity is back. She was only going to be with her mother for the winter holidays. She normally stays with me. I guess I got a taste of being single without the responsibilities when we met." He gives me a sad smile. "I love that my daughter is here. We lived in a state of upheaval, moving from one crisis to another, when Jena was living with us. I got away from that life, not just for my daughter, but I can't do it again."

He's comparing me to his ex-wife again. It hurts and it's unfair.

I was the most boring person on the planet until I came to Drachen. I pull my hands away to swipe at my tears. "So, this is really over?"

He nods. "We can be friends?"

I cringe. But what else can he offer? We work for the same company. Better to be civil than making life miserable. It won't be easy. This is something that should have been and now it's over. This is going to hurt for a long time.

"Work friends," he adds hopefully. "I'll still support you at Drachen. I think you're one of the best recruiters I've known."

I want to scream at how unfair this is, but I can be an adult too. "Haley will be promoted to a recruiting position soon. She can be the onsite recruiter for Dark Star. I can help her if she needs it."

He rises slowly to his feet, still having a difficult time looking at the bruises on my face. My stupid tears are streaming again, and I don't bother to wipe them away. He's standing near the curtain, erasing any chance that he'll change his mind. "Goodbye, Kellis. I'll always..." He stops, avoiding my gaze. "I'll always help you if you need me. I hope you can be happy." He parts the curtains and disappears.

I pull the sheet over my face and sink deeper into my bed. I've lost Matt, but at least I've accomplished my goal to stay at Drachen. It's small comfort when I know Matt won't be in my life.

"Is it my turn?"

I lower my sheet and sit up. Kurt stands at the end of the bed with an enormous bunch of flowers, grinning like an idiot.

I grab the first thing I can find on the side table and fling it at him. The small lotion bottle bounces off his chest. "Get out!"

"Bad time, or is it the meds talking?"

"Chloe, are you out there?"

My sister pokes her head inside. "What's wrong? Should I get the doctor?"

I point at Kurt. "No, I want him gone."

They look at each other. "You know this is Kurt. He wants to make sure you're alright"

"I'm not alright because of him."

Pain washes over his face. He hands the flowers to Chloe and walks out.

My tests were fine. I have no side effects from my injury, but Chloe still watches me to make sure I don't lapse. My face looks like I've been in a fight, but the bruising is fading. I'm lucky I have the weekend to heal.

Sunday arrives and I realize I won't be ready to face work the next day. I call Nina to ask if I can work from home for the week if I need to. She asks how I am and gives me an okay to stay home. Monday is the day Kyle Okobi will sign his offer letter. When I receive the approval from Drachen, I'll call him to present the offer. That victory lap I plan to take better be worth it after everything I've been through.

My face still isn't ready for visitors. I'm up at my usual time placing a cup in the dishwasher. I catch sight of Kurt coming back from his jog. He's stretching, watching my house. We haven't spoken since the hospital.

Chloe comes in. "Spying on Kurt?" She leans into the window and waves. He grins and waves back.

"What do you think you're doing?" I walk away so he doesn't see me.

"I'm being nice to our neighbor. I got a text from him. He says he'll arrange his rides from now on, that he doesn't expect you to drive him. He's also canceling our breakfasts. Shame, I really enjoyed looking at him in the morning scrambling eggs while wearing his pristine striped apron."

After Chloe leaves, I move my laptop to the dining room and

work most of the day. I become concerned when noon arrives and there's no word about the offer approval.

I punch in the number for Abby, the compensation analyst that's working on the offer. "How's it going?"

"Fine, maternity leave can't come too soon. What can I do for you?"

"I'm looking for a status on the Okobi offer."

"Yes, I remember that one. That's been on Allison's desk for the last three days."

I call Nina for advice.

"I have a meeting with her in ten minutes," she says. "I'll ask her then."

I'm staring down three o'clock, pacing the floor. The offer has to be presented by 5 p.m.

At four, Nina rings. "I spoke to Allison. She says she still had questions. I walked her through it and reminded her about the deadline. If you don't hear from her in 30 minutes, call me and I'll hike back to her office."

At four thirty I call Nina.

The minutes are inching up as I wait. At ten to five, Nina rings back out of breath. "Allison's not in her office. I've been searching for her. Security just told me she left for the day."

I stare at the phone. "I've got to call him now."

"Okay, call me and let me know what happens as soon as you finish. I have to report to Allison."

I take a few seconds to compose myself, then dial his number. I don't have a clue what to say. I'm just trusting I'll say the right words to convince him to come to Drachen.

"Kellis, how are you this fine day?" It sounds like he's driving. Road sounds are coming through the phone.

"I'm fine, Kyle. How are Gracie and the kids?"

"Excited about returning to California. What news do you have for me?"

An alert pings on my phone. "Will you excuse me? I need to take this." The offer letter is sitting on the SharePoint. Some of the pressure around my temples is lessening. I download the offer and send it to Kyle. "I'm back," I sigh. "It's been an interesting day. I've just sent you the offer. We can go over it together and I can answer questions if you have them."

"That's great. I'm walking through the door." I hear kids playing in the background. "Give me a minute while I go to my office." There's light tapping. "I'm pulling it up now...I have it."

I place my phone on the table and engage the speaker. I'm accessing the letter on my laptop. I begin my rote presentation that we are pleased to extend this offer. Then I scroll down to the compensation portion of the letter. The numbers haven't changed."

"Is this a joke?" Kyle says. "This is the original offer."

"There's seems to be a mistake. I must have overlooked the revised proposal. Give me a minute to search the SharePoint. I'm frantically tapping, but there's nothing in the folder. This can't be right. Allison had plenty of time to do her review and even get approval from Munich. "I don't have an offer at the moment. I'm sure it will be ready tomorrow. Could you give me an extension?"

He takes a few seconds to respond. "This is very concerning. We discussed this at great length. If there was an objection, it should have been raised at that time."

"I know and I understand, but we've known each other for a long time. Can you trust me?"

"Normally I would, but I feel Drachen has placed me in a difficult situation. If I don't take the offer on the table from the other company, I could lose out completely. I won't do that to my family."

"Kyle--"

"I'm sorry, Kellis. I have another call."

Nina is sympathetic when I tell her, but we both know this is not good. Maybe if I had asked about the offer earlier. "I need to call Allison," she says, distracted. "Don't worry, we'll talk tomorrow and figure out what happened."

The next day I get a call from Candice, my recruiter. "There's no way to sugarcoat this. I got a call from Nina Madrone. She wasn't happy about this decision, but the company has terminated your contract."

I fall hard into my seat. I'm unemployed again? "Did they say why?" Like hearing I failed would make it alright.

"I'm sorry, Kellis, you're a contractor, and you know they don't need to give a reason. Do you want me to find something for you now, or do you want to take some time off between jobs?"

I wasn't going to look for another position. I'm racking up too many failures to have the confidence to try again. It's time to do something I was probably born to do and work for my mother. "Not right now," changing the phone to my other ear. "I'll let you know when. Thanks."

CHAPTER 24

Pity Party

I'm sitting on the couch with a bowl of heavily buttered popcorn on my lap, in my jammies, watching *The Price is Right*. Chloe walks into the living room in her robe. It has to be close to 9:30 a.m. "Why aren't you at work?" I say, watching a contestant guess the cost of a can of peaches. "You don't want to screw up the only money coming into this house."

She plops down on the couch, leans over, and scoops popcorn from the bowl. "I took the day off in sisterly solidarity. I also wanted to see if they can run the office without me for one day. If the office isn't burnt to the ground when I return, I'll consider that a yes."

This feels like a planned therapy session or an intervention. "You didn't work today so you can say *I told you so?* Do you ever get tired of being right?"

"No," she huffs.

I turn back to the TV.

"Sorry, that was a bad joke. I'm here for you. If my little sister

215

hurts, I hurt." She tugs at my sleeve, then scoops more popcorn.

I manage to return a weak smile and place the bowl between us. "Thanks. But, I'm fine. I just need a little time."

"No pressure, but how long do you plan to reside on this couch during the day?"

"I think I need something to drink." I push to my feet and head for the kitchen. Chloe waits a few seconds, then follows me. I poke my head into the refrigerator.

"You know the family decided to have our family day on Christmas eve. They took a vote while you were in the hospital. Mom's hoping it will spill over into Christmas. That's only a few days away."

I'm half listening. I don't want to think about my family in the holiday spirit. I lift up the jug of orange juice, asking if she wants some.

"No, I'm good," Chloe says, leaning against the counter. "Dad's flying in from Texas and the twins are coming from Oregon. Mom's been beside herself with planning."

It will be good to see Faith and Dan. They haven't been down since summer. I take a glass from the cupboard and pour the juice over the sink. A cool breeze flutters the curtain. It feels good. This close to Christmas the temperature should be cold, but instead it's perfect. An SUV pulls up in front of Kurt's house. The trunk pops open and a woman gets out of the vehicle. She's pulling a sign and a big hammer out of the trunk and drags it to the lawn. Seconds later she's pounding a 'for rent' sign in Kurt's front yard. "Chloe. Did you know about this?"

She looks out of the window. "Yes, didn't you know? Kurt's been called back to Germany."

"Why would I know that?"

"He told me he's been texting you since you left the hospital. Don't you ever look at your texts?"

"You talk to Kurt?

216

"Nearly every day. He asks about you."

This I don't believe. He's been a pain ever since I met him.

"He's not the ogre you make him out to be."

"Kurt's arrogant, stubborn, thick...and those are his good qualities," I snap back.

"No one is perfect. I'll admit he needs to work on his social skills, but he's—"

"What? Sadistic, controlling—"

"What he is," Chloe interrupts, "is in love with you."

This is coming from her *everything happens for a reason* philosophy. I have no words, so I head for my room.

"Don't act like it hasn't crossed your mind," Chloe yells at me as we move through the house.

"Matt," I'm shouting. "Matt is the one I want."

"Okay, fine," she cuts me off and halts in front of me. "Let's talk about Matt Westmore."

I fold my arms and lean against the door, waiting for her assessment of how I screwed up a promising relationship because I was nice to Herr Heinrich.

Chloe is giving me that *you need to listen to reason* vibe. She's so agitated with me she's resorting to counting her points on her fingers. "He didn't want anyone to know you were dating. He freaked out when you cut your hair. You tell him you need to go to Las Vegas for work, but he doesn't trust you and shows up. He wasn't pleased when he saw you dancing at the Christmas party." Chloe throws up her hands. "My God, he doesn't want you, he wants someone that lives a dull existence."

"That's not true," stretching the words out.

"Really," she says in disbelief. "These last years, after you closed your company, you were becoming that person, but that's not you; it's never been you. He dumps you over drama? He couldn't wait until you're out of the freakin' hospital? If you had patched this up, you would have continued to fold yourself into his ideal until there was nothing left of Kellis. I have news for you: everyone's life is messy, that's what makes you interesting."

I walk inside my bedroom and pick up my cell from the desk. I scroll through my texts. There are too many messages to count from Kurt asking: *How are you? I'm sorry. Can we talk?*

I glance up from the phone. "How can I love someone, when all I want to do is smash his face in?"

"This isn't funny, Kel."

"Do I look like I'm laughing?" I toss the phone on the bed.

"You said you had a good time with him in Las Vegas. What's the harm? Talk to him. He's leaving right after Christmas."

Nina, Haley, and Riku are giving me pity stares across the table. The restaurant is quiet. It's a little after 5 p.m. I'd agreed to meet Nina to give her back my company equipment and was surprised when Haley and Riku decided to tag along. Nothing romantic appears to be happening between them. At the Christmas party, he looked at her like she was a free buffet and he hadn't eaten in days. Disappointing; they're so cute together, but it looks like they're stuck in the friend zone.

"I suggested we find the Cheese Rebellion truck and eat there but I was vetoed," Riku says, frowning at the menu.

"It wasn't practical, Haley protests, "the truck was in Burlingame. Have you seen the traffic on 101? I'd have agreed if we were going by helicopter." Haley runs her finger down his oversized menu. "There's a tuna melt; you can have that."

He shakes his head.

"I don't want to think Kellis and I are the only adults at the table," Nina says.

Haley and Riku are watching one another like two siblings at the dinner table. I think this is worse than the friend zone.

"Thanks for meeting us." Nina cuts into my thoughts. "I know coming back to Drachen to return your equipment would have been awkward. I wanted you to know that you have our support. Several of the hiring managers were not happy when they were told you were gone."

"What excuse did Allison give? Or did she just send around a memo with all my imagined failings?"

"You know she can't do that." Nina's stilted response doesn't sound convincing. "She cited budget cuts and your contract ended. It's normal to cut personnel before the end of the year."

"Have you resumed the search for Kurt's second-in-command?" Allison probably had another agency picked out, knowing that I wouldn't get the hiring done.

They nervously glance at each other. Dread is already twisting my insides. There's something they don't want me to hear.

Nina slides her hand over and places it on mine. "They didn't restart the search. Okobi accepted the offer."

I jerk my hand away and sit back. The pity stares are back. "What happened?"

"It's taking me time to piece this together," Nina says. "Allison sent out a memo the next day to everyone announcing Kyle Okobi as the new second-in-command for R&D. I was excited. I thought something happened after we talked and you were able to convince him to come on board. I walked into her office to discuss the good news when she tells me to call your agency and let them know your contract had been terminated. She instructed me not to leave a review of your job performance."

"She gave you no explanation?"

"Allison said, and I don't believe this, that you bungled the offer and lost the candidate. That she called him and was able to persuade him to accept."

"This is a fairytale. You're telling me he accepted the original offer?"

"I saw his paperwork. I sign off on new hire information before Janet inputs it into the system. The compensation was what he requested, and she upped the sign-on bonus. Allison is taking credit for the hire."

"The revised letter was not on the SharePoint when I retrieved it from the server."

"She's insisting that it was. I don't know Kurt very well to discuss this with him. I called Matt. He was livid when I told him what happened. He said he'd look into it."

Matt agreed to help? I foster a glimmer of hope that he might change his mind about us, until reality smashes it to pieces. What the hell am I thinking? I gambled and lost everything. Why would he want a pathetic loser in his life?

"Kellis?"

My focus swings back to Nina, her face pinched with pain. Haley and Riku sit stunned as a silent audience.

"I'll know more in a few days," Nina assures me. "We can talk again when I know something. Everyone agrees this doesn't make sense."

"There's something else." Riku glances at Nina and Haley for approval. They give him silent permission to speak. I've never seen him more serious. I brace for more bad news. He lets out a breath. "Everyone knows what happened after the party."

Great, more good news. I flag down the waitress. "Can I get a drinks menu?" She nods and scurries away. I don't allow Riku to start talking until we all have a beer in front of us.

Riku pushes his beer to the side and folds his arms on the table. "I was leaving the party. I must have taken a wrong turn because I was on the other side of the building when I saw you, Matt, and Kurt talking in a tight group. It looked like Matt was talking to you and gave you something. Then that quick, Matt's fist flies out at Kurt. Matt misses. But the punch goes wild and crashes into your face. You fall back and hit your head with a loud ugly thump."

I'm embarrassed and morbidly interested in what happened. Matt and Kurt were the only witnesses and I wasn't going to ask them to fill me in. "How did I get to the hospital?"

Riku's brows draw together. "You weren't moving after you fell. Matt tried to get to you, but Kurt catches him and yells not to touch you. Kurt takes a swing at Matt and connects. Matt shakes it off and goes back after Kurt, shoving him against the wall. They were busy, so I pulled out my phone and called an ambulance."

"Haley interrupts. "When we arrived, they'd pretty much stopped abusing each other. They were just staring at you and breathing hard."

"That's when the ambulance showed up." Riku squints at me. "You look like you're healed. How are you feeling?"

I touch my face. "The bruising is almost gone. My make-up is a little thicker than usual, but I'm okay."

He nods still staring at my face. "You had me worried, until the EMTs came. I felt better when you regained consciousness."

"Was Allison there?" A new dread overtakes me that she'd witnessed this disaster.

"No, I saw her leave with Rogers after we finished the performance," Haley says. "Allison told me later she was proud of what we'd done and that I would be in charge of the HR Christmas entertainment."

I glance at Nina, who waves away my concern. "Oh, no you won't get any complaints from me. I hated that job. In fact, they had a small ceremony where HR was awarded a trophy for the best act. We pass it on to another department if we don't win next year. Accounting says they're gunning for us and not to get too comfortable with this win. They're taking singing lessons."

I blink. Despite the sorry state of my life, I howl and they join me in an uncontrollable, no holds barred laughter. God, I miss them. They're my friends, people I really care about.

CHAPTER 25

Slipping Away

Chloe pushes a tin of homemade cookies into my hands. "Staring at his house isn't going to make him come out. Kurt is the last one to get our Christmas cookie tin. You can deliver it to him."

I was actually staring at the inflatable manger and cartoon characters outside his house. I think he added the Santa and sleigh off to the side, but I can't be certain. The decorations for the rest of the court are subdued. Since this outrageous homage to the season began, we've had a steady stream of cars and some pedestrians coming to see his display at night, until he cuts the lights at midnight. Chloe is tapping her phone. "What are you doing?"

"I've just texted Kurt that you're coming over." Her phone dings. "I got a smiley emoji back," she sing-songs, holding up her phone. "The family should be coming in by dinnertime. I forgot to tell you, we had another vote. Everyone is staying for the weekend."

I place the tin on the counter, open it, and steal a cookie. "Where am I when all this voting is going on?"

"You need to look at your texts," she admonishes. "I'm going over to Mom's to help. Remember to bring the poinsettias."

"I will." I promise, crunching the last of my cookie. I follow her to the foyer. Chloe slips her bag on her shoulder and grabs her suitcase. She brushes crumbs off my shirt. "I know you're nervous. There's a lot you don't know; give Kurt a chance."

"Bye, Chloe."

"Have you packed your bag yet?"

"Goodbye, Chloe." I give her a nudge out the door.

"I have your garage door opener," she calls over her shoulder. "Mine's on the blink. I need to get some of Mom's presents for Dad and the twins. She asked me to stash them here, so I might come back later."

I'm gripping the cookie tin, while I lean into the doorbell. Kurt appears in the doorway, hesitant. That's new. I shove the tin into his hands, mumble 'Merry Christmas' and walk past him.

"Come in," he says to my back.

The house is still in over-the-top Christmas mode. The floor plan is the same as my house, so I have no problem finding the living room. How he can stand to live alone in this Christmas nightmare is beyond understanding.

He joins me, watching as I stare at the gaudy seven-foot tree fully loaded with presents. "Can I get you something?" he offers.

I want to say I won't be here that long, but I remember I promised my sister I would talk to him. "Sure, why not? I'll have a cola."

He hands me a can and we sit on the couch. I push away the reindeer and Santa cushions and wedge myself into the corner. "I guess you heard I was fired from Drachen."

That was a definite ice breaker; his brows raise. "Yes, I was told. I'm sorry. Allison said you overlooked a revised offer letter and lost the candidate. She followed up with him and was able to save the hire."

He shrugs. "It happens; we all get nervous."

This is how he rationalizes my failure. But in the end, he got the candidate he needed. If he didn't, this would be a different conversation. "Allison had three days to do the final sign-off on his hire documents." I'm not happy that I have to explain something I've been obsessively going over in my head for days. "Nina spoke to her on the day I was to extend the offer and reminded her of the deadline. There was no revised letter on the server. I'm not surprised that Allison was less than truthful."

He considers this. "I didn't think to question it during my debrief with Allison, and Kyle didn't mention anything when I called him to welcome him to Drachen."

"Kurt, you've been working with me for months. Have I ever appeared nervous?"

His brows furrow, but he doesn't respond to my question. I try a different tactic. "Look, I've been in this business a long time. I've extended countless offers to candidates. Okobi and I are friends. I know his family."

It's important he know I'm not a screw-up, that I did everything I could to succeed. "When I discovered there was nothing to offer, I asked Kyle for an extension. I was desperate to make the hire and did something I've never done before, because it was a gamble. I asked him to trust me on the strength of our relationship, but he refused. I don't blame him. His family is looking forward to moving back to California. If he had waited, refused the offer from the other company, and there wasn't another offer from Drachen, he would have been left with nothing."

"How would I know this?" he shoots back. "You haven't bothered to return my texts. I haven't spoken to you since the hospital. Why didn't you contact me immediately when he refused?"

"You know Drachen is a stickler for chain of command. I worked with Nina to get this done. You can talk to her about what happened."

I take a sip of my cola, then set it down. "Allison got what she wanted. Me out for incompetence and Haley in my place. Game over." Sitting here in this house with him suddenly feels restrictive, and I'm not sure I can be civil. This is only one of many things that has gone wrong. My working life would still be in shambles even if I'd been successful with Okobi. The love contract and Allison's dislike for me would have created more problems to overcome. Kurt has taken a wrecking ball to my life and I'm supposed to smile and be Zen about it. I stand.

"Are you leaving already?" He's alarmed and scrambles to his feet.

"I've got errands to run. I'll tell Chloe we talked."

"Don't go. I'll be gone in a few days." His tone is pleading. "There's more to discuss. I won't have another chance to talk. Please."

I'm edgy. I can't think in this house. I'm trying to find a way out of this meeting, but there might be an alternative. "Why don't you come with me on my errand? I'm going to the nursery to pick up poinsettias for my mom. We can talk and you can help me get the plants into the car." At least there will be space between us.

He's relieved by the suggestion. "I'll get my jacket."

"Meet you outside."

I'm dragging my suitcase behind me. Kurt steps to the back of the car. He grabs my case and places it in the trunk. Driving him seems familiar and we talk about general things but not the stuff that really matters. Traffic's light today. The drive isn't very long to the nursery.

I love this family-owned business, but it doesn't look as colorful as my spring or summer visits. Winter colors are subdued, like a photo that's a little out of focus. I have a discussion with the nursery staff. They'll need time to pull the order. Kurt and I walk out among the row of plants and stop at a display they've abandoned while they help us.

Kurt leans against a potting table. He folds his arms. "I think we're done with small talk."

I nod, looking off into the distance. Neither of us knows how to begin. "Why?" I say.

He tilts his head. "Why what?"

"Why do you enjoy torturing me?"

"I." He stops. "I didn't think I was doing that. I seem to irritate you, but I thought we were getting past it in Vegas."

"You're manipulative. You're always playing a game. No matter how I try to avoid you, you always manage to entangle me even more."

"I admit I did some things that kept you in my life, but it wasn't malicious. You could have said no at any time."

He really doesn't get it. "You're a VP, rumored to be the next head of Drachen. Someone once told me that if you're low on the food chain, corporate life can be like an episode of Survivor. How long do you think I would have lasted being a pawn between you and Allison? How could I have said no to you and kept my job?"

His lips form a tight line. "Your job was never in jeopardy from me and I never demanded sex."

"Tell me Kurt, was that coming? Were you just going to appear in my bed like you do everywhere else?"

"Ah, Kellis?" Joey says. He's the youngest of the family, a tall, lanky teenager who looks like he's blushing. I realize we must've been shouting.

"Hey, Joey," I say, trying to smile. "Is the order ready?"

"Yeah, are you alright?

"I'm fine," I say, like having a heated argument in the middle of a nursery is an everyday occurrence. "Kurt and I enjoy political debates. I know we shouldn't, but we get into them anyway."

He glances at Kurt, who tries to look friendly. "We got the plants out front. If you'll give me your keys, I'll load them."

I pull the keys from my coat and hand them to him.

"I'll help," Kurt says. "It's Joey, right? I'm Kurt." He extends his hand and the boy shakes it. They're talking as they head to the car.

I walk deeper into the rows of plants, pushing down my anger or the old irritation, I'm not sure which one. I'm feeling flushed. I pull off my cap and gloves, stuffing them in my pocket. It's cold and gray today, more like the season. There's a small pinpoint of pain just above my left eye that I've been trying to ignore for the last twenty minutes, and I hope it's only a headache.

Joey's slamming the trunk. I walk by him as he hands me the keys and I head for the driver's side. Kurt slides in. He frowns at me as he fastens the seatbelt. "Are you alright? I didn't mean to upset you. If this is too much, I'll find my way back."

"No," I say, pulling onto the dirt road. We're a few miles from a city street. "I've got to learn to listen more. I can do this." He's talking, saying something back, but it's distant. The pain in my head has increased. The light is too bright, and the radio and his voice are grating. I pull over to the side of the road and turn off the engine.

"What's wrong?" I hear through my fog.

My hands drop to my sides and I lean my head against the rest. "I can't drive. We'll have to call a car to take us home."

"You don't look well. Is it the flu?"

I close my eyes. "I can't function right now. I have a migraine. I need to take my medication."

He glances at my bag. "Can I get it? Do you have it with you?"

"It's in my suitcase. I can't take it now. The pills knock me out for a while. I've got to go home." I dig into my bag and hand him my cell. "Use my phone to call a car. The app is already set up."

He opens his door and gets out.

I'm barely registering this. I'm thinking he's going to flag down a car. "Kurt, listen to me for once." He appears at my window.

"Let me help you to the passenger side."

I give up arguing his logic and walk with him around the car. He probably thinks I'll be more comfortable there while we wait.

He moves under the wheel, turns the engine, and pulls the car onto the road. In my haze, I realize what he's doing. "You're driving?"

He adjusts the rear-view mirror. "You'll need to direct me. I'm not familiar with this part of the city."

The landscape is whizzing by. I sink down further in my seat and close my eyes. "You said you didn't drive."

"You're right, I don't drive; it doesn't mean I don't know how."

Jesus fricken Christ, when this is over, I will kill him and it won't be pretty.

Every bump and bounce on the road is amplified. Relief sets in when he finally pulls into my driveway. "I'll help you inside. Which is the house key?"

"I lost it a week ago. Open the garage, the door to the house is unlocked inside."

His glance flicks around the car. "Where's the opener?"

I moan, frustrated that I'm left without a way into my house. "Chloe has it; hers is broken. I don't think she ever had a key. Can we go to your house? I need a place to sleep for a few hours. The couch will be fine."

"I can try to get into your house through a window or call a locksmith?"

I'm surprised he doesn't say yes. The pain is increasing, and I need my medication. I don't want to miss my window or the pill won't be effective. "I sleep too deeply when I take the pill. It's irrational, I know, but I need someone with me while I sleep. Please."

We amble past the living room. I stop. "Here is fine," I say, trying to break away for the couch."

He doesn't let me go. "Stop arguing and let me take care of you." I'm off my feet cradled in his arms, traveling down the hall. I melt into the strength and the warmth of his body. I'm willing to let him help me if I can rest. He walks into his room and deposits me on the bed. "I knew someone who had migraines. You need a dark room and quiet." He moves to the dresser and pulls out pajamas. "You'll be more comfortable in this. Change while I get your medication."

I say nothing. I watch him exit the room, closing the door. I'm in no state to check out the room, but there are no Christmas decorations here. I change and get into the enormous bed. My head on the pillow, I sink into the thick cotton of the sheets. I breathe in his scent and relax.

A light tapping.

"Can I come in?" His voice is muffled by the door.

"Yes," I say and sit up.

Kurt hands me the pill and water. He watches me, concern creasing his brow as I pop the pill in my mouth and chase it with water. I lean back, grateful that I can rest. "I won't be far. I'll hear if you call out for me."

I'm in an unfamiliar place. Mild panic sets in. "Stay with me," I blurt out. "I mean, until I drop off. It won't take long."

He takes a step toward a chair.

"No, Herr Heinrich, here." I indicate the bed.

He settles his big body next to me, unsure what to do next.

"Tell me a story," I say. "My dad made up stories when I couldn't sleep."

A smile pulls at the corner of his mouth. There's disbelief at my request, but he opens his arms. This is the Kurt from Vegas, my sweet fake husband. Right now, I need to feel safe. I move to him without protest.

He holds me close. "I'll do my best, but I've never had to soothe a little girl." He's quiet for a few moments, then lets out a sigh. "Once upon a time, there was a boy who never heard the word no."

I don't hear more of the fairy tale as the world slips away.

CHAPTER 26

Storming the Castle

I wake slowly to Kurt's soft breathing and my head against his chest. I look down at unfamiliar PJs until I remember why I'm here. "The poinsettias," I moan.

He gently unwraps his body from mine and raises up on an elbow. He's wrinkled from sleeping in his clothes. "I called Chloe earlier." He rubs the sleep from his eyes. "She knows what happened. Dan and Faith came over and took the plants to your mom's."

The twins would be curious about him. They might subject him to an uncomfortable grilling like any good Ivarsson. "Did you talk to them?"

"No, I waved at them from the window. I didn't want to risk not being here if you needed me." His fingers graze my hand, and his touch tingles. I feel guilty that he stayed holding me while I slept. "You've been sleeping for almost three hours. How are you feeling?"

"No pain, just groggy."

He untangles our fingers. "Are you hungry? I can make you

something."

I sit up. The dark room is like floating in a vacuum. There's nothing to anchor me in time. I don't see a clock and my phone isn't here. "I really should leave, or my family will start Christmas without me."

He remains on his side, assessing me. "Chloe said to stay as long as you need to and not rush to your mother's house, that the family understands. I'll drive you over when you're ready."

"Thanks, I'm not hungry, but I'll take something to drink." It's the only thought I can get my head around.

"I've got a fridge in the walk-in." Kurt disappears into the closet. "Is water okay?" he calls out. "Or I can get something else from the kitchen."

I swing my legs over the side of the bed and the grogginess hits me.

"Where are you going? You said you're still groggy. Slow down until you're feeling stronger."

This is the concerned Vegas Kurt. It's surprising how he can go in and out of character. "I'm fine." I reach for the bottle of water. "I just need a few minutes."

"Alright," he says, disappointed. "I'll wait outside while you change. Let me know when you're ready."

I take a drink and remember my promise to have a talk with him. I'm in a better mood; it helps when there isn't relentless pounding going on in my head. "Don't go," I say for the second time. "Let's have that conversation."

He's hopeful in his wrinkled shirt. I wonder if he knows he doesn't look impeccable. "Are you sure? I don't want to cause another migraine. I realize it was me that brought this on."

I scoot back to the headboard and draw my knees to my chest. He joins me. We sit together, our hips touching.

"I have a rare form of migraine," I say to a captivated Kurt. "At least that's what I was told at a migraine support group I attended. I only get migraines after an extended period of stress, when my body thinks it's over. The last time this happened, I was working on a string of hires for one of my biggest clients. I knew I had to finish everything before my vacation. I powered through it and finished everything up. When I walked through my hotel room in Maui, I was hit with a migraine. Luckily, it only lasts a couple of hours and then I'm good."

"I was right, I did cause this--"

"You've been a part of my stress for the last few months, but I can't blame it all on you. It happens. The pain was talking to you earlier. What do you want to discuss?"

He leans back, throwing his arm along the headboard. "I realize that I handled everything wrong. I'm not used to this."

"Used to what exactly?"

"Dating, pursuing a woman." He flings a hand out to nothing. "This is new territory for me."

"What we were doing was not dating. Pursuing me? That was more like borderline stalking."

"Chloe did say I needed to work on my social skills."

"This is true. You're brilliant but not all warm and fuzzy."

No response that he wants to explore this revelation. Okay, time to talk about the elephant in the room. "Really, you're saying you're interested in me?" I think he's fascinated with me, like some weird oddity he can't explain. No, this is not love. God, I hope this isn't what passes as love with him.

He stares at me for a long moment. "I thought I made that clear to you."

I rest my head on my knees. I'm dying to hear how he figures I should know he's interested. "When did this declaration happen?"

He's astonished but attempts an explanation anyway. "I convinced Allison to reinstate you on the second-in-command recruiting. I moved in next door. I asked you to come with me to Las Vegas," he says, naming all the things that irritated the hell out of me. "I treated you to first-class accommodations during our Vegas trip.

So, that's why the travel department had no record of a Vegas itinerary for me when I inquired.

"And I asked you to marry me," listing the last point.

I lift my head from my knees. "Hold on, cowboy. You did not ask me to marry you. You skipped that part and went straight to the honeymoon."

He thinks about this. Like he has to remember that far back. He'd been drinking that night, but he was sober enough to remember. "I might've done that," he admits. "When we were in the helicopter and the pilot asked if we were newlyweds, I saw something in your face. I know it was there. You wanted me, us. Was I mistaken? I didn't hear an objection from you."

He did see the attraction. It was dark in the helicopter, and I thought I'd hidden it. Something seems to spark between us when we're together, but he always does something to screw it up. That night in Vegas was the longest we'd spent without arguing and we had some really sweet moments to remember. I push my legs out in front of me and smooth the pajama fabric. "I didn't want to contradict you in front of that couple, Kaylie and Wyatt, or the pilot. You were having a good time. I didn't see the harm." I look at him pointedly. "Something was bothering you that night, and you looked like you needed the distraction. Your worries started before we left for Las Vegas, but you've never said what happened."

Pain creeps across his face at the reminder. "I'd rather talk about my lack of social skills."

I place my hand over his. "That might take longer than either of us have." He almost smiles. Maybe we're reaching some understanding.

"Maybe it was the way I was raised. I've been famous since I was twelve. I told you my parents sent me off with a minder and a tutor. Employees want to make you happy when they find out you're paying their salary."

"You're the boy who never heard the word no."

"You were snoring; I didn't think you heard anything."

"I don't snore."

"You do. And how would you know? You're sleeping."

"Finish the story."

He slips onto his elbow, looking up at me. "I shouldn't say I was allowed to do anything. My minder Maria was a surrogate mother and kept me in line, but I got my way most of the time. When I grew older, I noticed women."

"You mean girls? You found them attractive, interesting?"

"No, I mean women; they were much more fascinating than girls my age. I was sexually active early. I've never had this much problem with a woman. They're usually pursuing me." He gives me the devil's grin. "Who's going to say no to this?" He's trying to do a muscle flexing pose but manages to look more constipated than sexy.

I think it's a joke, so I laugh and he joins me.

He rolls from the bed. "You look like you're back with the living. Are you ready to see your family?"

I nod, surprised that we're done. "Is this what you wanted to talk about?"

"I wanted to say I'm sorry. I thought if I admitted to what I'd done..." he hesitates, searching for the words. "To get to know you, you'd understand. Kissing you in the hotel before I left was my awkward way of saying..." he trails off again. "It doesn't matter. I hope you'll forgive me for the pain I caused."

I'm surprised at the confession. Had Chloe known this?

He leans against the door frame. His face grim, determined to finish. "The love contract was not my idea; that was Drachen's management, but I didn't need to taunt Matt with it. I came between the two of you. I shouldn't have done it. Jealousy is no excuse; you weren't interested." He glances down at his clothes. "I'll change in the bathroom."

That was probably the most self-aware conversation we'd ever had.

CHAPTER 27

Traditions

Mom is standing at the door with Dad behind her. Dad turns to shout into the house that I'm here. Chloe, Dan, and Faith join them, crowding the door too. Kurt comes up beside me with my suitcase. I introduce him to my curious family.

"Have a Merry Christmas," Kurt says to everyone, then faces me. "I'll leave the car in your driveway." He gives a final wave before heading into the night.

"Where are you going?" my dad's voice booms above our murmurs. "This is Christmas eve. I hope you're not refusing our hospitality. You're staying here."

Kurt turns to face us. He stands a few steps from the porch, chin tilted up. "Sir?" he says to my father.

"Reny has more than enough room in this castle she calls a house. We'd like the opportunity to get to know the man who took care of our little girl. Chloe has filled us in, but I want to talk to you myself."

Kurt's face lights up. "Thank you, Mr. Ivarsson, I think I'd like that."

They all file back into the house except for Chloe, who steps out onto the porch. "How did it go? I didn't see any scratch marks on his face."

"He just wanted to say he was sorry. Nothing more."

"He talks non-stop about you like a lovesick teenager and all he did was apologize? I guess he realized it wasn't worth it."

"What do you mean I'm not worth it? Worth what?"

"You know, he's a good guy and a real hottie. If you're not interested, maybe I'll take my shot," she says, looking a little dreamy-eyed. "I wonder what it's like to live all year around in Munich?" She muses.

"Chloe, really?"

She laughs. "No, I'm joking." She gives me a playful punch on the shoulder. "He's way too perfect-looking for me. I like them a little rougher around the edges." She wraps her sweater tighter around her body. "Come on, it's freezing out here. Let's go have some Christmas cheer. Mom's been passing out mulled wine."

I follow my sister inside. She walks past me into the great room. The smells of food mingled with the scent of Christmas are enough to make me nostalgic and starving. Dan and Faith are on the couch firing questions at a relaxed Kurt, who's accepting a mulled wine from Chloe. She takes a seat next to him.

I'm treated to Chloe and my family hanging on Kurt's every word. I finally have enough of my relatives finding him more fascinating than me. I go to my assigned room to unpack.

It's a few hours until someone notices I'm gone and comes to check. It's Chloe; I'd know her banging anywhere. "It's almost midnight; we're about to open presents."

We're seated around the enormous, elegant tree. The entire house is decorated like a scene out of a home designer's showcase, but it manages to be cozy. Disjointed, living miles away from one another, we are still close, still a family.

Kurt smiles at me, happy and sad at the same time. I don't know if he's ever experienced a celebration like this, but I know this is what that little boy all those years ago wanted when he picked up Christmas ornaments for his tree.

We tear into our presents, oohing and awwing over our gifts, and thank everyone profusely over what we're given. My mom's generosity is endless. She's made this moment perfect for all of us, even Kurt. Somehow, she managed to find beautiful, thoughtful gifts for him. I suspect she had one of her minions research him and make a run to the shops to find the presents so he would feel welcome. I've told him about our family time. He knows being here is an exception to our family time rules. My fake Vegas husband has returned. Kurt is participating in our games, jokes, and laughter as if he's part of the family.

Dan begins to yawn, and we know it's time for bed. We'll sleep in, but we'll be up for Mom's Christmas brunch. They drift off to their rooms until Kurt and I are left. He joins me by the fire. "Thank you for sharing your family with me." The room is dimly lit, only the firelight illuminates his face.

"You took charge and made sure I was safe and comfortable. Thank you."

"Glad I could help," he says stifling a yawn. "I think I'm ready for bed. Will you show me to my room? Your mom forgot to let me know where it is. I don't think she'd appreciate me wandering around this place."

We stroll through the kitchen entering a long corridor. "I know my dad calls this place the castle, but Mom uses this house as a retreat for people who come here to enjoy the spa. She lives in a cottage on the estate. This house is built like a horseshoe with a wing on either side of the great room. We're in this wing; my parents are on the other side."

239

He glances over his shoulder. "I thought you said your parents were divorced."

"They are. About the time I turned sixteen, Chloe and I figured out that it didn't stop them from their conjugal visit every year. That's why there's a no girlfriend/boyfriend rule at family time."

A soft chuckle vibrates from Kurt as we move along the hall. "I knew I liked your parents," he mumbles to himself.

"This is your room." I push the door open. "Let me check if it's ready. If you need towels, pajamas, toothbrush, or anything else, I can find whatever you need in the storage room at the end of the hall."

The bedroom is bathed in soft light from a lamp on the table. I head for the main switch on the opposite wall. Kurt is at my back. I reach out to turn on the light source, and his hand is over mine. "Don't turn on the light yet," he says in a low murmur. He's in shadow when I face him. "Not just yet. I want to talk." He's near enough to touch. I take a breath. The air is crackling around us like the night we spent in Vegas. "You never answered my question about the helicopter ride and what I saw in your face that night." He presses closer. "Was it true? Did you want me?"

I'm drawn to him, surprised at the doubt in his eyes that he might be wrong. "You were different that night, playing my besotted husband." I smile at his uncertainty. "I kept my distance, while helping you get through whatever was troubling you that night. I didn't want to make the mistake of hoping that our fake marriage could be anything more."

He studies me, searching my face for the truth. "I'd have cut the evening short, if I thought you would have said yes to me. I'd have dragged you back to the hotel for you to have your way with me."

I shift my arms to his neck, pulling his lips to mine. "I might have let you, if you had asked nicely," I say, to his shock. I wasn't willing to admit even to myself, that by the end of the night I was thoroughly captivated by Kurt and thought he felt the same. When he walked me

240

to my door, I expected an invitation to share a bed and was surprised when he left me standing at my door shouting my good night to his retreating back.

My lips brush his mouth, catching a little stubble for my effort. "Why don't we have a do-over of our last Vegas night together?" Warming to what should have been.

His fingers play in my hair. "If that's what you want, I can have us flown back there tonight."

"I forgot that you're probably a gazillionaire and can do that kind of stuff. I was thinking closer to home."

He latches on to my waist, lifting me up to kiss me. I don't relish the feeling of my legs dangling like a rag doll and protest a little. I land on my feet and he presses against me while his hands run down my sides. His heat pushes through the wool of my shirt and I'm burning for him. We begin a passionate kiss, his hands at my shirt, my fingers at his belt, neither making headway. I'm moving him to the bed. One push and we topple, hitting the mattress with a bounce. Kurt's on his back, I'm on top straddling him, pulling off my top. He urges me off of him to discard his clothes, both of us in a hot frenzy to free ourselves to get at each other to do the dirty. I'm down to my bra and panties; he's naked, golden even in this dim light, all sleek, taunt muscles like something out of a wet dream. Come here," he says, holding out his hand. "Don't make me wait."

His big body against the headboard, I let him pull me onto his lap. Strong fingers run along the edge of my bra, taking his time to tease his way under the lace to play with my nipple. His free hand moves slowly, caressing my other breast. I close my eyes, exhaling a soft moan.

"Take this off." He gently tugs at my bra, urging me to show myself to him. "I want to taste you, love," he says. I quiver at his hoarse whispered plea that just turned the heat between my legs wet. All I want is his hot teasing lips and me writhing under his touch. I slowly slide each strap off my shoulders, prolonging the moment. His attention is on the blue satin and lace that holds me. He doesn't wait for me to tease him with the reveal. He pulls the cups down, exposing me. "You make me crazy, wanting you," he says, extending his hands around to fully release me. I'm aware of air cooling my warmth.

His palms circle my waist, urging me further up his body, until his hot mouth finds my nipple. He sucks, nips, and teases until my nib is erect and I'm moaning with the pleasure. We twist to our sides as he continues to lick. I'm vibrating from the sensation, while I run my fingers through his short-buzzed stubble guiding him. I'm hungry, ready for more, when his hands settle over my behind, tugging at my panties. I finally reach down, pull them off, and toss them to the side. "I want more," I say in a loud whisper.

The devil's grin slides across his face. "I can do that." He moves me to my back and positions himself between my legs. He kisses my belly, moving down slowly, taking his time to savor until his lips are at my pussy. He parts me, his tongue sliding inside my folds, torturing me with unbearable languorous licks. I shudder, barely holding on as my release builds. I fight the urge to come while his tongue is leading me to distraction. I urge him away from my throbbing clit, determined to have his hard cock thrusting inside me. I want his solid body pinning me to the bed. I want to see his crystal blue eyes at the moment he comes.

"Is this what you want?" he says in a hoarse whisper. He drags the head of his cock through my wetness. I lift my hips, wild for him to enter. My breath catches when he suddenly thrusts deep. The movement shoves the bed forward, the headboard bangs against the wall, and I gasp.

His drives are wild, the bed's squeaking, and the headboard is slamming against the wall with each advance.

"We have to stop; we're going to wake everyone," I say, desperate to dislodge myself and wiggle away. He tries to stop me, but we're a tangled mass of arms and legs. The bed is a twin, not big enough to handle two adults. We roll off and crash to the floor, blankets on top of us.

I push on Kurt's chest to still him while I listen. I hear nothing, only the heater kicking on. Kurt pulls the blanket around us. We both take a breath and sit with our backs against the bed. His wistful face is close to mine when he reaches out to smooth my hair back. "You're sexy," he says, delight flashing in his eyes. "I didn't know you could be more beautiful."

"You're a hottie." I grin, embarrassed by his comment. I run my fingers along his stubbled jawline, admiring his male beauty.

He cradles me in his arms and I place my head on his chest. "It's hard to believe you're here with me, schatz," he sighs and gives me a squeeze.

"Schatz?" I whisper, "What does it mean?"

He pushes a length of hair behind my ear and I stir. "It means treasure. You're my treasure, love."

I warm with the compliment. My feelings for him still frighten me, but I'm anxious for him to want me again. I glance at his eager face and he finds my lips. His kiss is slow and sensual. He plays with my clit, drawing circles and building my need for him until my body is ready to move under him again. He maneuvers me on my back. I'm captive as his powerful body hovers over me, his appreciative gaze memorizing my nakedness. I squirm, arching my back, pleased that he approves but uncomfortable with the stark attention.

He touches his forehead to mine as his hard cock slips inside and I moan as he fills me. He grinds, my clit pulsating with each pass. I dig my fingers into the flesh of his biceps, holding on to his mass, moving my hips to meet each drive. He watches me as my pressure builds until I can't hold on. I come first, wanting to release with a scream instead of a whimper. Moments later Kurt's eyes widen and his irises darken as his orgasm rocks his body, coming with a gasp. His heavy, inert body covers me completely until he finally lifts up on an elbow. His serious face makes me want to giggle.

"No laughing," he warns. "What we did was sacred." Teasing in his eyes.

"What we did was hella good," I chide. He laughs as he settles at my side and pulls the blanket around us. I'm content enveloped in his scent, protected by his massive body and basking in his unwavering attention. I look into the laughing crystal blue eyes of Kurt Heinrich and I think that I might like this new normal.

I'm alone, waking up slowly. It takes me a few seconds to remember where I am. Then memories of the night before come back to me in vivid images and sensations. I sit up, stretching. The clocks says that I've only been sleeping for a few hours. It wasn't practical to sleep in his room; there wasn't enough bed for both of us to relax or sleep. I'm deciding if I should explore the kitchen when I'm aware of light scratching on my door. I push out of bed, still not fully awake. I open the door to see Kurt showered and in clothes he wasn't wearing yesterday. I take a step into the hall to see if anyone is around, then I pull him into the room.

"You've got a regular-size bed." He says this like an accusation. "Why didn't you say something? I slept on the floor last night."

I returned to my bedroom in the pre-dawn, I didn't want to be caught in his room. I don't think my parents would have cared; it's the ribbing from my siblings I want to avoid. My bed is still unmade and stuff is tossed around. "Mom has families here for retreats, and your room is in the kids' quarters. You drew the short straws on a room. I'll talk to her about another bed."

"Or you can invite me to sleep with you."

I like his suggestion but this is still my mom's house. Better to go home when he starts to get the urge to play again. "We can talk about that later."

"Can you be ready in ten minutes? I want to show you something. I promise we'll be back before brunch."

I'm looking around for proper clothing to replace this T-shirt I'm wearing. "What is it?"

"A surprise; I didn't mention that part."

I can't figure out if it's a real surprise or if he's luring me back to his house for some fun time. I decide it doesn't matter. "Give me twenty minutes to shower and change." I move toward the bathroom, but he catches my hand and pulls me to him. I'm only wearing a T-shirt and his hand is creeping the fabric up my side. He gives me a minty kiss. If he keeps this up, we're going to end up on the bed again. I gingerly pull away. "I've got to change."

"Can I watch?"

"No! Wait for me in the great room."

He's picking up my jeans and a sweater from the floor. "Then put these on and let's go, we won't be gone that long." He spies my bra and hands it to me. "You're going to need this as well." He says this with a grin. "At least for now."

I rip it from his hands and head to the bathroom. After a quick sink wash, we're heading out the door. I don't argue when he insists on the driving duties. I've chauffeured him around enough. We stop at a grocery store. He runs inside and returns with a large bag and continues his cryptic journey. "Where are we going?" My patience is waning.

He looks over at me, excited about something. "We're almost there. I'd say it's about ten minutes away."

The landscape is familiar; we're riding through our neighborhood. I'm about to raise another question when he pulls the car into his driveway. "Did you forget something?"

"The surprise is inside."

Kurt guides me to a stool in the kitchen. Talking to his virtual assistant, the lights blaze on, the heater rumbles to life, and seasonal music drifts from unseen speakers. The benefits of a wired home. I'm in this Christmas explosion again. Santas are greeting me, fake snow and holly are everywhere. The unending pin lights strewn above us are strobing. I ask him to stop the manic points of colored light, fearing it would trigger another migraine.

He's contained excitement moving about the kitchen, pouring a quart of eggnog in a pot and singing the end of a carol. I've never seen anyone project hot and dorky at the same time.

He catches me watching him. "I shared your Christmas traditions last night; I want you to be here for mine."

We sit in front of his enormous eclectic Christmas tree with our steaming mugs of nog. Presents are piled high, some appearing to be giant Jenga stacks. This gift display is larger than what I've seen under my family's tree, even when relatives came to visit.

"Merry Christmas, schatz," he says and gives me a slow, soft kiss that has me melting.

"Frohe Weihnachten suiisse," I say back to him, nipping at his lip.

He gives me a surprised chuckle. "Merry Christmas, sweetie. I like that. Are you studying German? I know an excellent tutor that'll give you lessons. He works on the barter system."

"You know, the internet is a wonderful place; you can translate any word into any language." I look at him coyly. "This guy who tutors, you say he likes to barter? What will he take in exchange?"

"An exchange of something intimate is best."

I can't stop the image of him screwing me senseless while demanding I conjugate a German verb. "What's your Christmas tradition?"

We sit among the presents. "First, I want to give you my gift." I think he's leaning forward for a kiss; instead, he reaches for something behind me. He produces a box wrapped with snowman paper and a big silver bow.

I'm embarrassed, looking into a boyish, happy face, that I have nothing for him. We've been together since yesterday. He hasn't had time to shop and wrap a gift. He must've bought this for me some time ago. I resolve to find something for him later. "Thank you," pushing my fingers through the paper. The white tissue inside reveals a pink plaid cashmere scarf and leather gloves. It's something I would have bought myself. The gift is surprising. If I was willing to bet, I would say that Herr Heinrich would have given me a peekaboo nightie. I brush my fingers over the soft material, lift it out of the box, and place it around my neck.

"Beautiful," he says. "Now let's get to the tradition. It's time to open presents."

Has he gotten me more gifts, or is he expecting me to exchange something? He reaches to the side and places a stack of five gifts in front of me. He grabs an equal number of wrapped boxes. "Were going to open presents," he says in a deliberate manner.

"Do you mean all these boxes?" gesturing to the nearest pile.

He nods.

I rip into the first box; it's a tea set. The next is a Barbie and other items only a little girl would dream of receiving. Meanwhile Kurt has action figures, board games, and trucks that a small boy would enjoy sitting near him. "These are all toys. You bought yourself a mountain of toys?"

He's just ripped the paper off of a Spiderman action figure. "Yes, that's right, they're all toys. No, I take that back. This section contains toys for 6- to 12-year-olds. There's a separate section for infants and young adults. The young adult section is mostly electronics, music, books, with a few gift cards thrown in for movies and restaurants."

There's wrapping paper all around us and more presents to open. "Why so many toys?"

He slides another pile toward me from a different section. "I give them away to the local toy drive. I've always done that. I have my assistant find out from a shelter what the most popular toys and gifts are in all age groups. I have them bought and wrapped. Did you know that people mostly donate for infants or children and forget about the teenagers who would like a gift for Christmas? It's actually a win-win. I open several presents on Christmas day and disadvantaged kids get unwrapped gifts."

I can't figure out how many sides this man has, but I realize opening gifts is fun no matter what it is. We spend more than an hour and, in the end, there are stacks of unwrapped gifts and we're sitting in a pile of wrapping paper and bows. We rest against the couch, and I reach for my mug. "So, this's your tradition, egg nog and opening presents? I mean, it's the same in most households, but I think you do it on a grander scale."

He puts his arm around me. "You're right, it started off with a few presents because that's the only thing I could afford. But every year the stacks got bigger."

"You do this by yourself?"

"Maria, my minder, helped me open presents for the first two years. Then I pulled some teenage antics. My parents found out and decided Maria was not strong enough to handle a teenage boy and they fired her. She was replaced by a man in his 20s. You can guess how that turned out. He wasn't so much my minder; I was more his wingman. He stayed with me until I turned 18 and by then I didn't need a minder." He takes a final sip of his nog. "Last thing I want to talk about is my sad young life. I'm sure your parents are wondering where you are; maybe we should go back?"

I smile at him. "Not until I give you my gift." I pull my scarf from my neck.

"Really, you have something for me? Is it at your house?"

"No, it's here." I brush his lips, gazing into his eyes.

He holds my face. "A kiss from you is a gift," he says, giving me a real kiss.

I begin to unbutton his shirt starting from the bottom. He's passive, watching me with interest, preferring to wait for what I'd promised. When the last barrier is removed, I slowly run my fingers from the hollow of his throat to his tight abs. Then I push the shirt halves away, just enough to keep him exposed. He reaches for my sweater, but I move back out of his reach. "No," I warn. "It's my gift, remember?"

He tilts his head, trying to figure out my next move. I hold his gaze as I strip for him. Avoiding his hands when he tries to reach out for me. "Relax," I purr at him, "let me do this my way." I slide back to him, my hand fingering the button of his jeans. My quick fingers work his zipper. I yank his pants off before he gets the urge to help. I sit back to take him in. He's naked except for the starched white shirt that gives me a peek at his broad chest and his gorgeous cock that's waiting for me. I can't see anything that isn't camera-ready perfection as he reclines. But it's the way his ice-blue eyes smolder when he looks at me that makes my pussy ache to feel him inside me again. I wiggle between his legs and wrap my fingers around his growing cock, massaging it until it's hard and he's moaning softly. I flatten out onto my stomach, his cock still dancing in my hand. "Frohe Weihnachten, Herr Heinrich," I say, before my lips close over the tip of his cock.

His head lolls back as his eyes close. "Yeah, you're right. Mr. Heinrich is having a very merry Christmas so far."

I tease him with my tongue, guided by his moans. I suck, enjoying the control over his body. I'm relentless with my mouth until I take him in, pushing down the urge to gag. His cock wants to go further. I will myself to relax as I take more of him inside. His fingers are in my hair, guiding me, until he whispers, "Right there, yes, there."

I'm focused, attuned to his body. He's careful as he moves. I can tell he is holding back and wants to thrust my mouth harder, but he urges me away. I look up at him, wanting to finish. "On top so I can see you bouncing above me."

My knees are on either side of his hips. My pussy is slick with fluid as his cock slides deep inside. I clench, welcoming him to me. We're kissing while his hand plays with my clit, my moisture glazing his hand. He begins to thrust. I sit up and I move my hips. He's holding onto my ass, kneading his fingers into my flesh as he guides me. I'm riding him hard, enjoying him bucking underneath. I'm barely aware of my surroundings but realize only for a few seconds how we must look. Wrapping paper and toys everywhere and that God-awful tree looming above us. We climax in a frenzy of loud moans. I collapse on to his chest. I lift up to look into his eyes. "Kurt," I say, excited.

"Yes?" he says, running his hand over my arm.

"I realize I've just added screwing under the Christmas tree as one of my own personal holiday traditions."

He chuckles and pulls me back down. "I think I should rethink being alone with you." He's resting his hands behind his head. "meetings at work might have to be off limits."

"Did you have to mention work?" I say, easing my body to his side.

"I wasn't thinking. I thought Chloe said that you'll be working with your mother. Is that true?"

"I haven't decided. With all the craziness that went on with Drachen, I still enjoyed working for them. I'm considering working for another tech company."

He sits up. "You were happy? You seemed stressed every time I saw you."

I look up at him. "I seemed unhappy because I was always dealing with you."

He considers this. "I enjoyed working with you very much." He grins.

I look around the room and I still can't find a clock. "Do you have something against clocks?"

"No, I always have my phone with me. Aw, I understand. You're hungry and you want to go to your mother's brunch."

"I need to take a shower."

"Take your shower here. You can put on my sweats and we can go over to your house to change if that's what you want. You'll find clothes in the guest room."

I untangle myself, but he's reluctant for me to leave; he holds on to my hand until the last moment.

I run the shower in the guest room. I'm enjoying the cascading water over my head that's rejuvenating my tired body. The door slides open. I'm not surprised that Kurt has joined me. I get a kiss as he moves me to the side to catch the stream for himself. I'm thinking this is going to be round three as the steam rises around us. He reaches to pump soap from the dispenser and rubs the luxurious liquid on my body, the soap frothing into white foam, his hands gently reaching every part of my slick body. I'm shuddering as my need for him rises again, but he performs these as an act of tenderness. I close my eyes and relax as he tends to me. I'm realizing I've never had a man pamper me like this. He retrieves the hand nozzle and rinses.

Kurt takes the shampoo from the dispenser and massages the liquid through my hair. He's silent, concentrating on performing his task. He rinses my hair, the soap running over my shoulders and breasts. He turns to the dispenser again and repeats the process with the conditioner until it's done.

I reach around him for the soap. I lather him, his eyes close while my hands travel over his taunt muscles. Kurt's energy, is stilled, accepting my touch. I work slowly, methodically, mesmerized by my efforts. I realize I want to pamper him, that this is also my gift.

He's still drying off when I wrap a towel around myself and step into the guest room. I pull out a drawer, but notice a picture of a blonde woman on the dresser, his arm around her smiling for the camera. I pick up the photograph and inspect it. The woman looks familiar. Then I realize it's the blonde in the black Mercedes that stayed with him about a month ago. There are other things in the room like a brush, fashion magazines, female clothing.

Kirk appears in the doorway, a white towel wrapped about his waist. His eyes bright, grinning like sunshine until he notices the picture in my hand. A deep frown washes away any happiness. "I hadn't realized these things were in here." He says with sadness. "I haven't been in this room for more than a month."

"Is she someone from Germany?" Anyone would guess they were lovers, her arms around his waist, looking at him and not at the camera.

"You have nothing to worry about." He places a hand on my elbow and guides me to the bed. "You've been asking me what happened during our trip to Vegas. I got a phone call before the car came to take us to the airport. It was about Maria, my minder. She's been like a real mother. We've been close even after all these years."

"I received news that she was in a car crash and that they were performing surgery. I kept in contact with Maria's sister, who gave me updates all during that time. When we were at the beer pub she was still in serious condition. It became worse the next day and I decided to leave for Germany. "

I take his hand, hold it tight. "I understand your concern; it must have been awful when you received the news, but this doesn't explain the picture of you and this woman."

Kurt takes the picture from me. "This is Greta. I've known her since I was a boy. She's Maria's daughter. I've always thought of her as an older sister; she's only a year and a half older than me, but she's had a crush on me since I was a teenager." He gives me a proud smile, pointing at the photo. "She's a designer and was meeting with some clients here in California to work on a project. She called me at the last minute and said she would be staying with me." He glances around the guest room. "It's just like her to leave a picture of us or some of her things here as a joke. I knew she still had a crush on me when she visited. I didn't encourage her, but I was glad to see someone from home."

He's still not giving me the full story. I'm afraid there's some secret that he doesn't want to reveal. "Did Maria recover?"

He takes a ragged breath. He's near tears. "Yes, Maria survived the surgery, although she'll have a lengthy recovery. One of the reasons I'm returning to Germany is to be close to her. I've asked her to live with me, but she'd rather stay with her sister.

Greta was in the car with Maria when they were struck by a driver running a traffic light. She was serious for a while, but her condition stabilized quickly. They said because she was younger, that she would recover quicker. When I went back to Germany to see them there was something the doctors had overlooked; Greta had a brain hemorrhage and died before I arrived."

I put my arms around him, my head on his shoulder, feeling his pain, but his body stiffens, not wanting to let go. The texts I received while he was in Germany now make sense. They were mostly unrelated thoughts close to gibberish. He was probably in so much pain he didn't know what to say. He moves from the bed. "I'll need some time to get ready. Dress, and I'll drive you back to your parents."

I say nothing as he closes the door behind him.

CHAPTER 28

Bootstraps

We're late for the brunch, but Mom has saved us plates. Kurt is lively with my family. I think I'm the only one that can see he isn't fully present. When we stop stuffing ourselves, Mom shoos Kurt out and asks me to help her in the kitchen.

"Mom, why are you doing all this work? If you would keep one or two of your staff during the holidays, you could work less," I say, placing the last of the scrambled eggs in a container.

She leans against the counter, a spoon in her hand. "Our family time around the season should be similar to past Christmases when we celebrated with you kids. That's one of the reasons we agreed to no outsiders. We knew eventually that rule would be broken when one of you had a serious relationship or eventually got married. I just think it's important that we hold onto that time for as long as possible."

"But you asked Kurt to stay. We're not dating."

My mom raises an all-knowing eyebrow and I forget sometimes she's a psychic. "I don't need second sight to see that there's an attraction between the two of you."

I flash back to an hour ago and my face begins to heat. "I'll admit there might be something between us, but it's still too early."

"I know things were difficult after you were let go from Drachen. I haven't said anything up till now, but my offer still stands to work with me in Madre Luna. I would be overjoyed for us to be working together. But don't take the position if your heart isn't there. I'd rather you be happy."

I've thought of nothing else, but I still can't bring myself to commit. I need to make a decision. Right now, that seems more daunting than I can handle. "Let's start making plans after the holidays," I suggest. "Then you can tell me where I might fit into your organization."

Mom gives me a hug. When she releases me, she smooths a lock of hair behind my ear. "I need to tell you what's been coming to me for a long time. You still have two choices where men are concerned. Now go out and entertain that gorgeous young man or I'll do it for you."

"You've got to tell me more than that," refusing to be shooed out of the kitchen.

"Go talk with your father and Kurt. You know how predictions work. You get the meat and not a lot of details. Let me finish so I can work on dinner."

Kurt and my dad are the only ones in the great room in earnest conversation. I take that back, what is probably happening is that my father is deep into a bowling story and Kurt is politely listening. I walk up behind my father. Neither men have noticed me.

"Is it a win if it's been obtained through manipulation and half-truths? Bowling regulations stipulate that in order to qualify..."

I place a hand on my father's shoulder. "I asked you to keep the bowling stories down to a minimum."

"We were just having a really good conversation," he pleads his case. "Kurt here doesn't know much about bowling. I'm giving him the 1000-feet aerial view of my profession."

Kurt nods dutifully.

I'm not fooled. "If you don't mind, Dad, I need to steal him away from you. There're some things that we need to talk about."

"By all means. Have your confab. I'm going to see what your mother is doing in the kitchen."

I sink into my father's chair. Kurt is studying his hands. Him not looking at me is giving me concern. Telling me about Greta must've been difficult. "Do you want to talk about it? We don't have to stay here. There are lots of rooms in this house but the grounds are beautiful. We could take a walk."

"I'd like that, but I'd like a raincheck. I thought I would have tomorrow off, but I received a call that I'm scheduled for meetings for tomorrow. I'll need the rest of the day to prepare. I'll call a car to take me back home."

I didn't want him to leave in this mood. "No, I'm driving you. Let's go."

We say goodbye in the car. I think both of us are afraid that if we're alone in the house, he'd never get any work done.

"Something's going on at headquarters," he says, his gaze wandering to his disjointed Christmas display. "Normally they wouldn't call us back during the holidays. Execs like their time off too much." He gives me a kiss but doesn't linger. He swipes a finger over my cheek. "Thank you for the best Christmas. I'll keep in touch."

"When are you going back to Germany?"

"Not for a while." He smiles. "We have some things to discuss before I leave."

I wouldn't say that Kurt was not missed by my family. But we quickly resumed our Christmas family time without Herr Heinrich. But my mind continued to wander back to the last two days and what it meant going forward.

The next day came and went with only two short messages from Kurt that he was busy but fine. A car rumbled up to his house after midnight. I'd texted him but didn't receive a response until the morning. On the third day a crew came by and removed all of the outdoor Christmas display. The day after a moving van came. I continue to text him but receive no answer. Even Chloe confesses that she hadn't heard from him. I finally called Nina and she confirmed that he was already back in Germany.

The only thing I can assume is that after Kurt got what he wanted from me, he wasn't interested any longer. My father was right: don't get your honey where you get your money and when it doesn't work out it's the woman that gets the short end of the deal. Rejected by two men and fired by Drachen. Yeah, it's confirmed, the gods hate me.

The phone rings a few times before it's answered. She picks up her own line. "Madre Luna Spa and Resort, you've reached Reny Exton."

"Hi Mom," I force myself to sound upbeat. "How are you?"

"I'm fine, your sister says you're doing better."

I can't answer about my well-being. Most days I'm numb. Once the urge to hide from the world stops, I'll start healing. "I called to schedule a meeting with you so we can discuss the position you offered."

"Are you sure, dear? You don't sound very happy about it."

"It'll be great working with you. I'm just trying to get over the last few months."

"Well, remember what I say, it's not always as it appears. But then again, sometimes it is. Are you free on Wednesday?"

"Kellis," my sister shouts. "You have a package. I'm leaving it on the kitchen table. I've got to go."

I appear in the kitchen just as my sister is screwing the top on her water bottle and jamming it into her lunch bag. "I have a what? I couldn't hear you; I had the music up."

She points at the table. "Delivery. Package. For you."

The package is about the size of a shirt box. I rummage around in the drawer for a box cutter and start to rip the top open. Chloe is standing there with her lunch bag in her hand, waiting to see what's inside. The box is glittery gold with a hot pink ribbon. I slip off the bow and part the tissue paper inside to find a handwritten letter:

Dear Kellis,

This is my real Christmas gift to you. Your life, before we met.

1) You are reinstated to your position at Drachen. You will also be paid for the time you were absent.

We discovered Allison had placed the revised offer on the server but did not give you permission to access. I'm not certain of this and cannot prove it for a fact, but I think Allison gambled that you would not convince Okobi to wait another day for our offer. Once Nina informed her that you had lost the hire, she called Okobi immediately with the revised offer and even authorized a bonus that had not been approved by Munich. A formal complaint has been filed about her behavior and she has come under scrutiny about her management tactics. She will keep her job but will not be the VP of staffing.

2) Nina Madrone has been offered the position of VP of Talent Acquisition (formally known as staffing) and related functions. This will only be for the Americas at this time. Eventually I will propose that she take an executive role over the global Talent Acquisition operation. If she accepts the VP position, you will be reporting directly to her.

3) The love contract has been destroyed. Only a few people knew of its existence. This document was not public knowledge, and it will not follow you at Drachen.

4) I spoke to Matt Westmore. We had a long talk. I admitted to what I'd done and that you were not to blame. He cares for you. Call him; he wants to see you.

Someone once told me that it isn't a win if it's gained through manipulation and half-truths. I took something that wasn't mine, because I knew I could. I didn't mean that apology during our talk at my house. I wanted you, and Matt was in my way. I told you what you wanted to hear; it was more manipulation. Better to part now than hurt you further.

If this isn't enough to make you whole, tell me what I need to do and I will make it right.

Kurt

P.S. I'm no longer rumored to be the head of Drachen. I will take over the position in the new year.

I hand Chloe the letter. She puts down her bag and scans it quickly. She glances up at me. "Holy freaken shit."

Days go by in a blur, moving steadily from one to the other. We slipped into another year and I didn't even notice. I didn't think it was possible to lose weight, but I'm not hungry and pounds are dropping. I thought briefly about packaging this as a diet aid, but then who wants to be this sad? I sit with my trusty bowl of heavily buttered popcorn and watch the TV in my room most of the day until I muster enough concentration to play a video game.

There's banging on my door. It can't be anyone else but my sister and roommate. "Kel, are you ever coming out of your room or should I leave your meals by the door?"

I swing the door open. Chloe scrunches up her face at my appearance. I haven't looked in the mirror lately, but I can pretty much imagine what I look like. Hair uncombed in oversize pink wrinkled sweats that need to be taken off my body and thrown in the hamper. "And what is your problem, dear sister?" I say, offended.

She pushes past me, a basket on her hip, and makes a beeline for the window. Chloe takes her frustration out on the window as it bangs open. "My problem is you, and your downward spiral; it's getting old," she says, tossing an item from the floor into the small plastic basket. "I came in here to get your laundry; I'm starting a load, and by the way Dad will be here in about 10 minutes."

I land hard on the bed, spilling some of my popcorn. I'm shocked at what this means. "Why is Dad here? He's got a tournament in Seattle in two days; he should be up there meeting his fans."

Chloe sits down beside me, the basket at her feet. "What was I supposed to do? I told him that you won't listen to me, so I had to bring in reinforcements. Someone has to save you from this." She throws up her hands to plead with the heavens. "If this doesn't work, Mom is coming and she's the last person you want over here. Better to deal with Dad. I suggest you take a shower, comb your hair, and wear something that doesn't double as pajamas."

I barely have enough time to get dressed in a sweater and jeans and into the living room before my dad, Zach Ivarsson, strolls in, filling up the space with his presence. "Daughter," he says to me. I mournfully watch Chloe back out of the room. They'll be no support from that traitor.

"Hi Daddy," I squeak, angry at myself for reverting to age five. He sits in a chair while I take a seat on the couch. "You didn't have to come all the way down from Seattle. We could've talked on the phone."

My father gives me a parental glare. "I was told this was an emergency. That you've been moping around here, refusing to leave the house and have stopped listening to good sense. Is that correct?"

I nod. At this time, it's best to agree. The lecture will end quicker.

"And this has been going on for how long?"

"A few days."

"A few weeks." My unseen sister's voice sails into the room. I whip around to look, but she stays hidden.

"Thank you for your input, Chloe," my father's voice rumbles out, while his attention never wavers from me, "but I don't need your help."

"Sorry," comes the repentant voice of my sister.

"From what I can see, the reports I've been given are true."

I touch my hair, wondering if I missed something in my grooming. "You know Chloe exaggerates. I'm just taking a little time between jobs to decide what I want to do." Maybe I sold it, but his steel gaze is still on me.

He leans forward on the arm of his chair. "I know you got your heart broken…twice." He shows me two fingers in a weird victory sign, then waves it away. "But that's no reason on God's blessed earth to lay down and die over a man. Believe me, and I speak with some authority on this subject, they aren't worth it."

"That's not what happened." I try to joke it off.

He cuts me off. "Do I have my facts straight? Do you have a broken heart or is there something else I'm missing? No matter what, you'll get the help you need. I promise."

"It's a broken heart," I mumble, "but the pain is real."

He lets out a long, weary sigh. "I know, baby. I know the pain is real and it feels like you're never going to recover. And I know it's easy for me to say because I'm not the one suffering through it, but I have, and I can tell you there's something on the other side."

"It's my fault." I'm pissed that he was right. "You warned me, and I didn't listen. You said don't get your honey where you get your money. You said it would be a disaster."

My father frowns and shakes his head. "Kellis, I told you that when you were a teenager. It was your first job and you were boy crazy back then. I said it so you wouldn't get into trouble. I met your mother while we were on the job."

I leaned back in the folds of the couch, trying to decide if I could be any more pathetic than I am right now.

"I'm sorry I had to drag you into reality, but if I needed to shock you back to us I would do it again. Your family loves you. We don't want to see you in pain. I know you have to heal but you've got to let us help you. It's rough, but you've got to try."

I know they love me and what he's saying is true, but I just can't get to that place. Not yet. I look into the face of the man who's loved me all my life even when he wasn't here, and I let the barrier down. "The last few years have been difficult," I admit, close to tears. "I've been plowing through all of it but this time it's too much. I know you tell me to rely on myself and I do, but this time, both times, I thought I had someone I was going to share my life with. It's hard when you don't get the happily ever after."

My father sits next to me on the couch. His arms are around me while I cry softly. "Look, maybe that Heinrich guy was an ass, but he did do something for you. He gave you a do over. We rarely get something like that. Now you have to decide what you really want. The man you know or maybe a new man. You even have two jobs waiting for you. Hell, if you don't like those choices, go for a third. You know you can come with me on the tournament circuit. You were always good enough to go pro. In one tournament season with me training you, I know I can get you qualified for a pro spot. See, you need to look at all the possibilities."

You can't go back to the beginning when the race has already been run...or whatever metaphor you want to use. Matt and I needed time to build trust. We couldn't just pick up where we left off, but we're getting there. I told him everything and even admitted to sex with Kurt. I could see he was hurt even if it happened after our breakup.

I'm hesitating about Drachen, but it was an open return, which gives me time to decide. Nina did take the VP position and has been calling me about my start date. There's one decision I did make: I

263

gently turned down my mom's offer. We both knew it was not the right time to work together.

I'm driving to Matt's neighborhood. I'm nervous. Since I called him, we've been talking over the phone for a couple weeks, but this is the first time I'll see him since Kurt dropped that bombshell letter on me and left me to pick up the pieces.

Neither of us is at fault for wanting to put off this meeting. Matt's been busy working on a second-in-command for Dark Star. And I haven't pushed to see him yet because I'm still hurting over the events during Christmas. When I pull the car into the driveway, he walks out to my car. He's handsome with his dark hair and I notice that he's working on a beard. He still inspires the same feelings in me and now I'm glad we agreed to meet.

I emerge from the car and he doesn't hesitate to take me in his arms and kiss me. "You don't know how much I've missed you," he says, his forehead touching mine. He looks a bit worn. But I can't claim that on us. His daughter is with him and there are still the responsibilities from Dark Star.

The comfort of his big warm body makes me remember how I missed him as well. "I'm here now. Maybe we can start over," I say, as I remember the last time I was here. I was also asking for a do over.

We lean against the car, looking at the house. It's still nippy and we'll have to go inside soon. I touch his hand. "Are we good yet? Between you and me, are we good?"

He places his arm around my shoulder and squeezes. "We're as good as we can be for now. We'll figure out the rest." He gives me a quick kiss and I hug him around the waist. "Come on, let's get inside. I've got a fire going and Verity has been waiting to meet you."

CHAPTER 29

Four Months Later

I open my eyes to Matt's handsome face smiling at me. "Wake up, beautiful, we're landing, and they've just turned on the seatbelt sign." Matt and I are ending a 12-hour flight to Munich. I rake my fingers through my hair and adjust my skirt. I'll grab my jacket from the overhead once we begin to disembark. We're here for a string of meetings at Drachen headquarters.

We climb into the limo and I pull out my cell to find a signal. My texts come to life and I swipe through them until I find the response I'm looking for. I read it carefully and then smile at Matt. "We got a yes on our offer. Your second-in-command position is officially filled."

Matt is watching the scenery rush by. "That's one thing I can report to Heinrich when I see him."

I stiffen at the mention of his name. Matt and I are not in the same meetings, but I have an appointment with Kurt in his office at the end of the day.

"I was reluctant when you suggested Tim Cortez, your ex-boyfriend, for the second-in-command. I still remember that guy from the restaurant I took you to on our first date."

"If that was our first date, then it was news to me. You asked Hal and I out to celebrate hiring the night crew?"

"Is that right? I don't seem to remember that. I just remember you were anxious to go out with me."

I chuckle at his revised memory and let it go.

"Tim's cocky attitude didn't win him any points when he wouldn't leave his seat because he was talking to my gorgeous companion," he says, taking my hand. "After the stunt he pulled in the restaurant, he was lucky I spoke to him at all, but after talking to him in the interview I could see he was a good fit for the position. I need to trust your instincts more. Good job on a great hire. I'll need that sixth sense you have about candidates if we win this government contract coming up next month."

I let out my breath. "I was reluctant to tell you about that before the interview because I didn't want to prejudice his chances. He might be an ex-boyfriend but he's good at what he does, and I think your personalities will fit perfectly. He also said he'd like to take us out to dinner when we get back." I elbow Matt in the ribs and he swipes at me to protect his ticklish side, "He told me, last week, that he and Candy are getting married."

The enormous, gleaming headquarters of Drachen technology is a busy place. My day has been a blur of faces and presentations. I have one meeting left with Herr Heinrich. I haven't seen or spoken to Kurt since Christmas. He's a loose end I have to tie up before I can move forward.

I'm greeted by Ana Warner, Kurt's secretary, in the lobby to escort me to my meeting. We'd met each other through video conference but this would be the first time we've met face-to-face. "Good afternoon, Ms. Ivarsson," says Ana with a note of crispness.

I lean forward so she's the only one that can hear me. "Good afternoon, Ana, you know I'll be here for a few days. I'd rather you call me Kellis."

She gives me a sly smile that transforms her angelic features. "You know that isn't possible. I'm glad to finally meet you, Ms. Ivarsson. Maybe we can schedule a breakfast and I promise to call you Kellis."

There are people bustling around us, but I respond in a louder than normal voice. "Danke, Fraulein Warner."

Ana's hand flies to her mouth to stifle a giggle. "Your German is atrocious," she teases, "but I think you thanked me. If you don't mind, I'd rather we speak English. I need the practice."

We walk towards the elevator to the executive section of the building. It's later in the day and seems eerily quiet as the car passes floors to the top. "What kind of mood is he in?" I say to break the quiet. This is something I asked often when we talked while getting the equipment ready for an interview. It was more or less said as a joke then, but I genuinely want to know.

"He's different since coming back."

Before I can respond, the doors open to an intimidating ultramodern waiting room. "Please have a seat. I'll let him know you've arrived."

I enter his sleek, spacious environment of grays and blues. It screams power, wealth, and masculinity. And all I can think is it's good to be the king. There're no pictures or personal mementos anywhere in this sterile office. If I had to guess, I would say a designer was hired to select everything in the office. But it does reflect his rank and power in the company. Kurt is speaking into the phone, finishing up a call. He glances at me briefly enough that my heart catches. He's the same impeccably dressed, in control man that I first met when I peeked out from under the table to see his disapproving glare. There's no sign of Vegas Kurt; he has turned back time. I take a breath to strengthen myself for what I have to do. It's time to even the score.

"Kellis, why didn't you tell me you were coming?" He says

267

this like we're old friends who have just fallen out of touch. "I only discovered you were on my calendar today. If I had known…" he trails off. "Please sit. How was the flight over?"

"The flight was good. When Matt told me he was coming to Germany for a few days, I asked if I could tag along. I had helped headquarters hire a few American candidates in the early months of my contract. I wanted to meet with them and also your head of global Talent Acquisition."

"I want to congratulate you on reopening your company. I was happy to hear Nina put you on our staffing vendor list for the Americas. She says she's been pleased with your work. I'm disappointed that you decided not to come back to Drachen. Not as a contractor but as an employee."

Deciding between my mother's offer and Drachen was difficult. Matt and I had long, exhaustive talks over each position and he pointed out that I was the happiest when I was managing my company. For some reason, I didn't think I could ever open that door again, but I did and I'm thriving. I can say I have the best of both worlds. "In the end, it was the only logical decision. The recession was the reason I closed my company."

"I'm glad it worked out for you. I was told you were coming for a meeting, but Ana didn't give me a reason. Is there something I can help you with?"

"I think there is." I pull a leather folder onto my lap and retrieve a single sheet of paper. I place this on the desk. "It's the letter from you that I received after Christmas. It's what you wrote at the bottom of the letter that concerns me."

He doesn't touch the paper. He doesn't have to. He knows what's written on it and I'm sure he has copies. "What part of the letter concerns you?"

I take the paper back. Although I've memorized this part, I decide to read to him. "It's the last part 'if it isn't enough to make you whole, tell me what I need to do and I will make it right'."

"What is it that you want?"

I'll give it to him. He goes right to the point. "A couple of things. One, I want an exclusive contract with Drachen in the Americas to hire all of their engineering and managers up to senior level. That includes permanent hires and contractors. I also want first refusal on all other job titles. Right now, I'm only set up to recruit for engineering and management but plan to expand to other job titles. I want my contact to be Nina."

He sits back into his seat, contemplating. "And why do you think you deserve to have an exclusive staffing contract with a multi-billion-dollar company?"

"Again, I refer back to the letter. What you wrote here is binding. You really should have had it run through Legal. I was lucky that you were feeling remorseful and generous. You weren't able to make good on your promises as a VP for Drachen, but as the CEO of the entire company you do have the power to grant my request."

"What are your terms?"

I pull out a bound folder. "Here is my presentation with terms and costs. I've also done some projections. You'll find a copy of this proposal in an email attachment I've sent you. I'm not gouging you, Kurt. Your company will have cost savings with me as your agency. If I'm not able to fulfill a hire I'll give it to another agency, but I'll be your clearinghouse. I'll still get a percentage if their candidates are hired. It will be a win-win for both of our companies."

He retrieves the proposal and flips through to the projections. "You've decided to use Drachen to help you relaunch your company?"

"I put some feelers out. Most of my biggest clients are interested in working with me. Of course, Drachen is the only company I'll have an exclusive contract with."

"I'm the CEO, but I can't make this decision unilaterally. We still have a global head of talent acquisition and I'll need to speak with other stakeholders. You said you met with the head of global talent acquisition. I'm betting you've already discussed the proposal?"

"Yes, we did have a positive discussion and she seemed to like the idea." I get up. "I would be happy to pitch the idea to all the stakeholders. You're the last of my meetings, but I will be here for three days until Matt is finished. I'm open for the next two days. I expect to see something in writing for me to look over before I leave."

"And if I don't comply with your demands?"

I sigh. "Sexual harassment filings are not a pretty thing; it's been known to bring down empires."

"What was your second demand?"

"We can discuss that after I sign the paperwork."

Matt stands, waving at me from across the room. I weave my way through the diners to join him at a table. "The driver almost couldn't find this place," I say, pulling off my coat. "When he said it was down this alley, I almost asked him to take me back to the hotel. If it wasn't for the well-dressed people walking into that narrow space and that heavenly aroma drifting into the cab, you would've been eating alone."

"You're here now; relax." He helps me with my coat and hands it to the hostess. "I've asked the waiter to bring us a bottle of wine. "Tell me what Heinrich said? I bet he was surprised when you read his words back to him. Did he balk?"

The waiter arrives at the table with our wine and we're forced to go through the ritual until a bottle is sitting on the table and two glasses are filled with red wine. "No, he didn't seem angry or irritated; he could've given Matty Ice some pointers. He listened and had a few questions. Whatever he was thinking, he kept it to himself."

I play the conversation over in my mind. Somehow it seemed off. "I know we thought to use the harassment complaint as a last resort, but he asked what was the alternative if he didn't meet my demand. I don't think I even needed to threaten him with the letter."

"What are you planning to do now?"

"I offered to do a presentation to the stakeholders. If he doesn't take me up on my offer, I plan to tour the city and maybe get some spa time in."

"He knows you wouldn't have asked if you didn't think you could handle the contract. Don't lose your nerve and don't fall for his shit. Stay focused and you'll get everything you want in the end. Now let's order something; I'm starving. We need to get back to the hotel after dinner, my meeting schedule for tomorrow is brutal."

CHAPTER 30

The Reckoning

The end of the next day, I receive a text message from Kurt. He's requesting a meeting after work to discuss some of his concerns about the proposal before I leave tomorrow. He's in meetings all day and wants to see me away from the office. What caught my eye was the last line: Can you meet me at Dream Bowl Palace at 6:30 p.m.? Please come alone.

I know Dream Bowl Palace, and the request to come alone means he doesn't want Matt there. I have no choice if I want that exclusive contract with Drachen to go through their approval process without a delay, I'll have to meet him.

I call Matt and leave a message on his voicemail about the meeting with Kurt. I check the time. He said he would be in meetings until six. By the time he listens to this I'll be on my way.

Dressed in jeans, white shirt, sweater, and sneakers, I grab my coat; it gets cold in these places. Dream Bowl Palace is a bowling alley, it's like a bowling mecca. The World Bowling Association has held tournaments at the gigantic venue. My father has played there many times, but I've never been. He started playing in their tournaments after I stopped going on the road with him. To say that it's a bowling mecca is only part of it. It does have 52 lanes, but it also has an 18-hole indoor mini golf course, pool tables, bar, and restaurant.

Kurt steps outside just as I'm leaving the cab. He's dressed in something like a trendy bowling shirt and jeans. He's casual impeccable. I have to give it to him, the man can rock a bowling shirt. I just have to remember what Matt warned, to stay focused and don't fall for his shit.

"Good evening, Kellis."

Fine lines are showing around his ice-blue eyes as he gives me a ghost of a grin. I will myself not to get lost in them as I push the last good memories of him making love to me out of my mind. "Are we eating in the restaurant?"

"Yes, sure we can eat, if that's what you want, but it's early for me. I needed to get out of the office and I didn't want to go home to change."

That seems to be a stretch even for him. "You're telling me you always have a bowling shirt and jeans in your office or maybe an entire wardrobe for unexpected meetings?" Which would probably be more likely.

"I tried to think of a place where we could meet and discuss your proposal. I thought this was as good as any for a meeting. I asked Ana to find something appropriate for me to wear."

That's Ana, adaptable efficiency. I'd love to steal her away from him. The two of us would make a dynamite team. I'll make a point to talk to her about living in California. I'd even consider her working remotely if she'd say yes. "If we're not going to eat, where should we talk?"

Kurt pulls the door open. "I thought we could bowl a game. I've been taking lessons. Your father said you were good enough to be a professional. I'd appreciate it if you could critique my technique."

It's an unusual suggestion. I've never had a meeting in a bowling alley. It will give me a chance to use the facilities. "Fine," I push past him. "Where are the lanes? This way?" Fifty-two lanes is quite a sight. If I had to describe this place, it would be the Disneyland of bowling. Beautiful lanes, murals on the walls. After we get our shoes from the rental, I choose a lane and sit to finish lacing them. "How long have you been taking lessons?"

He sits beside me a little too close, but not uncomfortable. "I started when I returned to Germany. After bowling at a few other alleys, I settled on this place. It seemed like a good way to relax after work."

I leave the bench, searching for a way to order a beer and find a button near the score pad for service. I've already selected a ball on the way to the lane, but Kurt is walking up with his ball in his hands. "Looks like you're ready. You can go first."

He hesitates for a few seconds to test his grip, then glances at the lane. He paces off from the foul line, then turns toward the lane to ready himself to begin. He takes 4 ½ steps up to the line and releases the ball. It rolls straight toward the head pin for a few feet then veers off into the gutter and disappears. Kurt stares after the ball like he can't believe what just happened. "I was much better in practice with my teacher."

"That's okay," I say, "everyone is nervous on the first throw. You've got another chance, throw again."

The ball slides out of the feeder and Kurt scoops it up. This time his release is better. The ball rolls a little further down the lane before it slides off into the gutter without threatening one pin. He walks to the bench behind me without making eye contact and sits in a dejected heap.

It's been a long time since I picked up a bowling ball. My father always had more faith in my ability than I did. I pull my ball to my waist to begin my approach and let it roll. The trajectory is strong, moving between the first and second arrows. There's a familiar crash of pins and they all scatter as if they've been chased. The strike was textbook perfect. "If I were you," I say, returning to the ball feeder to wait for my ball, "I'd ask for my money back."

Kurt doesn't hide his amazement at my demonstration. "You see, that's why I need your help. Some of the employees would like to form a bowling league. They're even talking about an executive team. Of course, it would all be in fun, but I must make a better showing in front of my peers."

I work with him for an hour and by the end of it he's no Zackariah Ivarsson, but he's not throwing gutter balls either. With more practice he could be a decent bowler.

We finish our last game and return to the rental area to retrieve our shoes. We're seated on a bench putting them back on. "How's Maria?" I say. Kurt's reaction is slight, but he continues to lace his shoes.

"I'm happy to say Maria seems stronger every day. She doesn't mention Greta. I don't think she can trust yourself to talk about the car accident. We avoid it. We talk about safer subjects. How I was the perfect child, is her favorite topic." He looks over to see if he's gotten a reaction.

I shake my head. "You said you had some questions about the proposal. What were they exactly?"

"Let's have some food first. We can stay here or go somewhere else."

I'm in favor of getting this over as soon as possible. "We can eat here," I suggest.

"This place can be noisy. I know a café not too far by car where we can have a quiet talk."

I shrug. "Let's go."

The restaurant is quiet, and even quieter at the table we select.

The menus are placed in front of us. "I think we should start the discussion. I want to know your concerns. Is it the first refusal of job requisition or does this come down to price?"

Kurt pushes his water glass aside to clear a space to rest his forearms. He's in business mode, ready to deal. "I have no objections to the proposal. It looks sound. The compensation is a bit on the higher end of the scale, but in the realm of reasonable. I think you've figured out the reason I've asked you out was not for a business discussion. If I'd asked you for dinner you would've refused."

He's right; we both know the purpose of this meeting. I weigh how much to tell him, then decide just to get my questions answered. "Why did you leave me on Christmas? Tell me the truth. Not what you think I want to hear. And if you say it was you not me, I swear I will hurt you."

He leans back, resigned to answer the question that's been haunting me for months. "After I made my decision, I didn't have the courage to face you. I knew if I saw you again, that I wouldn't go through with my plan. I had a long talk with your father. He made me see that this was not a real relationship. After thinking about it, I agreed and decided to make it right. That's why I wrote the letter."

I rear back in my seat, disbelief blurring my senses. "On the strength of you talking to my father and not discussing this with me, you decided to break it off?" I stop. I'd rehearsed what I was going to say in response, but I'm going off script. I rage at him anyway. "Fucking me and leaving me, all on God damn Christmas day, says *I got what I wanted, you don't mean shit to me, have a nice life.* Up until you left, I wanted something real with you. You took care of me. You enjoyed my family's Christmas. Yet, you walked."

He turns away, frustrated but determined to win the argument. "That was always my intention to be with you. Your family's respect is important to me. I couldn't ignore your father's concerns and continue seeing you. By sabotaging you and Matt, I had robbed you of the person that might've been the best man for you."

"Was this enlightening conversation after we came from celebrating your Christmas tradition?"

"Yes."

"When my dad said: Is it a win if it's been obtained through manipulation and half-truths? He was talking about us?

He nods.

You threw everything away over a halfhearted comment?"

"You've got to admit my plan worked. You and Matt are together. I saw the two of you the first day you arrived. I saw how much you love him."

I don't get this. It makes no sense. "This is all over a misunderstanding?"

"This wasn't a misunderstanding." He's adamant, and his accent is inserting itself.

Finally, I'm getting to some underlying emotions.

"I was dishonest. I didn't ask you because I wanted to give you a choice. A chance to have a relationship with Matt. I love you, but I didn't want to be a poor substitute."

He's throwing the L word around. Herr Heinrich thinks he's right about everything. I'm done working through this nonsense argument. "If you have no problems with the proposal, then when can I expect to sign the contract?"

The change of topic doesn't faze him. He shifts easily into the next issue. "The preliminary contract has been drawn up, but it's working its way through Legal. It won't be ready tomorrow. Monday at the latest. You're welcome to wait here until Monday to review the document. But I'll send it to you on Monday to look over."

"Then I'll be leaving tomorrow with Matt. And I expect to see the contract on Monday. If we have nothing else to discuss about the proposal, then I'll be leaving."

"Is that how you handle everything? By dismissing it and

storming away? You're getting everything you want, Kellis, can't you give me some time with you? Even if it's to say I'm sorry. More than likely I won't see you again. I thought I might see you occasionally if you had accepted the position at Drachen. But with you contracting with the company, I see it's impossible."

"What do you want from me, Kurt? Why do we always end up in this place?"

"I can't have what I want, so I'm going to ask for what I might get, a little time with you. It wasn't all bad. I know I don't have any right to ask. But can I at least have your friendship? You'll always have mine. Even if you don't want it. I'll be there when you need me, Kellis. Please."

The contract was not ready for my review until the following Monday. I wasn't concerned. It's difficult for huge companies to initiate change quickly if it isn't urgent. There are too many channels to maneuver in the regular process.

Kurt flew to California and brought the final contract to my house that's doubling for my office until I find a space downtown. He said he was coming back anyway. He's decided to sell his house. He'd actually purchased the home shortly after he moved in.

Kurt sits at the kitchen counter, formal in his gray suit. His presence reminds me of our breakfasts when he was living next door. Matt was here when he arrived. The men still don't like each other. I don't think it will happen again, but I escort Matt to the door to avoid him taking another punch at Heinrich. I step out onto the porch with Matt and close the door behind me.

"You're two minutes away from getting everything you want. How does it feel?"

"I haven't pulled the last trigger. If I can get a yes to that, then

I've gotten everything."

Matt gives me a quick kiss. "I'll be up late tonight working on some reports. Call me when this is all over and let me know what happened. Better yet, Verity has a sleepover." He winks at me. "Come over and we can celebrate."

Kurt has pulled the papers out of his briefcase and placed them in front of my chair. I take my seat and pick up the pen he's provided. With a flourish, I sign my name to a contract that I actually endorse. Kurt is stoic. It took courage to come here and not have this delivered. He knows it's unlikely he will see me again. With formality, he rises to his feet, his emotions hiding behind a mask of indifference.

"If there's nothing else, then I'll go." He offers his hand.

I wave him back. "Please sit. We need to discuss my second request." I reach inside my pocket for a small wrapped package, no bigger than a couple of inches. I place the object on the counter.

"What's this?"

"It has to do with my second request. I suggest you open it."

He takes the tiny package and tears the paper, revealing a gold signet ring. "This is mine." Still puzzled, he rolls it between his fingers. "I don't understand."

"I want that God-awful thing melted down to form a ring that will fit me. That chunk of gold caused me a lot of grief. Every time I see it on my finger, I want it to be a reminder that I've won."

He tries to play it off that it's nothing. "Send me pictures of the style you would like, and I'll have a jeweler craft it."

"I want it formed into a wedding band. You see, Herr Heinrich, you promised to replace that ugly signet with a wedding ring. And that's what I want."

"Matt's a billionaire," He scoffs. "I'm sure he doesn't want you wearing a reconstituted wedding ring from me."

"That decision is up to me. Matt doesn't care as long as I wear a ring."

His shoulders tense; this has to be bruising that huge ego. It's what he deserves after putting me through hell. He slips the ring into his pocket and readies himself to leave. "Is that it? Will this finally make you whole?" I note the sarcasm.

It took me a long time to figure out this last demand. I'd almost forgotten I had that signet until I found it in a drawer. "Yes, this will do it for the first part of this request."

If I was punching him, this last bit would be the final blow and he would be face down at my feet, me doing my victory dance over his defeated carcass. This is so sweet; I just might break into one now. I square off with a man that's tittering on the brink, primed for me to deliver his final retribution. "By the way, I'm not marrying Matt the billionaire, I'm marrying pain-in-the-ass Kurt, the CEO of Drachen. You said that you'd do anything to make this right. This will make it right. I want to be Frau Heinrich, and I'll take the rest out in sex."

He's punch drunk. It takes him a few seconds to understand what I've said. "Is this a bad joke? He pushes off the chair to stand in front of me. "You're in love with Matt. Every time I've seen you together it's like you're in your own wrench-worthy happiness."

He takes a few steps toward the exit, but I catch his hand as he moves pass me. I don't release him, but he's still facing the door, determined to leave. "Kurt, listen to me. Matt and I discovered that we do love each other but more as friends. If you hadn't interfered when you did, or been honest about your feelings, we would've discovered this a lot quicker."

I hold his palm tighter, desperate to get through to him. "Matt and I are like family. I adore his daughter Verity, and we've become close, but she needs her mother. He and Jena have been talking. I think they might get back together again. I'm against it; I think she needs a lot of therapy. Matt's a good man, and I hope she realizes that before it's too late." Kurt pulls his hand free, his face creased with doubt. I move closer to him, irritated that he doesn't understand. "I wanted this contract signed before we're married. I didn't want anyone to say I won the contract because I was your wife. Your torment was just a sweet bonus. Do we have a deal?"

The muscles along his jawline tightens as he works out something in his head. He pulls the signet ring out of his pocket and places it back in the small box. He lifts his gaze to meet mine and pushes my last request toward me. "What if I say no?"

Disbelief suddenly drains my strength to respond. Is it possible I was wrong about his feelings and he's moved on with someone else? I take a ragged breath. "You promised to make me whole; you said you loved me."

His body tight; he shifts his weight. "I won't agree to anything until you say it."

I'm staring into his ice-blue eyes looking for the man I fell in love with in Vegas. "Say what, exactly?"

He takes my hands in his and mouths, "I love you, Kurt, you are a god to me."

I'm flushed with relief. I pull his arms around me. "I love you Kurt." I sing out, then scrunch up my face. "What was that last bit? Did you say it in German?" I give him a devious smile. "I didn't understand."

"There's a price to pay for ignoring my orders, he says lifting me onto the counter. Urging my legs apart, he moves between them. His kiss is slow and sensual and I melt, wanting him badly.

Kurt's lips trail to my ear. His tongue is teasing the sensitive opening, making me lose my mind. The heat from his throaty words sends shivers through my body and I'm helpless. "Heirate mich, heirate mich einfach. Ich liebe dich, schatz," he whispers and begins to slowly open my buttons.

"Translation," I say dreamily.

Kurt manages to undo all my buttons and slides one bra strap off my shoulder. He stops and I'm staring at his smitten face. I said:

"Marry me, just marry me. I love you, my treasure."

He's sliding my other bra strap off my shoulder. I bite my lip and glance at the door. I hope Chloe is late today.

The End

⫸────♡♡♡────⫷

German Phrases

Drachen	Dragon
Guten Morgen	Good Morning
Auf Wiedersehen	Good Bye
Herr	Mr.
Frau	Mrs.
Fräulein	Miss
Frohe Weihnachten	Merry Christmas
Ja, ja, ich verstehe	Yes, yes, I understand
Danke Sehr	Thank you very much
Frohe Weihnachten suiisse	Merry Christmas, Sweetie
Schatz	Treasure
Heirate mich, heirate mich einfach. Ich liebe dich, schatz	Marry me, just marry me. I love you, my treasure
Danke	Thank you

WORK Spouse
BOOK THREE

A LOVE@WORK SERIES NOVEL

Chloe's in trouble. Her boss, the politician she's worked with for too long, has unexpectedly lost his election.

She's a high-level aide who must work with the new city council member and keep him out of trouble. He's a brash billionaire and a rising star in the party who has his sights on the governor's mansion or a Washington senator. He's also Chloe's old crush who doesn't remember her… or their one night together.

She failed to make a lasting impression the first time around, but with the help of a hunky fireman, the newest city council member won't forget again.

Work Spouse will launch Spring 2020.
Sign up for my PaxWorld newsletter to be notified of the release date.
www.paxsinclair.com

About the Author

Pax Sinclair is a contemporary romance author that writes about love in Silicon Valley. Her characters are not always from the high-power tech community, you'll find other fascinating people who live in this valley as well.

She writes short stories, novellas and novels, that are funny, quirky, always steamy and sometimes erotic.

She currently has two series,

Sweet & Sultry

Love @ Work

Pax is a California native.
She lives and works in Silicon Valley.

BEFORE YOU GO

Thank you for reading Love Contract. If you enjoyed this book, please leave a review on Amazon, Bookbub and Goodreads.

Love@Work Series
Trinal – Book 1
(Available now on Amazon)

Love Contract – Book 2
(Available Feb 13th, 2020 on Amazon)

Work Spouse – Book 3
(Launch Spring 2020)

Working Girl Blues – Book 4

YOU MIGHT ALSO ENJOY

Sweet and Sultry Series
Someone Like You - Book 1
(Available now on Amazon)

Owe Me Something - Book 2

Check the release dates of upcoming books, read excerpts, see author interviews, or join my mailing list to receive my newsletter PaxWorld at paxsinclair.com

Visit Me
paxsinclair.com, Goodreads, Amazon Author Central, Bookbub
Facebook, Instagram, YouTube